KEEP ON LOVING YOU

Trickle Creek
Book 5

ELENA AITKEN

Chapter One

KAT

IT WAS A BEAUTIFUL DAY. If you liked being up before dawn on a Sunday.

I did not.

Unless, of course, I was on the trails on my mountain bike. When I was flying down the twisty dirt trails, with the blue sky overhead, and sun shining through the trees and creating pockets of sunshine, the early morning was totally worth it.

Too bad those days were far and few between lately. Business was booming and I was far too busy running my increasingly busy hairstylist business to take very many days off lately. Even for mountain biking.

Until today.

I had been planning this day for two weeks and had even rebooked a handful of clients so I could join my big brother

Craig on the trails for a day of sibling bonding and competition, as we would no doubt push each other on increasingly harder terrain until finally we were both streaked in mud and dirt, completely exhausted, with maybe a few bumps and bruises, and more than a few stories to relive when we finally collapsed on the patio of Brickhouse with a cold beer.

It had been years since we'd had a proper bike day. Between my shop, and Craig's ice cream store, the Sugar Shack, never mind his new fiancée and his little girl, our schedules rarely matched up. I could hardly wait.

I left my SUV with my bike on the rack, parked outside my brother's house, and dashed to the door. I only bothered to knock once before letting myself in.

"I hope you have coffee," I called out as I stepped into his entryway. Instinctively, I squatted and braced myself for the inevitable crash of my niece, six-year-old Meredith, whose favorite method of greeting her auntie involved running at full speed into my legs.

I waited, and when Meredith didn't arrive, I got to my feet. "Hello?"

"In here."

I followed the sound of his voice to the kitchen, where I found my big brother draped over the kitchen table, cradling a cup of coffee between his hands, his cheek pressed to the wood surface. He was wearing pajama pants and an old concert T-shirt. His hair was ruffled from sleep and in no way did he look ready to hit the trails with me.

He raised a hand in greeting. "Coffee's fresh."

"You're clearly not." I gave him a sidelong glance and

poured myself a cup before sitting across from him. "I'm afraid to ask." I lifted the steaming cup to my lips. "But I will." I raised my eyebrows.

Reluctantly, my brother sat up and ran a hand through his tousled hair. "I've been up all night," he explained. "Meri's sick."

That would explain the lack of greeting. "Is she okay? A cold or the flu?"

"She threw up about a million times."

I pushed out of my chair and stood, putting distance between me and what was very likely my germ-infested brother.

"Yes," he answered my unasked question. "I'm probably sick, too. Lucy just went back to bed." He waved his hand dismissively. "I probably should have texted you to give you a heads-up."

"Don't worry about it." I made a mental note to spray myself down with the hand sanitizer I kept in my glove box when I left. "That sucks that you don't feel good. I've been looking forward to this for weeks."

"Me too." Craig shrugged and dropped his head again. "I tried to rally, but…"

It was clear that the only place Craig was going was back to bed. "Do you need anything?" I moved to the fridge to take stock of its contents. "Soup, juice, maybe some—"

"We're good." He stopped me. "Whatever it is, I think it's only a twenty-four-hour thing. Meri stopped throwing up around five. Honestly, I'm just exhausted. I think we'll all spend the day on the couch, watching cartoons and sleeping. We'll be better soon."

"In time for the meeting tonight?" I looked at him sideways.

"Oh, that's right. Asher and Noa are going to be back."

"And I can't wait to see them."

After receiving a stipulation from our deceased father's will that he needed to take a forced sabbatical from the family business, our older brother took off for a six-month trip around the world. But not before accidentally kidnapping a runaway bride and falling in love with her. I had been following their travels on social media, but I was more than ready to see the two of them in person.

"You better be feeling better for the meeting." I tried to look stern. "I've been waiting a long time for this." It wasn't just the family dinner I'd been waiting for, and we both knew it. As the youngest sibling, it was my turn to hear what stipulation our father had left for me in his will. It wasn't whatever task he had in mind for me, as much as it was the letter I was sure he'd left for me that I was looking forward to.

It had been over two years since he'd passed away, and I still missed my dad with an ache I wasn't sure would ever go away.

"I know," Craig said. "I'll take as many vitamins as I can. I'll do my best to be okay for tonight, I promise. But I'm sorry about today."

I tried not to look as disappointed as I felt. After all, it wasn't Craig's fault we weren't going to get to go riding after all.

"We can just reschedule our bike date for another time." Even as I made the suggestion, I mentally scoured my calendar, and my next free day wasn't for weeks. If then. "I'm sure we'll find something that—"

"Oh no." Craig cut me off. "I know how busy you are, Kat."

I waved away his protest. "I'll make—"

"No." He stopped me again. "What I'm saying is that you're going riding today."

Taken aback, I gave my brother a look. "I am, am I?"

"You are." He grinned. "Because I totally forgot to tell you. Last night, before...well, before the puking started, I heard from Andy. He's coming to town for a bit. So I invited him to join us."

I worked hard to control my reaction to the unexpected news that Craig's best friend was on his way to town. The same guy I had secretly pined over for years, growing up. The first boy who I'd been totally and completely in love with, even if he had no idea. The man whom I'd fantasized about far more than was probably healthy, instead of pursuing actual relationships with men who were available and interested in me.

"Andy?"

Craig nodded.

If he'd noticed my reaction, he didn't mention it. No doubt he was too tired to notice much of anything. Which was definitely for the best in this situation.

"He should be here any minute. He drove most of the way last night and was going to head in early this morning."

"To bike?"

Once more, my brother nodded.

"With me?"

"No." Craig laughed. "Well, maybe. But just to ride in general. And since it's a ten hour drive, we can't leave him to ride alone. So, it seems like a good chance for you to get out there and—"

"I don't think so."

I started to back up in an effort to reach the door before Andy arrived. Not because I still had my schoolgirl crush on him. No, I'd grown past that. Way past that. In fact, the last time I'd seen Andy on a trip to Vancouver for a hair show, I'd been sure to pay a visit to him so I could once and for all put those feelings behind me.

"Why not?" Craig reached for my untouched coffee cup and helped himself to the extra caffeine. "You guys are friends. Didn't you go to his place for dinner when you were in Vancouver? When was that?"

"Just before Dad died."

"Wow. That long ago?"

I nodded. It had been a long time ago, but I remembered it as if it had been yesterday. But my brother did not need to know the details of that particular visit. "It just won't feel the same without you," I lied. "I promise we'll go as soon as you're feeling better." Determined to get out of there before Andy arrived, I spun on my heel and slammed directly into a hard chest. I swallowed; his familiar scent flooded my senses, threatening to overwhelm me.

The room spun around me, and if I didn't know better, I might have thought I'd come down with whatever germs my brother had. But I did know better.

Two hands caught me by the elbows.

There was no way I could get away now. I took a breath and looked up. His eyes sparkled and his mouth—the same one that the last time I'd seen him had been between my legs, doing extremely wicked and wonderful things to me— was twisted up into a very sexy grin that made my stomach twist into a tight knot.

Maybe those feelings weren't behind me after all?

As if I needed a reminder.

ANDY

I didn't usually need any excuse to catch up with my best friend, especially when that catch-up involved ripping down the mountain on a bike. Something there hadn't been nearly enough time to do since I'd started school, and then grad school to earn my accreditation as a physiotherapist.

Not that my schedule had cleared much since graduating either. After all, those student loans weren't going to pay themselves.

It had been way too long since I'd been back to Trickle Creek for any length of time, and even longer since I'd had the opportunity to have a little fun while I was there. I'd snuck into town for the grand opening of my best friend Craig's ice cream shop a few years earlier, but that could hardly be counted as a vacation of any kind, and I definitely didn't have the type of time to catch up with my buddy the way I would have liked to. Yes, going to Trickle Creek was always a good idea.

A sentiment that was only reinforced when Kat Carlson practically threw herself into my arms moments after I'd let myself into Craig's house.

Instinctively, my arms went up and around her. A mistake, judging by the way my breath was completely sucked from my lungs at the feel of her against my body. I held her for a moment longer than I probably should have, especially because the moment I inhaled her sweet scent, my brain betrayed me by instantly flashing back to the last time I'd been so close to her. Only, that time, we'd been naked, and Kat had fallen asleep in my arms.

A detail of her visit to my apartment for dinner on her quick trip to Vancouver that Craig never needed to know about.

Especially considering Kat and I had agreed that it would only ever be a one-time thing. She'd said some kind of bullshit about being *happy for right now*.

It *was* bullshit, because I was pretty sure I could be happy with Kat for a lot longer than that. Still, there was and always had been her big brother, my very best friend who was more like a brother to me, to think about. And that was a very big consideration.

I recovered from the shock of having Kat in my arms as quickly as I could and managed to paste a grin on my face before she looked up at me.

"Hi." I held her gaze for a moment. The urge to bend down and press my lips to hers was way too strong for two people who'd agreed to be just friends.

What happened between us was one night only. No repeats. Friends. That was it. That was all it would ever be.

"Hey," Kat said after another moment passed. She stepped back and pulled out of my arms. "Sorry, I didn't see you there. I was just—"

"Getting ready to go riding," Craig finished for her.

Craig.

I looked across the room to where my best friend was half sitting, half lying across the kitchen table. "You look like hell, man." I instinctively took a step back.

"Astute observation." Craig groaned and dropped his head again. "Did they teach you those skills in that fancy school of yours?"

I laughed. "That's exactly why they're going to pay me the big bucks one day. My mad observation skills." I tried to meet Kat's eye, but she was studiously avoiding me. "I have to say, man." I turned my attention back to my friend. "You really don't look like you're up for any...well, much of anything today."

"That must be those mad *observation skills* again," Kat muttered under her breath with an unexpected sarcasm that caught me off guard.

When I glanced in her direction, she was finally looking at me. Humor danced in her pretty blue eyes.

I nodded my head with respect.

"Kat's going to ride with you today." Craig pushed himself up from the table. "I am going back to bed."

"I told you, I'm not going to go." Kat shook her head. Her long red hair was tied back in a tight braid and hung down the center of her back.

I resisted the urge to tug on it, or more specifically, wrap my hand around the silky hair and use it to pull her toward me so that she was once again pressed up against my—no! I had to stop thinking of her that way. We'd agreed.

One night. That was it.

Never mind that the memory of her screaming out in ecstasy while my head was buried between her legs, teasing her, licking her, tasting her, had played on repeat through my brain every day since we'd last seen each other. That was, when I wasn't letting my imagination run away with thoughts of exactly what it would have felt like to sink myself into her sweet heat, if we'd allowed ourselves to completely cross the line.

"You need to go, Kat," Craig said. "Andy's come all this way, and if you don't go with him, I'm going to feel even shittier about screwing up our bike day than I already do. Besides, if Andy is going to spend the next few days at your place, you might as well go—"

"What?"

"*My* place?"

Both Kat and I spoke at the same time. I risked a glance

at Kat, who was not doing a very good job managing her facial expressions, which would have been a problem if Craig wasn't so out of it. After all, we'd been friends forever. Hell, I myself had practically been like another brother to Kat growing up. That was before. Still, there was no reason that Craig should think anything of me staying at Kat's place.

"Yes," Craig said, obviously growing exhausted by the conversation. "I'm sick. In fact, you're both putting your lives in your hands by being in this house one moment longer than you need to be. Go. Hit the trails. Be healthy. Have fun." Craig waved his hand randomly behind him as he moved toward the back of the kitchen and the hallway that would take him to his bedroom.

And then we were alone.

I exhaled slowly. "It looks like we're going to—"

"Come on." She pressed her lips together and shook her head with a resigned sigh. "Let's go. If we're doing this, then let's do it before it gets too hot out there."

As far as I was concerned, looking at Kat in her tight tank top and her bike shorts that hugged her ass, it was already plenty hot.

She turned and left, only stopping to glance over her shoulder with a sassy grin and add, "I hope you can keep up."

Chapter Two

KAT

BY THE TIME Andy moved his bike onto the rack on the back of my vehicle and we made our way up the mountain to the trailhead, I had managed to convince myself that despite the history between us, I was mature enough to put it behind me in order to have a day of mountain biking.

After all, I didn't get that many chances to get out and enjoy the beautiful place I lived, so I might as well make the best of it. And if it couldn't be Craig who accompanied me, Andy was a pretty good substitute. After all, I'd probably spent just as much time on the trails with him as I had with my brother over the years. Andy and Craig had been inseparable growing up. Andy had been like another brother to me.

Had been.

But that was *before.*

Before I knew exactly how good he was at making me scream with his tongue.

A rush of heat shot to my clit, making me squirm in my seat as I pulled into the parking lot. If I planned to make it through the day with him, I was going to have to put those thoughts out of my head.

Which was much easier said than done when he sat so bloody close to me, smelling so freakin' good, like cedarwood and citrus.

Damn.

"Ready for this?" Without waiting for an answer, I opened my car door and hopped out, putting some much-needed space between us.

I set to work, unclipping the bikes from the rack. "Dammit." I pushed and tugged on the back latch, but it wouldn't budge. "This stupid thing never works when I want it—"

"Here."

My breath caught in my throat when Andy reached around me. His front pressed up against my back and the heat of his body warmed me completely. I tensed, finding it hard to take a proper breath as he pounded his fist on the bike rack to pop it open.

"Got it," Andy declared before finally stepping back.

I turned slowly to look at him, but he didn't seem to be nearly as affected as I'd been by our nearness.

Probably because we'd agreed to be just friends and he had clearly taken our agreement to heart, unlike me, considering there was no way I could forget the way he'd pulled me close and run his hands up and down my body while his mouth—*no!*

"Thanks," I said somewhat lamely before I reached for my bike.

We spent the next few minutes checking the air in our tires and getting our packs ready before finally wheeling our bikes toward the start of the trail.

"I should be the one thanking you," Andy said as we walked. "I'm sure you weren't expecting to have to entertain me today and with everything that...well, I don't want things to be weird between us, Kitty Kat."

The use of my nickname, which only Andy had ever used since we were kids, caused a crazy flip and twist in my guts. I swallowed hard. There was no way to hide the flush I could feel burning on my cheeks. Still, I did my best to lie to him.

"Why would there be anything awkward between us?" I forced lightness into my voice. "We agreed to be friends, Andy. And that's what we are." I winked at him. "That's what we've always been."

"Right," he started. "But that was—"

"One night." I stopped him, determined to prove to him that I was just as unaffected by the sensual night we'd spent together as he apparently was. "And we agreed, Andy." I used my elbow to nudge him in the side. "Friends. Right?"

"Right." He glanced over at me, but I quickly looked away. "How did you put it?" he continued. "Happy for right now?"

"Exactly!"

It had been a silly thing to say when I'd come up with it a few years earlier, but maybe not that silly, because Andy had gone along with it. Ever since I'd first set eyes on Andy Fisher when my brother Craig brought him home after school one day, I had been in love with him. Well, maybe not in love, but there was a definite attraction and a massive crush that had only grown larger until Andy was literally the only man I could think of. Even after he moved hours away to Vancouver to go to what felt like a million years of school in order to pursue his dream of being a physiotherapist.

It had been clear from the start that there could never be anything between us romantically—nothing serious, anyway. And that's why, when I had gone to Vancouver for a hair-stylist's convention a few years earlier and Andy offered to cook me dinner while I was in town, I developed a plan to get him out of my head once and for all.

It was a simple plan: Convince Andy that I didn't believe in happy-ever-after, but *happy for right now*. Seduce him in order to get the thought of him out of my system for good and move on.

And it had worked, too.

Almost.

We'd spent a very hot night together. But we hadn't actually slept together. And the next morning, as if nothing had happened, we'd gone back to being friends. Just like I'd planned.

Only, instead of getting Andy out of my head for good the way it was supposed to, the exact opposite had occurred.

"You know," Andy continued as we approached the trail

map and he leaned his bike against a tree. "I had never considered the idea of happy for right now before that... well, before you."

He adjusted his pack, tightening the straps.

"And now?"

"I actually think you're on to something," Andy said. "Life doesn't have to be so serious, right?"

"Right." I nodded, not entirely sure what I was agreeing to.

We each mounted our bikes. "I guess what I'm saying is, I hope there isn't any weirdness between us now."

Weirdness? Not unless he considered the fact that it was taking all my self-control not to throw myself into his arms and feel his lips on mine again weird. Nope. No weirdness here.

"The only thing that you're going to find weird is how badly I kick your ass today." I flashed him a grin, and with a strong push of the pedal, propelled myself down the trail and into the trees before I showed him exactly how weird things between us could get.

ANDY

I could hardly believe the words coming out of my mouth were my own.

Happy for right now?

That had been Kat's bullshit line when she'd shown up

at my apartment for dinner, clearly determined for more. Not that I'd objected to it. Not at all. I'd lied to myself for years about my attraction to my best friend's little sister. An attraction that finally came to a head for one amazing night. Thankfully it hadn't gone any further than it had before I'd come to my senses the next morning.

Not that I even should have done what I had.

It didn't matter how attracted I was to Kat. She was Craig's little sister and that made her completely off-limits. Besides that, there were a million other reasons the two of us would never work. Most of which I'd had a very hard time remembering in the aftermath of our decision to be *just friends*.

Not that it mattered. Kat clearly wasn't having such difficulties. And that's exactly why I was spouting a bunch of bullshit I didn't believe. If she was okay with our decision to act like nothing had happened between us, then I could be too. Or, at least, I'd do a damned good job pretending.

I'd meant it when I'd said I hoped there wasn't any weirdness between us because more than anything—well, maybe not quite as much as I wanted to kiss those plump lips—I wanted to enjoy our day together. It had been years since I'd been mountain biking, but the moment I'd sat on the saddle of my bike, it all came back to me. Especially when Kat threw down the challenge to me that I wouldn't be able to keep up.

We chose a fairly easy trail to warm up on. Even though it was a starter track, I had to focus on the rocks, stumps, and tree roots to avoid making a fool of myself. It was the perfect distraction when otherwise I would have had my eyes locked on Kat's tight backside on the seat in front of me and how even though she was pedaling hard away from me, I could imagine exactly how her body felt naked under my hands as I explored every inch of her skin.

Yes, it was definitely for the best that I didn't let my thoughts drift into such dangerous territory.

We'd pedaled at a gentle pace down the easy track for a few minutes before Kat turned around and yelled over her shoulder. "Are you ready to eat my dust?"

There was no way I could see through her dark sunglasses, but I could picture the flash of a challenge that no doubt lit up her gaze. And I was ready for it. The words were hardly out of her mouth when I deftly changed gears and pushed down hard on my pedals before blasting past her on the trail. Behind me, I was sure I heard Kat mutter a string of curse words.

But I wasn't naive. She'd be right behind me in seconds, and there was a good chance she'd overtake me completely. Kat was a strong rider, but so was I. I was more than up for the challenge.

Sure enough, it didn't take long before I caught a glimpse of Kat in my peripheral and heard her call out a whoop of satisfaction as she caught up to me.

I saw the flash of red from her braid sticking out from her helmet as Kat cut in front of me and, with a spray of dirt, came to a stop a few feet up the trail. I maneuvered deftly so I wouldn't crash into her before coming to a stop with a laugh.

"Damn." I pulled my sunglasses down my nose, and she did the same. "You're pretty fast, Kitty Kat."

Was it my imagination that her eyes flashed when I used her nickname?

"Not so bad yourself," she said. "For a city boy."

I laughed. "Is that what I am now?"

She shrugged.

"Well, city boy or not, I haven't lost my edge. I think I've proved that."

"Seriously?" She laughed. "You're trying to tell me you think you've still got it? After that?" She waved behind us at the trail we'd just ridden.

"You don't think that's enough proof?"

"Not even close," she scoffed.

I looked around at the system of trails and tracks we currently stood at the crossroads of. I wasn't a stranger to Trickle Creek's extensive trail system, but it had been a while. If I wasn't mistaken, the only option besides the one we'd just ridden were black diamonds. The hardest and most challenging rides. There were massive trees and tight tracks to navigate, but when we were kids, those were the rides we liked the most. More than once, we'd placed bets, along with Craig, about who could ride them the best.

"Okay," I said, an idea formulating. "Why don't you give me a chance to prove it?"

She followed my gaze, picking up on my idea. "Oh yeah? You want to bet me? Like the old days?"

"Sure do." My lips quirked up into a grin. "But unlike the old days, let's make it interesting."

There was no doubt that I was playing with fire, but I couldn't seem to stop myself.

"Okay." She said the word slowly, each syllable sliding off her tongue. "What kind of interesting do you have in mind?"

Her sharp eyes flashed the way I knew they would, because she could only be thinking of one thing. The same thing I was.

It had only been one night, over two years ago. But I remembered every single detail—from the overcooked pasta, to the sensation of her fingers trailing down my back, to the deliciously sweet taste of her—as if it were yesterday.

Chapter Three

KAT

THE PASTA WAS OVERCOOKED, the sauce far too salty, and the garlic bread a shade too dark. But as far as I was concerned, it was the best meal I'd ever had. I helped myself to another piece of garlic bread, choosing one that wasn't quite as crispy as the others.

"Sorry about dinner," Andy said as I dipped the bread in the salty marinara. "I'm really not much of a cook." He shrugged. "Maybe I should have ordered something in, but it didn't seem right to treat you to takeout when you came all this way."

"It's perfect," I said with a full mouthful before reaching for the glass of wine I'd hardly touched since we'd sat down. "Honestly, Andy. It's been such a crazy week of going nonstop, I've hardly even had a chance to sit down and eat a meal. Let alone a home-cooked one."

I'd been in Vancouver for four days at an advanced hair-styling workshop I'd managed to wangle an invitation to. The entire workshop was totally out of my comfort zone, but that's exactly why I'd wanted to attend. The only way to get better at my craft was to push myself. And I'd done just that. I was completely exhausted. But not too exhausted to accept the invitation for dinner from my childhood crush.

I'd never be that tired.

"I'm just so happy to see you, Andy, and—"

I bit the inside of my cheek and silently cursed myself for being so eager. Truthfully, I was surprised it had taken me so long to say something stupid.

Sure, I might no longer be the awkward, flat-chested seventeen-year-old with braces, acne, and an unfortunately short haircut that made my orange curls frizz up around my head like a combination between an overgrown Orphan Annie and a clown straight from the circus. But even now, as an adult, with straight teeth, clear skin, and a generous C-cup, I was no less awkward. At least not when it came to Andy Fisher.

"I'm happy to see you, too, Kitty Kat." Andy flashed his signature smile.

The same one I used to pray he'd flash in my direction whenever he'd come over to my house to hang out with Craig, my older brother. And the nickname he'd given me… no one ever called me that. Only Andy. I could still remember with almost perfect accuracy the first time he'd said it. I'd been fifteen. It was the first time my brother had brought Andy home from school with him. He was new to our small town of Trickle Creek and had been assigned the locker next to Craig, the brother I was closest to growing up because we were only two years apart. All the other siblings, a mixture of step siblings and full siblings, were all quite a bit older than me, and to say we were a close family...well, it's not that we *weren't* close. But at any given time, there was a lot going on with the Carlson clan. It could be hard to keep up. Even for me.

"What's your name?" Andy had asked when I'd walked into the kitchen to find an after-school snack. The boys were sitting at the table, a plate of leftover fried chicken between them.

I hadn't been expecting to see anyone but Craig, let alone the most beautiful boy I'd ever seen in real life. His jet-black hair and sparkling blue eyes made him look like a movie star. And when he smiled...I was completely dumbstruck.

"Her name is Kat," Craig answered for me when no sound came out of my open mouth. "Kat the brat. She's my little sister. Ignore her."

My face bloomed in embarrassed heat, but Andy only smiled in my direction. It was the first time I'd felt important. Seen.

And a moment later, when he said, "Hi, Kitty Kat. I'm Andy. It's nice to meet you," I fell head over heels in love.

Just like that.

"No one really calls me that anymore," I said, in an attempt to remind him that I was no longer a kid. Maybe the curves in all the right places, the dress that I knew showed them off to their fullest potential, and the hair that I'd carefully styled in long, luscious waves over my shoulder wasn't enough to get that particular point across. I might have to up my game. Not that I had any. I had always been completely hopeless when it came to men. I reached for the glass of wine again.

"Right." He dragged out the word while he twirled his fork in his pasta. "But did anyone else ever call you that besides me?"

Ha. He caught me.

I ducked my head, but not in time to hide the small smile that crossed my face.

"I really am happy to see you, Kitty Kat," Andy said again.

This time he spoke slowly, his voice deepening. Or maybe it was my wishful thinking. Could it be, that after all these years, and the distance between us, that Andy might finally think of me as something more than Craig's little sister? It was probably too much to ask for that he might even think of me as a *woman*. Still, it wasn't going to stop me. I had nothing if not hope. Not when it came to my love life.

It had recently come to my attention from my best friend, Annie, that the entire reason I was still single was because on some level I was still comparing every man who crossed my path to Andy. At first, I'd blown it off, but then when I really let myself think about it, I'd realized Annie was right. And there was only one way to move past it: I needed to get Andy out of my system one way or another. Which was exactly what I was going to do.

I let the wine swirl around my mouth a moment longer than absolutely necessary before I looked him in the eyes and said, "I missed you. A lot."

He sat back in his chair and his mouth fell open.

Shit. It was too much.

I never should have said that. I never did know how to be subtle. I really should have taken Annie up on her offer for flirting lessons.

"I meant, it just hasn't been the same in Trickle Creek since you moved out to the coast." I shrugged as casually as I could. "I know Craig misses you, too. He even mentioned how maybe he could convince you to move back and scoop ice cream in the Sugar Shack instead of finishing your degree."

Craig hadn't mentioned anything of the sort. In fact, my big brother was ridiculously proud of how smart his best friend was and how Andy was putting all those smarts to good use by getting his master's degree in physical therapy. No doubt, if Andy even mentioned quitting in favor of working in Craig's candy and ice cream shop, my brother would drag him back to Vancouver himself and tie him to his desk if necessary.

But if Andy knew any of that, he didn't say so. Instead, he smiled slowly, his lips curling up in a way that made my stomach flip. "I sure do miss Trickle Creek," he said. "And everyone there."

He reached across the table and took my hand in his,

surprising me. I caught myself before jerking away from the touch.

My mind raced. He was holding my hand. My hand. He was looking into my eyes and holding my hand.

What. Was. Happening?

Certainly, I was dreaming. I had to be dreaming. But if I were, I had absolutely no interest in waking up anytime soon.

"How's the family?"

The last thing I wanted to talk about was my family. It's not that I didn't love all my siblings. I did. Mostly. But there was always something going on. Most recently, my father hadn't looked well. He insisted he was fine, but between me and my siblings, trying to get him to go to the doctor was exhausting.

"I don't really want to talk about it right now," I said with a small shake of my head. I wasn't going to let anything cloud my mood. Not when I was with Andy. Finally.

Andy nodded and moved on. "I'm really glad that Craig told me you were coming to Vancouver," Andy said, my hand still wrapped in his. "I think the last time I saw you was—"

"At the Sugar Shack grand opening."

His eyes twinkled, looking bluer than they already did, which was some sort of miracle of nature. "You're right. I had a break in semesters that worked out. I wouldn't have wanted to miss that. I'm so proud of what Craig has done."

I also didn't want to talk about my brother. Not when his best friend was holding my hand, and now…now his thumb had started to stroke small circles on my skin. I swallowed hard and willed myself to stay calm. It was a herculean task. I'd dreamed about him touching me. Fantasized about the way his lips would feel on mine. And gone over and over in my mind in vivid detail exactly what it would feel like to finally have him take me to bed.

Damn. Annie was right. No man stood a chance until I worked Andy out of my system. And considering there was no way a relationship between us would ever happen in a million years, there was only one way to do that.

ANDY

There were a million reasons why I shouldn't be doing what I was doing. What I *should* be doing was yanking my hand away from Kat's smooth, silky skin, tucking it into a pocket or running it through my hair or doing pretty much anything with it besides touching her in any way. More importantly, what I wanted to be doing—which was running my hands down her body so I could explore all those brand-new curves properly before pulling her in for the kiss I'd been wanting to take since I'd seen her the last time I'd been in town—could never happen.

It was only when I'd walked into the Sugar Shack for the first time that there, beside the display case full of fresh fudge, I'd laid eyes on Kitty Kat, all grown up—her red, silky hair cascading over her shoulders when she tipped her head back, laughing the throaty laugh that made every single thing in my body come alive.

And that's when I knew with a hundred percent certainty that the feelings of warmth and affection I'd always had for my best friend's little sister—the one I could never make sense of since we'd been kids and I'd helped her with her science project and defended her from Danny Paulson, who'd snapped her bra and pulled her hair one too many times—had been more than just brotherly protection. A lot more.

But just because I *had* those feelings didn't mean I should act on them. Hell, it probably meant the exact opposite.

No. I *knew* it meant the exact opposite.

But this woman had curves that would not stop, and the dress hugged each and every one of them, leaving just enough to my imagination that, from the moment she'd set foot in my apartment, I could not stop picturing what it would be like to run my hands down her body and pull her in close until she was pressed up against me.

Damn.

I needed to stop thinking about Kat that way. She was my best friend's little sister. Which meant, in no uncertain terms, Kitty Kat was off-limits. Always had been. Always would be.

Not a problem while she was safely in Trickle Creek, building her hairstylist business, and I was hours away in Vancouver, going to school. The distance might not make me forget about her, but it sure as hell helped when it came to behaving. But now...she was here. In my apartment, looking at me with those heavily lidded eyes, licking her lips to make them moist and so very kissable, and—

No.

I never should have invited her to my apartment. When I heard that Kat was in the city taking a course, there was no way I could let the opportunity pass to see her. In hindsight, I should have taken her to a restaurant. Somewhere we could have a drink, an easy, delicious—and public— meal, and not be tempted to scoop her up in my arms and take her to my bed to do all kinds of unspeakable things to her.

"Andy?"

I blinked and pulled my hand away, unsure of how long I'd been lost in my thoughts and fantasies.

"Sorry, I didn't—"

"I was just asking you how your classes were going and if you liked it here."

I tried to cover by taking a deep sip of wine. "Classes are good," I responded reflexively because, classes were good, if not a little mundane. "I'm ready to be done," I added more truthfully. "It's been a long haul. Only one semester, a practicum, and a few major exams left, and I'll be a fully licensed physical therapist."

"Oh." She grinned. "Is that it? Seems easy enough."

We both laughed and once again, I was brought into the moment with Kat.

"And you like it in Vancouver…" She held her glass of wine up, but didn't take a sip. "Do you have a lot of friends?

Someone to keep you company in between all your studying?"

"Someone? Like a—"

"Girlfriend," she finished for me. "Are you seeing someone?"

I needed to tread carefully. Of course there was no girlfriend in my life. Even if I had time in my busy schedule to date someone, I hadn't met anyone who was worth the effort. Not for a very long time. And the one woman I *had* found was completely off-limits, even if she was currently sitting in my one-bedroom apartment, looking very much like she would be worth every bit of the effort to strip her out of that tight dress and—

"No," I said quickly. "I'm not."

Her eyes widened with renewed interest. She set her wine glass down and looked me straight in the eye. "I think you probably know I've always had a crush on you, Andy."

Holy. Shit.

Obviously, I wasn't stupid. I'd known. Sure. But that was when we were kids and…

"I think when we were in school, I must have known, but you're Craig's little—"

"I don't know if we need to talk about my brother right now." She reached across the table and this time, she took my hand in hers.

Her long, slender fingers laced with mine until I was completely unable to pull away. Not that I wanted to. Quite the opposite, really.

"No," I agreed. "But I think it's fair to tell you that when

I saw you last time I was in town to visit, I may have also developed my own crush on you."

"But that was at least two years ago."

I nodded. "To be fair, it probably started long before that."

"A crush, huh?" Her eyelids fluttered and her tongue slipped from her mouth, just enough to moisten her lips in a way that had my entire body responding.

"Oh yes." I nodded slowly. "A crush that completely consumed me with thoughts of kissing you until you were begging me for more."

It was not what I'd planned to say. Hell, it was the exact opposite of what I *should* have said. And it was only going to lead to the kind of trouble I might not ever be able to come back from. What I really should have done was lied and told her how I always had and always would think of her as a little sister. But that would have been a lie because the thoughts racing through my mind at that moment were decidedly not familial.

Kat's breath caught in her throat, and her chest strained against her dress as she struggled to keep her composure. "And now?" She'd asked the question on a throaty breath. Her hand tightened in mine. "How's that crush now?"

I could still stop this from happening. I could pull away, tell her I didn't think of her that way anymore, and save us both from the moment.

"Kitty Kat, I think there's only one way to answer that question." I stepped up from the table, and with my hand still in hers, I pulled her up to follow suit until she stood in front of me. Before I could talk myself out of what I very much wanted to do, I ran one hand down the side of her curves until it rested on the delicious swell of her hip. It was only then that I released her hand to slide it through her silky red hair, cup the back of her head, and pull her into my lips for the kiss I'd been dreaming of every night as I'd fallen asleep for the last few years.

Chapter Four

KAT

HE WAS KISSING ME. Andy Fisher was *kissing* me. And it wasn't just in my fantasy. It was real. It was very, very real.

My entire body vibrated. If Andy hadn't been holding me—oh, and was he ever holding me—I might very well levitate straight off the floor.

Sure, I'd been kissed before. More than once. But never like this. Never before had there been so much...passion and electricity between me and a man. Yes, it was cheesy to think of it like that. As if Andy were some sort of hero in a romance novel who made me come alive after so many years lying in wait. But there was no other way to think of it, because that's exactly what was happening.

A low moan filled the air around us.

Was that me?

Oh, God. That *was* me. I might have been mortified if

Andy hadn't responded with a groan of his own as he tugged me even closer to him, as if he couldn't get enough.

Good.

Because I couldn't get enough, either. I wanted more. I wanted everything.

I had always known that a kiss with Andy would never be enough.

I could feel him hard and thick with need, pressing against my belly as he sucked gently on my bottom lip before he pulled back from our kiss.

"Why don't we take this into your bedroom?" I hoped I didn't sound too eager, but there was really no other way of telling Andy what I wanted from him in no uncertain terms. And I did know what I wanted. What I'd always wanted.

His eyes shut momentarily, and when they opened again, they were clouded. He took a step back from me, and his hands slipped down to rest on my hips. "Kat, I…"

"It doesn't have to be a thing, Andy," I said quickly. "I mean…that kiss was—"

"Fucking amazing," he finished for me, sending a surge of pleasure through my body.

I hadn't misread the situation at all. Not that I thought I had. It was true that I didn't have a ton of experience with men, but I knew enough. And judging by the way Andy looked at me, and the heat in that kiss, my feelings were right on track.

"It really was amazing," I said softly and took a step to close the distance between us. "But you know what else would be amazing?"

I couldn't even believe the words that were coming out of my mouth. Maybe it was the few sips of wine I'd had that had loosened my tongue. Not that it mattered. Not when I meant every word I said.

Andy didn't immediately say no. He didn't pull away or stop touching me, details that only fueled my resolve.

"Taking this into your bedroom would be pretty amazing." I leaned in and fluttered my lips over the sensitive skin just below his ear. Andy's scent overwhelmed my senses, and I sucked in a breath before catching myself. *Hold it together, Kat.*

"Kat...I..."

"You want this," I murmured in his ear. "As much as I do." As much as I always have, I stopped myself from adding.

His response came in the form of a groan. His body shuddered from my kisses. "Damn, Kitty Kat. I *do* want this, but—"

"No." I pulled back and looked him in the eyes. "There is no but, Andy."

"Ahh." He released his grip on me and stepped away.

I felt the loss immediately. Hot tears sprang to my eyes, but I bit my bottom lip to keep them from spilling over. I would not cry. He'd never see me as the grown-up woman I was if I acted like a child. *No.*

I watched as Andy battled with himself. He turned his back to me and scrubbed a hand over his face before threading his fingers through his hair. Still, he didn't turn around.

"Andy?"

He didn't move.

"It's okay."

"It's not." He spun back around and faced me. "It's not okay," he said, softer this time. "You're…and your brother…"

"Never needs to know."

Andy's face twisted with confusion, and I rushed to make my point.

"There's no reason Craig ever needs to know," I continued. "After all, it's not like we're going to have a relationship or anything. That's not what this is about. I mean, we don't even live in the same city. Like I said, this doesn't have to be anything more than…a friendly hookup."

It almost killed me to say the words out loud. It went against everything I felt inside, but I wasn't stupid either. I had always known that there would never be anything real between Andy and me. Even if he wasn't my brother's best friend, we lived ten hours apart. I'd already made peace with it.

"But you're—"

"A grown-up." I stepped forward, pressing my breasts out so they strained against the fabric of the dress I'd brought with me in the hopes that I saw Andy. With a boldness I didn't know I possessed, I ran a finger down the front of his shirt. "I'm not a little girl anymore, Andy." I kept my voice low and took a step closer. "I don't believe in fairy-tale endings of happily-ever-afters. I'm not naive enough to believe that's how life works out. I believe in happy-for-right-nows, and I think we can make each other very, *very* happy."

I stopped inches in front of him, bit my lower lip, and looked up through my lashes into his eyes.

Andy let out an animalistic half groan-half growl. And then everything was okay because his hands were gripping my face and his mouth was on mine, devouring me.

ANDY

Oh fuck yes.

We could make each other *very* happy. Of that, there was absolutely no doubt in my mind. The chemistry between us was absolute fire. And she was right. It's not as if there were ever going to be anything serious between us. Nothing more than one night, anyway. And if she was okay with that...

"You are so delicious," I murmured against her lips. Was one night going to be enough? It was going to have to be. Even if things were different and we did live in the same city, and she wasn't my best friend's little sister, I wasn't in a place with my life that I was looking for a relationship anyway. "Happy for right now. Is that what you called it?"

I needed to hear it again. I needed to be sure. After all, this was Kitty Kat. *My* Kitty Kat.

"Happy for right now," she repeated as she slid her hand behind the back of my head and threaded her fingers there, tickling the base of my neck, a move that sent a thrill through me. "We're not children anymore, Andy. It doesn't have to be all or nothing. Just live in the moment."

That was all I needed to hear. With another growl, I again caught her mouth in mine.

Fuck. She tasted good. So good. Sweet and spicy and like I needed another taste. A deeper one.

"This dress." I got the words out through gritted teeth.

"You like it?"

"It has to go."

Her eyes widened.

"Now."

I didn't wait for Kat to process what I wanted, or even to do anything about it. Instead, I spun her around, so her belly was against the kitchen counter. She put her hands out to steady herself, her ass pressed out toward me. I barely contained a moan at the sight of her presenting herself for me in such a way, and for a moment considered exactly how much I liked that particular position. But no, I needed to see her. I needed my mouth on those sweet lips.

I swallowed hard and tugged down the zipper on her back, revealing smooth, pale skin sprinkled with a smattering of the same delicate freckles that adorned her face. I'd always teased her about them but that's only because whenever I did, she'd reward me with that smile I loved so much. But now there was no teasing, because those freckles were the sexiest thing I'd ever seen.

Until now.

With a tug, I pulled the tight dress down and off Kat's shoulders. My fingers traced a pattern on the sweet sun spots before pulling her up against me so I could press my lips to the skin and kiss my way across the delicate marks I'd only ever admired from afar.

She squirmed under my touch, but I wrapped my arm around her waist and held her tight.

"You're so beautiful, Kitty Kat." With my free hand, I roamed around her body to the front of her thigh, where the hem of her dress landed. A small sigh escaped her lips, encouraging me, as I traveled up the sensitive skin there. I hesitated at the elastic of her panties, but only for a second before I ever so lightly fluttered my finger over the silky fabric.

Kat gasped and, at the same time, her knees buckled a little. I tightened my grip on her, pressed one last kiss on her shoulder, and spun her around once more so I could see the look on her face as I pleasured her.

And I was not disappointed.

"Damn, Kat. I had no...I never imagined..." Unable to finish my thought, I shook my head and reached for her. Once more, my mouth took hers into a deep kiss. I was beyond ravenous for her. I'd never let myself imagine what kissing her would be like. Not really. Because it could never happen. No matter what feelings I had for her, how strongly I was drawn to her, or how much my body responded from the smallest smile in my direction, I could never have her.

But now...

Maybe I still couldn't have her in any real way. At least not in any way that would go beyond tonight in my apartment. What if it wasn't enough?

It would have to be.

"Andy?"

I hadn't realized I'd stopped kissing her or pulled back at all.

Her eyes were wide with question, and she watched me warily. "Are you…if you don't want to—"

I shook myself out of the thoughts that threatened to screw up what promised to be a very good thing. "What I want," I reached for her, "is to make you scream." With no further hesitation, I scooped her up and set her on the kitchen counter.

She let out a squeal of surprise as I rucked up her dress and tugged her panties down. But the squeals very quickly turned to moans of pleasure the moment I buried my face between her legs.

Chapter Five

KAT

HIS TONGUE WAS pure freaking magic.

Never in my life had I felt anything like what was currently going on between my legs with Andy's attention.

My entire body felt as if it were going to explode. I could barely control the trembling that had started in my toes and was taking over my entire body.

"Andy?" My voice came out as a strained whisper. I swallowed hard and tried again. "Andy, I—"

He lifted his head and looked up at me from between my legs with the sexiest grin on his face. "Yes?"

"Oh my God, don't stop."

He laughed and dove back down to resume his hard work.

I wove my fingers through his hair to hold him there, but a moment later he did something with his tongue that made me cry out and throw my head back. I needed to use my hands to brace myself against the cool surface of the countertop.

"You like that, hmm?"

"Andy, don't…ohhh."

"Don't what?" He raised his head again and gave me a wink.

"Don't stop."

"Your wish is my command, Kitty Kat." He licked his lips, and if I hadn't already been completely lost with need for the man, that's all it would have taken. "I don't plan on stopping for a very long time."

But he did stop. I watched with disappointment as he got off his knees and stood in front of me.

"Kitty Kat…" Andy grinned and kissed me thoroughly. "Don't worry," he said when he pulled back. "I told you, I'm nowhere done with you yet."

Before I could respond, Andy scooped me up as if I weighed nothing. He pulled me close to his chest and kissed me tenderly. "But I think we're way past time that I need you in my bed."

A full-body spark raced through me. *Yes.* His bed was exactly where I wanted to be.

I reached out to cup his cheek and deepen the kiss, but he bit down on my lip ever so lightly and pulled back.

"Wait," he said. "First, I need you naked."

My body thrilled at his words. I'd dreamed about Andy speaking to me in such a way. Taking me to bed and doing all the things that would make my body light up. But now it was actually happening.

It. Was. Actually. Happening.

I had to concentrate. I had to hold it together and be the mature, no-strings woman I needed to be to finally have Andy. Even if on the inside I was screaming and waving my arms around in the air like a teenager at a boy band concert.

"I'm not the only one who needs to be naked." I worked hard to keep my voice low and controlled and hopefully full of sex appeal. His nostrils flared and his grip on me tightened as he moved through the apartment toward the small bedroom in the back, so I must have been successful.

"Strip," he commanded a moment later when he set me on my feet. "As much as I've enjoyed that dress, I think we're—"

His words died on his lips as I shimmied out of the fabric, pulling it all the way down to my feet before stepping out of it. Andy had already relieved me of my panties, and because the dress wasn't the right style for a bra, I stood in front of him completely bare. My long auburn hair fell over one shoulder, the ends tickling the top of my breast. My nipples hardened under Andy's gaze as he stood motionless in front of me.

"Damn, Kitty Kat. You are…"

I'd always loved when he called me that, but hearing the nickname with lust in his voice was without a doubt the sexiest thing I'd ever heard. It gave me more confidence as I stepped toward him and tugged at his shirt.

"Your turn. You're still wearing far too many clothes."

He let me pull his shirt off and over his head and waited while I worked the leather of his belt and then slowly undid the button and zipper of his jeans. I slipped my hands inside the denim, taking my time to travel down his smooth, hard muscles.

He groaned and shook his head, the only indication that I was driving him crazy.

"You're going to need to hurry this up, Kitty Kat."

I didn't need to be asked twice. I shoved his jeans down so he could step out of them.

I only had a second to take in the magnificent sight of him before he was moving toward me again.

"There's still something I need to take care of." His hands fluttered over my sides until they finally rested on my hips. He walked me backward until my legs hit the bed and I fell back onto the comforter. "And I'm going to make you purr."

I couldn't help it. A giggle slipped from my lips.

"Oh, you think that's funny?" Andy shook his head, but there was a grin on his lips.

A devilish grin that sent shock waves through my body, directly to my core.

"I told you I was going to make you purr, and that's exactly what I'm going to do."

Before I could react, Andy dove onto the bed and directly between my legs. I cried out when his tongue once more found my sweet spot and a moment later, the only thing I could focus on was the intense pressure building in my body that finally exploded in a kaleidoscope of color as my climax completely consumed me.

ANDY

She was beyond delicious, and making her come apart and lose control so freely was the biggest turn-on I'd ever experienced. Everything about Kat was more. And I knew exactly why.

She was my Kitty Kat.

I waited, giving her a moment to come back to herself before slowly pressing one more kiss to her core. She shuddered under my lips, and it took all the restraint I had to keep from tasting her one last time before I slowly moved up the bed until I was lying next to her.

I propped myself up with an elbow and gazed down at her. Her rich auburn hair was spread out on the pillow beneath her head, properly tousled and sexy as hell. Her eyes were closed, but she was still breathing fast. My eyes traveled down her body to her full, round breasts that rose and fell with every breath.

Her eyelids fluttered open and her beautiful lips curled up into a small, satisfied smile when she caught me looking at her. "I don't know about making me purr, but...damn."

I traced a finger up her front, between her breasts. "Oh, you purred all right."

She caught my hand in hers and held it tight. "Now I

think it's your turn to purr…" Her gaze flicked down to my now exceptionally hard erection.

I couldn't think of anything I'd like more than having Kat make me purr. But despite the teasing tone in her voice, I could see the exhaustion on her face, the way her eyelids fluttered with the need for sleep, and the lazy way she rolled to her side to face me.

Never mind how she'd only very recently finished telling me how busy her week had been and how little sleep she'd had. As much as I'd love to take things further, I was a gentleman. And considering I was already breaking about a million bro codes, maybe I should just quit while I was ahead.

"You're exhausted, Kitty Kat." She didn't object when I moved closer on the bed and gathered her up in my arms. I shifted her so she was sprawled over me, her head on my chest, her bare breasts pressed against me—a detail that was doing nothing for my increasingly painful erection—and her arm draped over me.

It was perfect. She was perfect.

"Rest," I murmured as I stroked her hair and her breathing fell into the easy rhythm of sleep.

Happy for right now?

Fuck yes. Right now, like this, I was immeasurably happy. And tomorrow morning, when Kat was properly rested…well, it made me even happier simply to think about it.

Chapter Six

KAT

I WAS HAVING the best dream.

Only it wasn't a dream. It was real.

When my eyelids fluttered open in the early morning sun, I confirmed it. Andy was sleeping next to me. His bare chest was turned toward me. His arm lazily draped over me and resting lightly on my hip.

Holy shit.

I blinked hard. And then again.

Yes. It was definitely not a dream. This was real. What we'd done was real. His mouth on my pussy. The way he'd pulled so much pleasure from me—and so easily, too.

My body shuddered just remembering how amazing he'd made me feel. But then...

I'd fallen asleep.

My hand flew up to my face, and I only barely stifled a

groan. How could I have fallen asleep after what we'd done? How was it even possible that my body would shut down at such a moment when the only thing I wanted was within my grasp? How could—

I knew exactly how. I'd been exhausted after all the early mornings and late nights at the styling conference. I'd been going nonstop for days, and then the wine... I hadn't had much. But then again, I hadn't needed much. No wonder I'd fallen asleep.

I let my eyes drift over Andy's body. His chest moved up and down as he continued to sleep peacefully, completely unaware that I was watching his every move. And memorizing every single one. The blissful memory of this moment would have to last me for years to come, because I'd meant it when I told Andy I didn't believe in fairy tales. And I certainly didn't believe in happy-ever-after. Not when it came to the two of us.

I wasn't surprised that my instincts had been right when it came to how he'd felt about me, too. My own crush on Andy had been building for years, but when I'd seen him at Craig's grand opening, I hadn't missed the way Andy looked at me. Like he saw me for the very first time. I'd noticed the way his nostrils flared, just a little bit. And the way his pupils dilated when I'd tossed my hair.

I'd seen every bit of it.

Because I'd been watching.

As much as I would have liked to lay there and watch Andy sleep all morning, the growing pressure of my bladder had other ideas. I'd take a moment to freshen up and then

I'd wake him up. After all, I wasn't anywhere near finished with him. We'd agreed on happy for right now, and as far as I was concerned, there was a lot more happiness to be had for both of us.

With a grin on my face, I slipped from the bed and padded out to the living room where I'd left my purse.

It wasn't until I was safely in the privacy of the bathroom that I pulled my phone from my purse.

Six missed calls and at least ten text messages. All from my best friend back home, Annie Darling.

I hesitated to tell my best friend what had happened, but only for a second before quickly typing in a text to Annie.

KAT:

You'll never believe where I am right now.

It only took seconds for Annie to reply.

ANNIE:

Andy's bed.

A laugh bubbled up from my throat, but I covered my mouth quickly. Annie knew me too well. As my best friend for pretty much my entire life, Annie had been subjected to far too many *I'm so in love with Andy* conversations and late-night text messages. She'd also been the one to encourage me to finally put my infatuation with Andy behind me. No matter what it took.

Which was a big part of why I had found the courage to…*well*…it was pretty much the entire reason I was there.

> His bathroom. I just woke up. Next to him.

I could practically hear Annie squealing from miles away. Still, I didn't want to give her the wrong idea.

> We didn't have sex. I fell asleep.

Seriously?

Annie's response came with a wide-eyed emoji.

> Kat: Can't talk.

Kat typed quickly.

> I need to get back.

I put her phone down and rushed through a morning routine in Andy's bathroom. I used a squeeze of toothpaste on my finger to freshen my mouth and splashed some water on my face. It was only when I was about to leave to return to Andy's side that I picked up her phone again and saw Annie's text.

> Maybe you shouldn't. Maybe it's not a good idea, Kat.

Not a good idea? It was the best idea. Besides, I was already feeling lighter, like I could successfully move on from the childhood crush that had held me back for far too long. That was the whole point of this, after all. I'd already managed to convince myself that I was fine never getting my happy ending with Andy, but that didn't mean I shouldn't see this through.

ANDY

The click of the bathroom door woke me up. I took a few minutes to blink the sleep from my eyes and come fully awake. I stretched my arm across the bed. The sheets were still warm with the memory of Kat's body.

Falling asleep next to her had been…too damn good. In fact, I'd fought sleep for hours so I could watch her and memorize the slight rise and fall of her chest, and the cute way her breathing got deeper until she woke herself up with a little start. Not quite a snore, but…damn, it was sexy.

Not as sexy as it would be to have her beneath me while I—

My phone chimed on the bedside table where I'd left it plugged in the night before.

The second I looked at the screen, I regretted it.

Craig. Kat's big brother. And my best friend.

CRAIG:

Hey. Were you able to see Kat last night?

Did I ever? *Shit.*

ANDY:

Sure did. Cooked her dinner.

There was no point to add unnecessary details.

Thanks, man. I know it's dumb, but I worry about her in the city alone. Glad she has you to look out for her while she's there.

I couldn't bring myself to respond. Instead, I put the phone down face-first on my nightstand as guilt flooded through me at what I'd done.

How had I talked myself into what had happened? I knew better. Dammit. I'd always known better.

But Kat had looked so damn good and so grown up and…we weren't kids anymore, and…

It didn't matter how I tried to justify it. I'd crossed a line with Kat, and I knew it. Hell, I'd known it when it was happening.

I couldn't change what had happened. But I could prevent the situation from getting worse. There were certain things I'd never be able to come back from.

Down the hall, I heard the toilet flush and knew I had to move quickly. My entire body was screaming to stay in bed and finish what we'd started the night before. But with Craig's untimely reminder that I'd just broken the number-one rule of best friends, there was no way that would be happening now.

I quickly grabbed a pair of jeans and a clean T-shirt, dressed in record time, and sprinted to the kitchen only moments before the bathroom door opened and Kat padded down the hallway. She had her back turned to me as she headed to the bedroom, which afforded me a very nice view of her backside. I swallowed hard, turned away, and busied myself by filling the kettle.

"Andy?"

"I'm in the kitchen." I forced my voice to be light and easy. The worst thing I could do now was make it a thing. We'd had an amazing night, but that was all it could be. Besides, hadn't she said it herself? Happy for right now.

If my throbbing cock was any proof, I was definitely not happy at the moment. But there didn't seem to be any other option.

Kat appeared a few minutes later, wearing one of my T-shirts. The fabric hit her upper thighs, barely covering her sweet pussy.

I swallowed hard and forced myself to look away. "Coffee?"

"I didn't think you were awake yet." There was a question in her voice that I chose to ignore. "I was hoping you'd be—"

"I'm starving." I cut her off. "And I'm dying for a cup of

coffee." I took the now boiling kettle and poured it over the grounds I'd prepared in the coffee press. "You still take yours with four sugars and three creams?"

She laughed, the sound filling the space between us. "Not since I was a teenager. I drink a much more adult, two sugars with one cream, now."

She'd moved so she stood next to me. Her hand reached tentatively for me, as if she were feeling out the situation in the light of day.

I couldn't blame her after my hasty exit from the bedroom. Still, I hated that she was questioning things.

"That is much more mature," I said as I turned to face her. With one hand, I cupped her chin and kissed her tenderly. I was way past playing with fire, especially considering I knew exactly what could happen if I wasn't careful. It was a fine line between throwing her over my shoulder and picking up where we'd left off, and the much more responsible behavior, concluding this little...whatever it was...in the best possible way. "I had a lot of fun last night, Kitty Kat."

"So did I." She pressed her lips to the tender skin beneath my ear and purred, "But I don't think we're done having fun yet." Her hands trailed down my side, and my entire body vibrated under her touch.

A groan escaped my lips, and I swallowed hard. Turning away from her would be the hardest thing I'd done in a very long time. But there was no other option.

I captured her hands in mine and held them between us. "I would love nothing more than to continue what we started last night, Kitty Kat." I closed my eyes for a moment and took a deep breath. "But I totally forgot I offered to pick up a shift at the clinic this morning. It's not my usual shift, but I need the hours and…damn. I'll call in sick."

"No." She stopped me, the way I knew she would. "Don't call in sick. Especially if you're covering for some-one. That's not fair. And I know you need the hours." Her pretty lips curled down in a frown, but she caught herself quickly. "Do we have time for a coffee at least?"

I once more pressed my lips to hers in a sweet kiss. At least until we stepped out the door of my apartment, we could have this. "Of course we have time." I released my hold on her and stepped back. "Go get dressed. It'll be ready in another minute or so."

KAT

I dressed slowly, taking my time to pull the skintight dress up and over my body before tugging my long hair back into a ponytail.

It's for the best.

I'd been repeating the same four words over and over since walking away from Andy, and I was finally starting to believe them.

Yes, I was disappointed. Beyond disappointed. Why had I fallen asleep?

It would be a question I'd be asking myself for a long

time, I was certain. Still, it had been a fun night. And even if it hadn't happened exactly the way I'd fantasized about, my girlhood dream of being with Andy Fisher had come true. And that really was something. Besides, now it was done and out of my system, and I could move on.

Andy would always hold a special place in my heart. He'd forever be the standard I held all men to. If we'd actually made love, I couldn't imagine that I'd ever be able to find a man who could come close to meeting the expectations he would have set for me.

"Yes," I told my reflection. "Definitely for the best."

With a smile on my face, I left his bedroom and joined Andy in the kitchen.

He handed me a cup of coffee. "You know what? I've always thought you had the best smile." His hand brushed my arm and lingered for a second. "I noticed it the very first time I met you."

"You did not."

"I did." He sat down across from me. "And then every time I came over after that, I made it a point to make you smile. Especially if Craig upset you."

"He always upset me." I shook my head.

"That's what big brothers do."

"I guess." I shrugged. "And that certainly hasn't changed."

"I bet it hasn't." Andy's voice dropped. "And I'm sure he's just as protective of you as always."

There was something in his voice I couldn't quite read.

"He is." I set my coffee down and looked Andy in the eyes. "If you're worried about him being upset about what happened..." I started. "Don't. He never has to know. In fact, he never *will* know." I waited until I saw the acknowledgment on his face. "I meant what I said last night, Andy. We're all grown up now and this...last night...that's all it ever needs to be. All it ever will be. I'm not looking for the fairy tale."

Not with you, I almost added, but bit down on my bottom lip to keep from blurting it out.

Andy reached across the table and took my hand in his. He threaded our fingers together. "How did you put it... happy for right now?"

I grinned and nodded. "You got it."

"And are you?"

He looked at me with so much expectation on his face, I wasn't sure what he was hoping the answer would be.

"I am," I answered honestly. I waited for his response, hoping that he was all right with what had happened between us. But even if he wasn't, for any reason at all, I would be okay. I'd made my decision long before accepting his dinner invitation, and no matter what Andy's response would be, I would be fine with it because I really and truly was good with it.

After a moment, Andy's lips curled up into a smile. "Me too."

He squeezed my hand one more time before releasing it, and I knew that signified the end of our time together.

I left my coffee, abandoned on the counter, and prepared myself to leave. "Thank you again for dinner, Andy. After a busy week in the city, it really was the best way to end my trip." And then, feeling a little wicked, I added, "And dessert was truly delicious."

He laughed out loud. "You're nothing but trouble."

"You have no idea." I winked at him and blew a kiss in his direction.

Andy walked me to the door and opened it. Right before I moved to walk out, he grabbed my hand and pulled me back into him.

I was breathless while he kissed me.

"You really are something special, Kitty Kat."

"I know."

We both laughed.

"You are, too, Andy," I added more seriously. "Honestly. Thank you for...well, thanks for the great night. Next time you're in town, ice cream at the Sugar Shack is my treat."

He shook his head, and I laughed again.

If I were being honest, it surprised me a little how okay I was with the way things were being left between us. But I was. It felt right and like it couldn't have happened any other way.

"Bye, Andy."

I turned and stepped into the hallway of his building.

"Kitty Kat?"

I turned slowly to face him.

"I get the whole happy-for-right-now thing," he said

softly. "But I really hope that one day you do believe in happy endings, because you deserve nothing less."

I let the smile lift my lips as I took his words in. "You never know, Andy." I blew him a kiss in an effort to hide my true feelings. "Anything could happen."

stepped into the hallway of his building.

Chapter Seven

KAT

WE WERE JUST FRIENDS.

We'd decided together. It was one night. No strings. Happy for right now.

Friends.

Which was why there was no way Andy could be suggesting what I thought he was.

Even if that's exactly what it sounded like.

"Are you suggesting what I think you are?"

I refused to look away from his gaze. Andy's pupils dilated; his tongue darted out and licked his bottom lip.

Oh yes, he was absolutely going to suggest what I thought he was.

And if he didn't, maybe I should. Because…Why. The. Hell. Not?

The connection between us was still as strong as it had

been two years ago. Stronger, maybe. And if I was feeling it, I most likely wasn't alone.

I swallowed hard as Andy reached a hand toward me. "Interesting as in—"

"Hey, kids!"

A shower of dirt sprayed up next to us, and it took me a moment to realize the creator of the mess was my oldest brother Chase and his fiancée, and my best friend, Annie.

I slipped my sunglasses back into place, using the opportunity to come to my senses. Whatever Andy had been about to suggest—even if it was exactly what I'd hoped for—it was probably for the best that he didn't. The situation wasn't any different. He was still my big brother's best friend.

I risked a glance at Andy, who thankfully wasn't looking in my direction. When I finally turned to Annie, my best friend was watching me with a very knowing look.

Probably because no matter what I'd told Annie after my trip to Vancouver, my friend wasn't stupid. Despite the fact that I insisted I was well and truly over Andy, Annie knew me better than that.

I raised my eyebrows in Annie's direction and pressed my lips together before looking at my oldest brother. "What are you guys doing here?"

"Craig texted and said he was sick. He felt bad about your bike day being thrown for a curve."

"But it seems you bounced back, no problem." Annie wiggled her eyebrows.

I shot Annie a look, but my friend only laughed. "I didn't know he was coming."

"It was kind of last minute." Andy shrugged. "But I'm always glad to get out for a ride. Too bad Craig had to miss, but Kat graciously agreed to keep me company."

"I'm sure she did." Annie grinned, and I muttered under my breath.

I would kill my friend if she mentioned anything to Chase about the whole *situation* with Andy. Fortunately, my big brother appeared to be just as oblivious, and I would know, because Craig wouldn't be the only brother pissed off to know the truth.

"Well, how about riding a few trails with us?" Chase asked. "I'm probably not nearly as good as you, Kat. But I've been pushing myself a little lately. It could be fun."

It probably would be fun. I couldn't remember the last time I'd ridden with my oldest brother. He'd moved away when I was pretty young and besides a few forced family holidays throughout the years, we hadn't spent much time together at all. I was definitely in for a little sibling time. "Sounds good to me." Besides, having a few people around to act as a buffer between me and Andy wasn't a bad idea. "Is that okay with you?" I glanced at Andy.

The intense look in his eyes from a moment ago was gone, replaced with a look that could only be described as indifference. Had I imagined whatever had transpired between us a few moments ago?

I must have, because Andy not only didn't look bothered by the interruption of Chase and Annie but happy about it.

"The more the merrier."

Oh yeah, any connection between us must have been imagined.

"Besides." Andy winked. "Having you both here might not make Kat feel quite so bad when I kick her ass on this next one."

"You wish." I tightened my helmet and rolled my eyes behind my sunglasses.

"Don't go too crazy," Chase said. "Nobody's allowed to get hurt before the family meeting."

My chest tightened at the mention of the meeting. I'd been waiting for what felt like forever for this meeting.

"If Craig's sick, won't you have to postpone the meeting anyway?" Annie looked between us, and my heart sank.

"He promised he'd be better." I blew out a breath as I accepted what my brother's illness meant. The waiting would continue. At least for a few more days.

"Sorry, Kat." Chase put a hand on my shoulder. "I know you've been waiting for your—"

"It's fine." I shook off my brother's touch. We all knew how much I'd been looking forward to my chance at hearing the terms our deceased father had set out for me in his will. "There's nothing we can do about a stomach bug." I straightened my shoulders and pasted a smile on my face that I hoped made it look like the delay didn't bother me. "Now, are we going to ride or just stand around all day on our bikes?"

Andy was the first to move. He winked at me and

nudged me with his elbow, almost knocking me off-balance. "See if you can keep up, Kitty Kat."

Before I could react, Andy was gone in a cloud of dust. Without further hesitation, I jumped on my seat, pushed off on the pedals, and headed down the trail.

Behind me, I heard Chase and Annie's laughter, and I knew they would be right behind. Not that they were likely to catch me. It may have been awhile since I'd been on my bike, but my skill was so deeply embedded in me, that it didn't matter. I leaned into each turn like a pro and pumped my legs hard on the flats, lifting at the right moment to jump over a rock or tree root.

It was harder than I expected to catch up to Andy. He was just as good a rider as he'd always been. His skill only fueled me.

I made a split-second decision to try to overtake him on the trail. It was risky since the path was narrow as it cut through the trees. But I knew there was an opening coming up where the trail widened just a little. But I'd have to be quick.

I pumped my legs harder, narrowing the gap between us until my front wheel was close to his back wheel.

There was no way I was going to let him beat me. Not when…well, when it was so damned easy for him to pretend like there was nothing between us.

The truth hit me like a brick.

That was exactly what was bothering me. Despite the fact that it had been my idea and we'd agreed to just be friends. That was before. Before I'd seen him again and annoyingly still had the same feelings for him.

I pushed myself harder, knowing even as I did that I should ease up and let him stay in the lead. But before the thought could take root, the path widened, and my opportunity presented itself.

Before I could think better of it, I pushed hard on the pedals and surged forward. I risked a glance at him as I passed Andy, and was just about to cut back onto the trail in front of him when I noticed a fallen tree in my path.

Shit.

I was going too fast to stop. There was nowhere to go. I jammed on the brakes, but it didn't matter. A second later, my front tire crashed into the tree, and I was flying through the air.

It wasn't until I was airborne that I second-guessed my plan, but then it was too late. Worse, a moment later, when I landed—hard—I realized that my little plan to overtake Andy had likely just cost me first place in the race only I knew we were having.

ANDY

When Kat appeared in my peripheral, I couldn't believe my eyes. Not that I should have been surprised. She always had been competitive, and I recognized the flash in her eyes as I'd taken off. No doubt, she was determined to beat me down the hill. And we hadn't even made our wager. It was too bad, too, because I was pretty sure that each of our terms of engagement would have been more than worthwhile.

Sadly, that line of competition vanished when the others showed up, which was definitely for the best. After all, Kat was still Craig's little sister. And Chase and Asher's, too. That hadn't miraculously changed. They'd all accepted me like family. My job wasn't to pursue her or lead her on with false hopes for something I couldn't give her, even if I wanted to. My job was to protect her. Just like a big brother would.

Only I was not her big brother.

Still, that was exactly why I eased onto my brakes when I realized what she was trying to do, which was to make a very dangerous pass on a trail that wasn't designed for overtaking. And she was going way too fast to safely handle any obstacles that might come up.

Including the fallen tree that we both saw at the same time. Fortunately for me, I'd already slowed enough that when I slammed my hands down on my brakes, I had just enough time to stop before hitting it. Kat wasn't so lucky. Or maybe she really did think she was invincible. Either way, she hit the log straight on and went ass over teakettle over her handlebars into the trees and brush.

"Kat!" I dropped my bike on the path, leapt over the log and dropped to my knees next to her. "Holy shit. Are you okay?"

She was lying facedown in a bush, her head dangerously

close to the trunk of a pine tree. I put my hand on her shoulder, and she groaned.

"Are you okay?"

She tried to roll over, so as gently as I could, I helped her to her back. I didn't miss the wince of pain as she changed positions. Her sunglasses had flown from her face in the crash, and she had chunks of mud and dirt on her cheeks and eyelids as she slowly fluttered them open and looked up at me. "What just...did I..."

"I think you thought you might be able to fly," I said with a chuckle. "And for a moment, you did. It was the landing that wasn't so hot."

She scowled and moved to smack me, but gasped in pain instead.

"Where does it hurt?" I instantly went into caretaker mode. I scanned her body with trained eyes.

I pushed the memory of the last time I let my gaze track over her naked body out of my head. If there was ever an inappropriate time to let my mind wander into that dangerous territory, this was it.

"Is it your wrist?"

"I think so." She nodded and held out her left hand. "I must have landed on it."

I tugged my gloves off and cradled her arm gently in my hands. "What about the rest of you? Anything else hurt?"

She shook her head. "I don't think so."

Without removing her biking glove, I prodded her wrist gently. She gasped, and when I looked at her, I saw the glisten of tears in her eyes. She was trying hard to be brave, but I could see how badly it hurt.

I glanced around, but Chase and Annie obviously had the good sense not to follow us down the trail we took and no doubt were waiting for us at the parking lot.

"I can call for EMS," I suggested. "Or if you think you can walk down, we—"

"I can walk." Her lips were pressed together in a line.

She was stubborn, that was for sure. It was one of the things that was so great about her. Still, I wasn't about to let her walk out of the trails if she had other injuries.

She must have seen the hesitation in my eyes, because she quickly added, "Honestly, Andy. Nothing else hurts. Just my wrist. I can walk just fine."

I contemplated calling EMS anyway, but ultimately, I decided to try it her way. "Okay," I said reluctantly. "Let's get you on your feet before we make any decisions."

A few minutes later, I had gathered up her bike—which miraculously didn't have nearly as much damage as its rider—pulled her out of the bushes, and dusted her off. I wouldn't admit it, but I took full advantage of the fact that she had a sore wrist to help her brush the dirt off her.

With her cradling her injury, I was left to negotiate both bikes out of the trails. Neither of us moved quickly, but fortunately, we weren't far from the parking lot where the others were likely waiting. As soon as we got close enough, I abandoned one of the bikes, jogging one ahead, before circling back to grab the other.

I directed her to sit on an overturned log while I quickly

went to tell Chase and Annie, who were already loading their bikes onto their bike rack, of the accident. It took a bit of convincing, but finally, they agreed to let me take her to the medical clinic to have her wrist looked at without making a big deal of the crash so she didn't feel embarrassed.

Judging by the way Annie winked at me, I was fairly sure that Kat had told her friend all about our *happy for now* night in Vancouver, and that Annie obviously did *not* disapprove. Not that I had time to think about what that might mean. I had one thing to do now, and that was to take care of Kat.

Chapter Eight

KAT

"I CAN DO IT," I said for what had to have been at least the eighth time since walking through the front door of my condo. We'd been at the medical center for most of the day, waiting first to be seen by a doctor, and then for the results of my x-ray that told me I'd have to wear a cast for the next few weeks.

"I'm sure you can." I didn't miss the trace of laughter in Andy's voice as he continued to hold his hand out so he could help me out of the sweater he'd lent me and that I was currently struggling with. "I was merely offering to help," he said. "You know, because of your newly cracked wrist and the fact that you're on heavy painkillers." He shrugged casually and chuckled. "But if you don't think you need me…"

He grinned broadly, then slowly and dramatically turned

away, holding his arms out, until I finally sighed heavily and gave in.

"Okay, fine." I mumbled the words under my breath. "You can help me."

Andy turned to face me, his grin even wider, if it were possible.

I'd never had an easy time accepting help from anyone. Ever. Maybe it was the fact that I was the youngest of five siblings, but I'd always had an intense urge to prove myself, in all ways. Even so, I couldn't deny how nice it felt to have Andy there with me today. I'd tried to hide how much pain I was in on the trail, and then again when the doctor examined me. If Andy had noticed, he thankfully hadn't mentioned it. Instead, he'd reached for my good hand and squeezed while the doctor did his thing.

He pulled the sweater gently from my good shoulder and stepped back.

"It's not broken," I said. "It's only a tiny fracture."

"Kat?"

I watched while he visibly tried to bite back his laughter.

"That's the same thing."

"It's not." I shook my head vehemently. "It's only a tiny little crack. I'll be back to new in no time." I didn't have much of a choice, because I had clients waiting for me. Fortunately, it wasn't my dominant arm. It would be clumsy, but I was pretty certain I'd be able to work with a cast on for a few weeks.

"If you say so." The laughter was gone from his voice.

I blew out a breath. "At least the meeting was already

postponed. I would have been so mad if my stupid accident was the reason we had to push it back." A few hours earlier, Craig texted the group chat to let everyone know that he still wasn't feeling up to a family meeting.

"You're really looking forward to your turn, aren't you?"

It was ridiculous, but I felt the sudden urge to cry at his simple question. I nodded and bit my bottom lip, not trusting myself to speak. All my brothers and my sister had their own special relationship with our father, but I was always Michael Carlson's baby girl. We'd had a bond unlike any other, and I'd been particularly devastated by his death.

I'd spent the last two years watching while all the others took their turn fulfilling our deceased father's requests in order to keep the family inheritance intact. It wasn't the challenge that I was looking forward to, but what went with it. If Chase, Charli, Craig, and Asher's experiences were anything to go by—and I was sure they were—there would be a letter written just for me, from my dad.

I'd spent months imagining what he'd written to me and what message he wanted to pass on to me. It kept me up at night and now, I was finally so close to having my turn.

"I am." I finally managed to speak. "More than I can properly express."

Andy reached out and squeezed my shoulder. The look in his eyes was one of tender care. "It will be your turn soon, Kat. Just another day or two. And I know you'll want to be one hundred percent before then."

He wasn't wrong.

I nodded and swallowed hard. It had been a long day

and no doubt the drugs they'd given me at the hospital were making me more emotional than normal.

Too soon, Andy removed his touch. "Why don't you go get settled on the couch and I'll make you a grilled cheese—"

"I can do—"

"I know you can," he said gently. "But I want to, Kat. When was the last time you ate?" He held my eyes for a moment.

Maybe it was the painkillers I was on, but I couldn't help but feel warmed by his gaze.

And I *was* hungry.

I nodded my acceptance and started to move into the living room. The idea of cuddling up on the couch with a full belly and a glass of wine was suddenly very appealing. I hadn't even managed to complete one full ride, but my body was sore. I felt like every part of me was bruised, and a chill was settling over me now that I'd removed Andy's sweater. I was still dressed in my bike shorts and spandex tank top, and I was cold.

Maybe a bath would be a good idea?

A glance behind me told me that Andy had gone into the kitchen as promised. I should probably ask him for help running the hot water and getting the bath ready, but how awkward would that be, given our history?

No.

I could do this myself.

Once upstairs, I didn't waste any time getting the water running. It wasn't until after I'd added a generous pour of scented bubble bath to the water before I attempted to strip out of my tight clothes. The shorts were awkward, but doable once I managed to shimmy one leg down and then the other. It wasn't until I tried to get my tight top off that I ran into trouble.

The medic had pushed up the sleeve to my elbow in order to get my cast on, which at the time had made perfect sense. However, now that I was trying to figure out the logistics of removing the skintight layer, an entirely new situation had presented itself.

"This is so stupid," I grunted as I channeled any and all acrobatic skills into shimmying my top off my good arm and over my head. Only my shirt didn't go easily over my head and managed to hook itself somewhat inside out on both of my arms and my head, trapping me in the tight fabric.

The water was still running in the tub, and no doubt was getting closer to the top, but I couldn't see to turn the taps, or even to point myself in the right direction.

"Dammit." I wiggled and struggled futilely for another few minutes and was just about to admit defeat when Andy beat me to it.

"Kat?"

I heard him call from my attached bedroom. The last thing I needed after the day I'd had was for Andy to see me completely naked, trapped in my shirt, but there didn't appear to be any other choice.

"Are you okay?" He knocked on the door. "You've been taking a long time."

I swallowed my pride. "Can you come in?" My voice

was muffled by the shirt. Still, I added, "Please. I need your help."

A moment later, I heard the door open, and the chuckle Andy didn't bother to hide.

"It's not funny."

"I don't know," he said. "From where I'm standing, it's actually very funny."

I dropped my chin to my chest. "Can you help me, please?"

ANDY

I didn't answer right away. I couldn't. I was way too taken aback by the sight of Kat's curvy, mostly naked body in front of me. She was every bit as gorgeous as I remembered. Maybe even more so. Either way, she took my breath right out of my body.

I was thankful for the fact that she couldn't see the way I was staring at her, because we weren't supposed to be looking at each other in any way besides a friendly way. And the feelings rushing through me—directly to my dick, which had very much taken notice of the mostly naked woman in front of me—were definitely not purely friendly.

I took a moment to pull myself together, swallow hard, and set myself to the task at hand, which was helping Kat out of her predicament before she hurt herself even more.

"Of course." I moved to the tub first and turned the

water off before reaching for the tight shirt that she'd somehow managed to twist around her head in what had to be a very uncomfortable way. "Stop struggling." I put my hand on her bare hip and stilled her. Heat shot through me and again, I was glad that she couldn't see my reaction. I was really going to have to get myself under control, and quickly.

"It hurts," Kat moaned through the fabric. "Get it off. I don't care if you have to cut it."

"We're not going to have to cut it." Reluctantly, I moved my hand from her hip and started to work on the fabric. Gently, I tugged the shirt first off her good arm and then, when that was free, I moved my attention to get her head free. She pulled in a gasp of air as if she were being suffocated by her clothing, and I had to fight the urge to laugh. "Better?"

"So much." She held out her bad wrist, and I pulled and shifted the fabric until I was able to stretch it over her cast and free her completely from the self-imposed trap she'd found herself in. "Thank you. I just decided that I wanted to warm up with a bath, and I didn't think it would be so hard to get out of my—"

She broke off and glanced down at her mostly naked body, as if realizing for the first time that she was only wearing her bra and panties.

I did my best to keep my eyes to myself, so when she looked up again, I was staring straight into her eyes. "Let me help you into the tub," I said gently. "I don't want you to slip and hurt yourself further."

I expected her to object, but to my surprise, she nodded. "That's probably not a bad idea."

I waited and watched while she tested the water and deemed it just right before I held out my hand.

She stared at me for a second before a blush crossed her entire body in a very sexy flush.

"What?"

She squeezed her eyes for a second before opening them on a sigh. "I need to take my underwear off."

Oh.

The blush made sense now.

I swallowed hard in an effort to control my own response to what she was implying. "I've seen you naked before, Kat."

"That's not helping, Andy." She shot me a look and turned her back to me. "Just don't look, okay?"

That was a promise I was going to have a very hard time keeping, so instead of making it, I said, "Let me help." And reached for the clasp of her bra when she finished shimmying out of her panties.

Her breath hitched as my fingers skimmed the smooth skin of her back, and I let my fingers linger a little before I unclipped her bra.

Friends.

I had to keep reminding myself that whatever had happened between us had been one time only. We were friends. And not the kind with benefits.

But maybe—

She shivered, reminding me that she was cold. I did my best to keep my eyes averted as I held out a hand and helped her sink into the tub full of bubbles, taking care to keep her cast out of the water.

Only when she was settled did I once more risk turning around. I was having a harder and harder time remembering the terms of our friendship, and seeing her wet and naked was definitely not going to help matters. Fortunately—or unfortunately, depending on how I looked at the situation—the thick layer of bubbles covered her completely.

"I should probably—"

"Stay."

"Stay?"

She nodded. "I mean…it'll save me from hollering for help when I'm ready to get out."

She bit her bottom lip and glanced away from me, but not before I saw the shimmer of tears in her eyes. She was usually so tough and independent. It wasn't until a few moments earlier when she'd mentioned the family meeting that I'd noticed how bothered by the postponement she was.

And with everything else that had happened, maybe the events of the day had impacted her a little more than she was letting on.

"That's a good point." I nodded and sat on the closed toilet lid across from her. "And I really wouldn't want you to try anything that might cause another shirt incident."

She laughed and shook her head. "Do you have any idea how annoying a cast is?"

I shrugged. "We did a unit in school where we had to train with a cast on to see what the patient experienced."

"Really?"

I chuckled. "No. Not really. But that would be a good class, wouldn't it?"

I watched her struggle not to laugh, but finally, she did, which had been my objective all along. I'd do anything to see that smile.

"It actually would be a good class," she said as she reached for a large poofy sponge thing on the side of the tub. She made a few attempts to wave the sponge around in an effort to get her shoulders before I moved to the side of the tub and took it from her hand.

Everything about it was a bad idea, but there was no way I couldn't. "Here," I said. "Let me."

Chapter Nine

KAT

HE'D SEEN me naked before.

He'd touched my naked body before.

Hell, he'd done a whole lot more than that.

Yet, somehow the way Andy moved the wet sponge over my back was a new level of intimacy.

It was probably a bad idea to have him in the bathroom with me, and it was absolutely a bad idea to have him washing my naked back. But I didn't care. I'd finally allowed myself to take a day off and it had pretty much turned out to be the worst day ever. If I wanted a little company after the shitty day I'd just had, that didn't seem like such a bad thing.

Besides, Andy was obviously able to compartmentalize our past a whole lot better than I could. So even if I did want to pull him into the tub with me so he could rub that wet sponge all over the rest of my body while also kissing me until I could no longer feel the pain in my wrist, well, that didn't matter.

A girl should be allowed to have her fantasies. Especially after a day like mine.

I moaned a little and leaned forward to give him better access to my back. "That feels so good, Andy. Don't stop."

"I won't." His voice was low and controlled.

We sat in silence for a few minutes while I let myself sink into his touch.

Finally, Andy broke the silence. "You know, technically, I think I won."

I spun around so quickly, I sent a wave of water over the edge of the tub. "What?"

"I mean…" He shrugged. "Technically."

Something in the way he looked at me heated me more thoroughly than even the warmest bath could. "Too bad we didn't get a chance to make that bet."

Andy's nostrils flared, and his eyes darkened. "You have no idea."

A shot of desire hit me directly between the legs. "So tell me," I said. "If we had made the bet, what were the stakes?"

He lifted the sponge from the water and let the water drip as he squeezed slowly. "You really want to know?"

Oh yes. More than anything, I wanted to know.

"Tell me." My words were little more than a whisper.

The sponge stilled momentarily before starting another slow slide over my shoulders. "If I won," Andy said slowly, "my prize would have been to finish what we started."

My breath hitched in my throat.

"Assuming you were agreeable, of course."

"Of course." I worked hard to keep my breathing level. "I would have been."

It was his turn to take in a sharp breath.

"Assuming you would have won," I added with a grin he couldn't see. "But you didn't."

When his movements with the sponge paused once more, I turned slowly in the tub so I could look into his eyes.

The way my body vibrated with need, I no longer cared who won or lost, as long as he picked up that damn sponge again and put his hands back on my body.

"I totally won." His voice deepened as he spoke.

"Nobody has won anything yet, Andy."

A low growl escaped his throat, and he leaned forward until our lips were only inches apart. "Are we doing this again?"

"There doesn't seem to be any reason not to." Except for all the reasons I wasn't about to mention. "Besides," I added. "It's not like it's anything serious, right? Just friends?"

"Just friends," he agreed. "Happy for right now."

It was me who had come up with the stupid concept in the first place. At the time, it was a means to an end. A way to get him out of my system. Now it was...

I swallowed against what I really wanted to say and nodded.

Andy closed the gap between us so his lips were on mine in a soft kiss, but after that build-up, I needed a whole lot more than soft. With my good arm, I reached up and threaded it behind his neck, pulling him down to deepen the kiss, my tongue slipping between his lips.

Andy groaned in response and held my face between his hands. Water trailed down my cheek. "Is there room in there for two?"

I'd never shared my tub with anyone, but there was no doubt about my answer. "Absolutely."

ANDY

Seconds later, my clothes were in a pile on the floor, and I'd slipped into the sudsy, hot water. My cock was painfully hard and throbbing between my legs the way it had been from the moment I'd seen Kat in only her bra and panties. No, that wasn't true. I'd been in almost a constant state of arousal since seeing her that morning in Craig's kitchen.

Not that I was about to let thoughts of my best friend interfere with what was about to happen. Not again.

The only thing I was focused on was Kat. And her beautiful, wet, and soapy body directly in front of me.

I slid my legs as far as I could to the edges of the tub, so we were sitting in a V.

"I had no idea you could fit two people in here." Kat flicked some bubbles in my direction.

"So I'm your first then?"

"You wish."

I did.

It didn't make any sense at all, but a surge of jealousy shot through me at the idea of Kat being with any other man. She was my Kitty Kat.

But she wasn't.

No matter what I might want, she'd made it perfectly clear that it was a *for right now* arrangement.

"If you don't get over here and kiss me, Andy, I may have to—"

I moved like a shot, lifting myself up and over her in the bath so water sloshed over the sides of the tub to the tile below. But I didn't care because, a moment later, my lips were on hers, my body was pressed up against her slippery, wet body, and I was kissing her as if my life depended on it.

She groaned under me and wiggled her legs to the sides, so I slipped between them. My hard length pressed up against her belly, and it took all my self-restraint not to take her right there in the tub.

I used one hand to hold myself up, while the other explored her body under the water. "Kat, you're so damn sexy." I breathed the words against her ear as I moved my kisses down her neck. I nipped and sucked and for the briefest moment worried that I might be leaving a mark on her skin. But I let the concern float away in the suds as my hand squeezed her breast and pinched her nipple, just enough to make her gasp and arch up into me.

Her good hand moved over my chest and, reflexively, I closed my eyes and memorized every inch of her touch. Her fingers felt so good on my skin as they ventured lower until finally— "Oh my God, Kat."

She squeezed my cock in her hand and began to slowly slide it up and down until my entire body vibrated, and I was only barely holding onto the little grasp of control I'd started with.

"If you keep that up, I'm going to—"

"And that would be bad because?"

I tore myself away from her neck and lifted my head so I looked directly into her eyes. "Because as good as this feels...and damn, does it ever feel good...more than anything, I want to be inside you, Kitty Kat."

Maybe it was the use of her nickname or the detail of what I'd just said, but I felt her tremble beneath me.

A moment later, her hand was gone, and her legs moved up and locked around my waist, holding me against her. My cock was poised at her entrance. "So, what are you waiting for then?"

Chapter Ten

KAT

IT WAS a good thing I was in the water because I thought I might completely self-combust. It had only taken the very slightest touch from Andy before I was squirming with need and desire. Never before had a man been able to make me feel the way this man did… Even after my trip to Vancouver, when I'd been so sure I would put him out of my head once and for all, I'd found myself comparing every man who asked me out on a date to Andy Fisher.

And if they did manage to get past dinner and drinks and were brave enough to try for a kiss…well, nobody came close to making me feel the way Andy did.

Which meant actually having sex with Andy could go one of two ways. He would either live up to the impossible standards I'd somehow made up for this sex god of a man to make me climax over and over again with his impossibly

huge cock, and completely ruin me for any other man. Or…
Andy would turn out to be a mere mortal after all, and the
many, many fantasies I'd had about him over the years
would be just that: fantasies. The idea that there was a man
made just for me, who knew exactly what buttons to push,
how to touch me, and where to kiss me, would turn out to
be nothing more than a silly dream. And I'd be freed from
the idea that despite the fact that Andy was completely
untouchable to me for anything more than the little trysts
we'd somehow managed to excuse, he truly was the *happy-
for-right-now* man, and nothing more.

Either way, it didn't matter because the only thing that
did matter at that moment was having Andy's hands on my
body, his lips on my mouth and, as promised, his cock
inside me.

I arched my body up against him, but he hesitated. My
eyes flew open in question.

"Birth control?"

I groaned, and my head fell back against the tub. I
wasn't on birth control because, well, there hadn't really
been any opportunity to need it.

Until now.

Reluctantly, I shook my head.

Immediately, Andy moved away and sat back against his
side of the tub.

I instantly missed the feel of his body against mine.
"Maybe it's a sign." I used a bubble-covered hand to push
my hair off my face.

"Sign for what?"

Before I could answer, Andy reached for me and, taking care of my injured wrist, spun me around in the tub so I was pressed up against him, nestled between his legs. His still-hard erection pressed up against my back when he pulled me tight against him.

Andy dipped his head and kissed my neck. One hand splayed across my belly, holding me in place; the other one slid lower and lower between my legs until finally, one finger circled my clit.

"The only thing I think it's a sign of is that we need to play a little bit more right here." He whispered the words as his fingers danced between my legs, and my breath hitched in my throat. "And then I'll carry you to your bed, where I know I will find a condom in the pocket of my pants."

My heart thumped wildly in my chest. He held me firmly, but I pressed back against him as much as I could until he groaned and pressed a finger inside my wet heat. I gasped as he added another.

"And then," he began to move his fingers inside me, "we will finally finish what we keep starting."

I couldn't formulate words. Instead, I let my head fall back against his chest. I groaned and wiggled as his thumb once more found my clit and pressed. "Andy! Oh."

"Oh yes." He growled against my ear. "Come for me, Kitty Kat."

He increased his pace until I was positive I was going to explode. The sensations ripped through me, and I cried out as the orgasm washed over me in waves. My body sagged against his, but Andy held me firm to keep me from slipping under the water. As I regained my senses, he once more pressed kisses along my neck, down to my shoulder.

"You are absolutely incredible, Kat. That was the sexiest thing I've—"

"Kat? Are you here?"

My eyes flew open at the same time that Andy shot straight up and out of the tub, sending water sloshing over the sides and onto the floor in huge waves.

There was now more water on the floor than in the tub, which normally would be cause for concern. But, at that moment, the only thing I was worried about was who the hell was in my condo, calling my name.

"Kat?"

The voice again. "Charli," I said, hissing my sister's name. "I don't know what she's doing here."

Andy groaned. "Your family," is all he said as he shook his head and moved for a towel. "They love you. No doubt Chase told her about your crash, and she's here to check on you."

I closed my eyes and sank down into the bubbles, stopping just before going underneath the water completely. For a moment, I considered ignoring my sister, but there was no way that would work. "Hide in the closet." I waved toward his pile of clothes. "Take those."

Andy nodded, scooped up his clothes with his free hand, and, right before slipping into the closet, blew me a kiss and wiggled his eyebrows, making me giggle.

"Kat?" My sister's voice brought me back to reality. "Are you—"

"I'm in the bath." I knew better than to think the idea of being in the bath would give me any kind of privacy from my sister.

Sure enough, a moment later, without knocking, Charli burst through the bathroom door and stopped short. "What on earth happened in here?"

I used my good arm to pull the bubbles, or what was left of them, around me. "By all means, Charli. Come on in." I rolled my eyes.

"Seriously, Kat. What happened in here? Are you okay?"

"I am…" I surveyed my bathroom and the massive amount of water on the floor. "I was…" I lifted my casted arm, which had somehow miraculously managed to stay dry, in the air. "I couldn't get out. I guess I made a little mess in my attempts."

Charli shook her head in wonder, but fortunately for me didn't push the issue any further. Instead, she gathered an armful of towels, laid them on the floor and, only once she'd deemed it safe, reached an arm out and helped me out of the tub and into a fluffy towel.

"I thought Craig's friend, Andy, was staying with you tonight?"

News certainly did travel in my family. "He is," I said as casually as I could manage. "I think he went to the guest room to change and freshen up."

Charli nodded. "It's a good thing I came by then. I can't imagine you'd want Craig's friend helping you out in this situation." She laughed at the idea of Andy seeing her little sister naked.

I managed to laugh along with her while I risked a glance toward the closet door.

"No," I said. "I'm glad you showed up when you did. I don't know what I would have done if you hadn't."

ANDY

I knew exactly what Kat would have done if Charli hadn't shown up. Right about now, she'd be lying on her back on the soft duvet of her king-sized bed, with her arms over her head, her red hair splayed over the pillow, and her pretty mouth open in a moan of ecstasy as I finally, mercifully pressed my painfully hard dick into her soft, inviting heat.

When we'd originally agreed to this ridiculous concept of *just friends*, I had no idea it would be such a torturous process. Not that I hadn't enjoyed every second with Kat, teasing and playing. But when it came to actually doing the deed, well, that was proving to be a whole lot more elusive than I'd ever expected.

"You're freezing, Kat. You need to get dressed." Charli's voice grew closer. "Let me grab you something from the—"

The door opened a crack at the same moment that Kat hollered.

"No!"

"No?"

Kat covered with a laugh. "No," she said. "Don't go in there. I know you'll freak out because it's totally unorganized. And besides," she continued, "my coziest sweatpants are downstairs in the laundry room. Do you mind grabbing them? I think there's a hoodie down there, too."

I was pretty sure I was standing right next to a shelf full of hoodies and cozy-looking clothes, but it wasn't as if I were going to offer any of them as suggestions. If Charli found me naked in her little sister's closet, there would be questions. Too many questions. And with a family as close as the Carlsons, there was no way that news of my naked presence wouldn't get back to Craig.

And if my best friend found out I was fooling around with his baby sister, well, there wouldn't be any coming back from that. I'd lose Craig, who was more like a brother to me than a friend, and there was no way I could risk that. After my parents died, Craig was the only real family I had. I couldn't lose him. Especially considering we were only having a little fun.

It wasn't serious with Kat. It was a silly little arrangement between friends. Nothing more.

I'd almost convinced myself of that, too, when the closet door flew open to reveal Kat, wrapped only in a towel, standing in front of me.

Despite the tenuous situation we were still in, I reached for her, unable to keep my hands off her, especially when she was half naked and her hair was dripping wet around her shoulders, but she stepped out of the way.

"Go," she hissed. "To the spare room. When you come

out, pretend you were in the shower or something. She can't know."

I nodded and did as I was told, because she was right. Charli couldn't know.

Thankfully, Kat lived in a two-story unit over her hair salon, with the bedrooms on a separate floor, which meant that I could slip into the spare room undetected while Charli was downstairs.

I took the opportunity to have a shower—a cold one—before getting dressed and joining the ladies in the living room, thirty minutes later. Kat was cuddled under an impossibly huge, fluffy blanket. Her sister had brought takeout and a selection of pastas that were spread out on the coffee table.

"Hey, Charli," I said as I entered the room. "I didn't hear you come in."

She greeted me with a hug.

"I see you've come to look after our little patient."

"I sure did," I said.

Charli gave me a strange look. Or maybe it was just my imagination.

"But she tells me that you've been taking very good care of her."

That was an understatement. If given half the chance, I'd take even better care of her, too.

"I only did what any good friend would do."

From the couch, Kat lifted her eyebrows and shook her head.

"Well, it's nice knowing she was being looked after,"

Charli said. "I brought dinner in case you haven't had a chance to eat. But I was actually going to head out soon and check on Craig, Lucy, and Meredith next. Poor things have been so sick."

"It sounds awful," I said. "I'm sure they appreciate you looking in on them."

"It's what I do. If it's not my baby and husband, it's the rest of this family." Charli grinned before turning to Kat. "Are you okay? You have everything you need?"

"I do," she said. "Thank you for rescuing me from the bathtub."

Charli laughed. "I'm just glad I was here." She looked at me. "That would have been awkward, wouldn't it?"

"So awkward." I tried to sound unaffected but wasn't entirely sure I was pulling it off.

"Okay," Charli once more focused on her little sister, "you ate, you're warm, and that pill I gave you will help you get a good night's sleep. Hopefully, you feel better in the morning."

"Pill?" I asked when a few minutes later I walked her to the door.

"A painkiller," she explained. "It will knock her out so she can get some solid sleep and heal. Hopefully, everyone is feeling better for the meeting tomorrow."

"I'll be fine." From the couch, Kat lazily raised her good arm and dropped it down.

Charli chuckled. "It looks like you might have to help her up to bed."

"Don't worry," I said. "I'll take good care of her."

Charli stood up from grabbing her bag and stared at me. "I know you will, Andy."

She looked at me so intently, for a moment I was certain she was going to call me out on exactly how well I was caring for Kat.

Instead, Charli smiled her trademarked bright smile. "Symon said he's been chatting with you about the job as the head trainer and staff physiotherapist for the ski team."

I glanced behind me, but Kat was out of earshot. "I didn't want to say anything until it was official." I nodded. "But, I'm hoping we can work out the details. It would be really nice to be back in Trickle Creek after all these years."

"Sorry." Charli reached for my arm and squeezed. "I didn't know it was a secret."

"It's not." I shrugged. "But until I know it's official—"

"Say no more." Charli held up a hand. "Your secret is safe with me. But I do hope it all works out. Craig will be so pleased to have you back, not to mention how excited a certain young lady would be."

It took me a moment to realize Charli was talking about Craig's daughter, Meri, and not Kat. Although I couldn't help but hope that Kat would also be happy to hear I was moving back to town.

The job would be a huge career move for me. But the fact that the position was in Trickle Creek, where Kat Carlson was, had only sweetened the offer.

"I'd love to be able to see more of little Meri," I said smoothly. "And of course, Craig, too." I chuckled, and Charli laughed.

"Of course." She flashed me another bright smile. "And hey, I know the real estate market can be kind of tricky in town right now. I have a good friend who is a top agent. She'll be able to find you something absolutely perfect. And she's pretty cute, too."

Charli winked, and I shook my head with a laugh. "I don't know if I'm really in the market." I didn't bother specifying whether I was talking about a house or a girlfriend.

"Trust me," Charli said. "She's perfect for you. Her name is Jess. She's brunette, attractive and fun. She's really involved in a beach volleyball league, too. I think you'll really like her."

It definitely sounded more like a setup than a real estate connection. Still, I didn't want to be rude to Charli. And it wasn't as if I could tell her that the only woman I was interested in dating was asleep in the next room. "She sounds great."

"She is." Charli beamed. "I'll text you her number, okay?"

I nodded. "I think I'd like that."

"Promise me you'll call her."

"I will." Hopefully, things would be finalized soon, and I truly would be looking for a more permanent place in Trickle Creek. Not that staying with Kat wouldn't have some benefits, too. Another shot of desire at the memory of what we'd been about to do in the bathtub earlier raced through me, and I worked hard to keep the reaction off my face.

Charli reached behind her for the door handle. "Take

care of our girl, Andy. I'm sure we'll see you soon." Charli gave me a quick hug, and she was gone.

My head spun in her wake.

It took me a moment to regain my senses and pull my thoughts together before returning to the living room. I leaned up against the door and took deep breaths, exhaling slowly.

That had been close. *Too close.*

And for what?

The little game I'd been playing with Kat put everything at risk. As an only child, I never had a close family growing up. My mother died when I was young, and my father might as well have died when she did. He spent the next fifteen years drinking and hiding from his life until finally, the year after I graduated, he drove his car into a tree, an empty bottle of whiskey on the seat next to him. My family had always been the Carlsons. All the siblings had adopted me as one of their own, and I valued that connection more than anything.

If any of the Carlsons ever found out about my situationship with their baby sister, they'd be beyond upset. And I knew exactly who would lose if that happened.

For the first time, I thought about it reasonably. I'd been insanely attracted to Kat for far too long, and in recent years, that attraction had grown to a whole lot more than just a physical one. But that didn't matter, because Kat had made it clear on more than one occasion that she didn't believe in happily ever after. And even if I could change her mind—and that was a big if, with a strong, independent woman like Kat—there was no reason for me to believe that she felt the same way about me.

It was a game to her. *I* was a game.

And as much as I wanted to, maybe it was no longer worth playing.

Not if it meant losing everything.

Chapter Eleven

KAT

WHATEVER CHARLI HAD GIVEN me for pain had worked.

I certainly didn't notice the throbbing in my wrist. In fact, I didn't feel much of anything anymore. It was getting harder and harder to keep my eyes open, and I'd already periodically nodded off a few times. But when I heard Charli and Andy talking in the other room, my eyes flew open.

"Trust me." I heard Charli say. "She's perfect for you. Her name is Jess. She's brunette, super cute and fun. She's really involved in a beach volleyball league, too. I think you'll really like her."

Perfect for him?

I knew Jess. She was super cute and fun. And there was no doubt that Andy would really like her. But it didn't mean

Charli should be setting him up with anyone. He didn't even live in Trickle Creek.

And if he did…

I strained to hear what they were saying. Charli was known for her history of playing matchmaker, so it probably wasn't too far-fetched that she should try setting Andy up, too. As far as Charli knew, he didn't have any other opportunities.

Not that I was an *opportunity*.

Besides, it's not as though Andy would actually take Charli up on her offer.

"She sounds great." Andy's voice was muffled, but I heard what I'd heard.

I tried to sit up, but my one good arm couldn't hold me.

"Promise me you'll call her?"

I held my breath at Charli's question, and a moment later exhaled with a deflated sigh when Andy said, "I will."

So that's how it was?

Not that I should have expected any different. He didn't owe me anything. It's not like we were a couple or anything.

If he wanted to date other people, that was none of my business. Besides, it was probably for the best, I thought as my eyes drifted closed again. Nothing was ever going to happen between us. Not in any kind of real way. Not beyond a secret rendezvous here and there. I'd always known it. And now I knew for sure that he felt the same way, too.

ANDY

Kat was sleeping when I finally made my way back to the living room. Her red hair was spread over the pillow, her mouth open just a little, and a soft snore escaped her lips.

She looked incredibly cute.

Something in my chest tightened.

I watched her for a moment before shaking away the dangerous thoughts that threatened to take hold.

I moved carefully, using special caution with her sore wrist as I scooped her up in my arms. Kat shifted and cuddled into my chest. Her face nuzzled against me, and she murmured something I couldn't quite make out.

"Ssh," I murmured as I made my way slowly up the stairs and into her room.

I shifted her into one arm as I pulled her comforter back and, as carefully as I could, set her down on the sheets. I tucked her in and brushed a strand of hair off her cheek.

It wasn't at all the way I'd thought the evening would end. And if I was being honest, it wouldn't have been my first choice. But, in the long run, it was probably the best ending for everyone involved.

Still…walking away from her was turning out to be harder than I'd expected.

I pressed two fingers to my mouth before lightly touching them to Kat's lips.

"Andy?" Her eyelids fluttered a little. "Is that you?"

"It's me." I reached for her good hand and squeezed a little. A dopey, drugged smile crossed her lips as she finally opened her eyes to look at me. Whatever Charli had given her was strong. "I'm here."

"Thank you," she said.

"You don't need to thank me." I spoke softly. "Go to sleep, and you'll feel a lot better in the morning."

"Will you be here when I wake up?"

I didn't want to lie to her, because the truth was that it would be better for both of us if I left and found somewhere else to spend the night.

"Don't think about me, Kat," I said instead. "Just get some sleep now." She closed her eyes, so I slid my hand out from under hers and took a step back. But her voice stopped me.

"I do think about you, Andy."

My gaze searched her face, but her eyes were still closed.

"I think about you a lot." Her words were slurred, only barely comprehensible. "A lot, a lot."

"Ssh, Kat. You're just—"

"I love you, Andy."

I froze.

She's medicated, I reminded myself.

"I love Charli, too," Kat continued. "And Craig and Asher, even though he can be…" She lifted her hand a little and dropped it again. "And Chase," she added after a moment. "And you."

Right.

"You're on some pretty good drugs." I grinned. "Go to sleep, Kat. I'll see you…I'll see you soon."

I waited a few more minutes until her breathing evened

out, signaling she was asleep, before I slipped from her room. I was in the guest room, packing up my overnight bag, still unsure where I should go, when the text from Charli came in with her friend's number.

Charli: Call her!

It felt like a sign, and not just because I needed a place to stay. Maybe it was time I grew up and moved on. I was too old to play these *happy for now* games. Especially with Kat, when there could never be a future with her.

I finished packing up my bag and was about to slip out the front door when another text message from Charli came through.

Charli: I'm glad you're there with her, Andy. It's good that she has family to take care of her.

Family.

Right.

It was another reminder that Charli and the rest of the Carlson clan—with the very notable exception of Kat—thought of me as family. And that was important. Really important.

I locked up and shut the lights off in the kitchen and the living room before once more heading up the steps to the guest room. I glanced at Kat's bedroom door but resisted the urge to poke my head inside, lest I be unable to walk away again.

Instead, I dropped my bag on the floor, flopped down on the guest bed, and picked up my phone to call Charli's friend.

She answered on the first ring.

Chapter Twelve

KAT

THE NEXT MORNING, when I made my way downstairs, besides a lingering ache in my wrist and a few bumps and bruises, I was surprised to find that I didn't feel nearly as rough as I thought I might.

The dream I'd had featuring Andy in my bed finally doing all the things he'd promised me while we'd been in the bathtub probably had something to do with the smile on my face as I walked into the kitchen.

"It looks like someone is feeling better." Andy crossed the room toward me, a cup of coffee in his hand. "You slept well?"

"Those pills Charli gave me really knocked me out." I stopped short of telling him about my dream.

He handed me the cup of coffee. "Still one sugar, two cream?"

I nodded. "Thank you. I can't remember the last time someone made me coffee."

Andy hesitated, and for a moment I wondered whether he was thinking about how many men may or may not have spent the night in my house. Of course, I was probably over-thinking it. Andy wasn't like that. *We* weren't like that.

"Well, I guess it pays to have me as a roommate." He winked at me before moving a safe distance away. "At least, a temporary one anyway."

I had no problem with having Andy as a roommate, especially if it meant that my dream might actually become reality. Finally. "Have you heard from Craig this morning? I hope they're feeling better. I'm sure you'd like to visit them too while you're in town." I shook my head and laughed a little. "I mean, I didn't mean to imply you'd come to visit me. I know that's—"

"You know I always like to visit you, Kitty Kat."

Something inside me melted a little the way it always did when Andy used my nickname.

"But I was thinking." His voice suddenly turned serious. He leaned up against the counter and crossed his arms. "This…thing we're doing. I…" He dropped his head and took a breath while I held mine.

I knew what was coming next.

"It's not a good idea, Kitty Kat."

And there it was. I'd known from the very first time we'd kissed in his apartment that this conversation was inevitable but secretly I'd been hoping maybe we could put it off a little longer.

I took another sip of my hot coffee and let him continue.

"It's dangerous," Andy said. "I mean, if Craig were to find out…if any of them found out, I…well, you know they'd freak out."

I nodded, because it was true. Shit would well and truly hit the fan if any of my siblings, but especially Craig, found out that I'd been fooling around with Andy.

"I just think maybe we should cool it a little bit," he continued. "Especially because—"

"Is this about Jess?" I hadn't meant to blurt it out, and once I did, I wished I could take it back, especially when the grin crossed his handsome face.

"So you were listening last night?"

I shrugged, trying a little too late for casual. "I was in and out of sleep. But I heard you promise Charli you'd call her."

Andy nodded slowly and chuckled a little to himself. "Well, it's not about Jess. Not really. But—"

"It's okay if it is," I added quickly. "Because you're right. We need to stop…" I waved my cast between us. "Whatever this is. We don't need Craig losing his shit over something that doesn't mean anything."

For a moment, I thought Andy might say something else.

Instead, he nodded once and clapped his hands together. "Good. I'm glad you agree. Because I did call Jess, but it's not what—"

The sharp ring of my phone interrupted us. It was probably for the best because despite how I was trying to pretend otherwise, I did care if he called Jess, and the last thing I needed was to hear all the details.

I pulled my cell phone from my back pocket. "It's Charli." I pressed the button to accept the call and put a smile in my voice.

"Good morning, big sis."

"Someone sounds like they're feeling better."

I looked directly into Andy's eyes. "I feel great."

"Well, that's good news because I just heard from Steven."

Steven had been our father's right-hand man, and along with William, the family lawyer, he had been responsible for administering Michael Carlson's will. "Steven? Is everything okay?"

"Yes and no," Charli said. "Apparently there's been an emergency in William's family, and he needs to leave town later today, so the family meeting has to happen today."

"Today?" A thrill of excitement shot through me, followed quickly by a spark of fear.

"Are you feeling up to it? Because we can—"

"Of course." Even if my arm had been cut off, there was no way I was going to miss the meeting. "I feel great. But what about Craig? Is he feeling up to it?"

"Craig said he's fine. I just wanted to make sure—"

"I'm fine," I said again. "What time do I need to be there?"

ANDY

My quads burned and I could feel the sweat trickling down my back, but I wasn't done yet. No, I wasn't going to be done until I got Kat Carlson out of my mind once and for all.

Even in my fatigued state, I knew that was never going to happen.

It didn't matter how many squats or lunges or burpees I did—I was never going to get Kat out of my head. The best I could hope for was pretending long enough that I might start to believe it. Even a little bit.

"Man, you are on a mission."

I spun around to see Symon Scott, Charli's husband, with their six-month-old baby strapped to his chest. "Hey." I raised my arm in greeting and continued to squat. "You found me."

With the rest of the Carlson clan meeting up at the big house, the family home, for the big meeting, I needed to find a way to keep myself busy for a few hours, so I'd reached out to Symon to meet me for a workout. After all, it looked like we'd be working together before too long.

"You started without me."

"Sorry, man." I finished my last set of reps and reached for my bottle of water. "I needed to get moving." There was no way I was going to volunteer why I was feeling so restless. "This must be Poppy." I smiled at the little girl, who responded with a smile. "I've heard a lot about this little cutie."

"She's pretty sweet." Symon pressed a kiss to the top of his little girl's head. "And she has the added benefit of adding weight to my workouts. You think you can manage a baby-friendly training session?"

"No problem." I chuckled. "I'll even hold her while you do your burpees."

Symon shook his head with a laugh and after a quick warm-up, joined in with my workout.

Poppy lasted twenty minutes before she demanded to be let out of her confinement. Symon spread out a blanket on the grass, and I joined him for some stretching while the baby kept herself busy with a stuffed toy.

"I heard a rumor that a contract was being sent your way later today," Symon said while we stretched our quads. "I'm not going to lie, Andy. I really hope you're going to sign it. I think you'll be a great addition to the ski team. Your expertise, never mind your personal experience with the hill and the sport, will be a huge asset to us all. Besides, it would be good to have you around a bit more after so long."

I laughed. When we were kids, I'd been on the ski team with Symon for a few years, although it became clear pretty fast that Symon Scott had talent far beyond any of the rest of us. A talent that eventually won him multiple world titles and medals at the Olympics. He was still a force to be reckoned with in the ski world, but had recently retired from competition and had taken on the role of head coach, which worked out perfectly considering the national ski team had recently chosen Trickle Creek as their headquarters and main training facility.

"You're just saying that because you want to kick my ass again on the slopes."

"Obviously." Symon winked. "But truly, it'll be good to have you back in town." He narrowed his eyes. "Assuming you accepted the job?"

"You would think that the head coach would be the first to know."

"I gave the committee my professional opinion." Symon shrugged. "And as amazing as that is, it only goes so far. But I did hear that they were offering you the job."

It was true. The contract and official job offer had come through in my email earlier that morning. I was ninety-nine percent sure I was going to accept it. After all, being the head trainer for the national ski team was a massive career move. Never mind the fact that the job was in my home-town, which meant I would finally be able to get out of the big city and back to my roots, and the only family I'd ever really known. *And Kat.*

"They did offer," I said after a moment. "And yes, I'm going to accept. Why wouldn't I? It's an amazing opportunity, and I can't thank you enough for letting me know about it so I could throw my hat in the ring."

"Like I said. It'll be good to have you around again." Right on cue, Poppy giggled and threw her toy. "See? And I'm not the only one who thinks so."

I reached across the blanket and danced the toy back toward the baby. "You're going to be happy to have me back in town, are you?"

Again, Poppy squealed, clearly delighted by me.

I couldn't help but think of Kat and whether she would be just as excited at the prospect of having me around more. Just as quickly, I pushed the thought from my mind because it didn't matter. It couldn't.

"Have you told Craig yet?"

Symon's question pulled me from my thoughts, and a flash of guilt raced through me. Here I was thinking about Kat and how she'd feel to have me around more when I hadn't even considered how my best friend would react to the news that I'd be moving back.

I really did need to get my priorities straight and get out from under the spell of the redhead. It was never going to happen.

"I haven't had a chance." I put the toy in front of Poppy and sat up on the blanket. "Now that he's feeling better… maybe after the family meeting, if you don't think it'll be a bad time."

Symon had way more experience with these Carlson family meetings because he'd been with Charli through most of them—including when it was her turn.

"Nah." Symon replaced Poppy's toy with a teething biscuit. "I'm sure it'll be fine. Usually, it's only kind of hard on the person who's impacted, and that'll be Kat." He shrugged. "And from what I understand, Kat's been pretty excited for her turn, so I'm sure everyone will just be relieved that it's almost over."

"I bet they will. It's been a long process."

"But not an entirely bad one." Symon raised an eyebrow. "Maybe don't tell them I said that." He laughed.

"But if you think about it, I don't think any of the Carlsons would disagree. After all, they've all met the loves of their lives because of all of this."

It was true. All four of Kat's older siblings had found love during the process of carrying out their father's wishes. I hadn't thought of that before. "Do you think the same will happen for Kat?"

Just voicing the question out loud gave me pause. It was true that I could never be with Kat. Not more than a few hookups that should have never happened. But it was equally true that the idea of her being with anyone else did not sit well with me.

Symon finished his bottle of water and screwed the top back on before crushing it with his hand. "I mean, I don't see why not. She's a catch, and if history is anything to go by...time will tell." He glanced at the clock on his phone. "They should be finished soon. I should probably get going. Why don't you come back to the house with me, and you can tell Craig and the others about the job?"

"Isn't this like a family-only kind of thing?"

"Andy. You *are* family." Symon shook his head with a chuckle. "Besides, the meeting will be over by the time we get there, and everyone will be happy to see you and hear the good news."

KAT

"You look like you might throw up."

I swallowed hard, not entirely sure I wouldn't, and turned to look at my brother. "Shouldn't I be saying that to you? Are you sure you're even healthy enough to be here?"

"I could probably use some sleep." Craig shrugged. "But I'm fine. Whatever it was that we had was only a twenty-four-hour bug or something. I'm just sorry I missed the ride yesterday."

I held up my cast and lifted my eyebrows.

"Okay, maybe I'm not totally sorry I missed the ride. How's it feel?"

"Like I cracked my wrist." I laughed. "It'll be fine. It wasn't that bad, and the doctor said the cast should come off in a few weeks and then I can wear a brace. I might have to move a few clients around, but it won't be too big a deal hopefully."

"Assuming you're still going to be working." Asher sat down on the couch next to me and pulled me in for a side hug. "Don't forget what happened to me. Dad pulled work right out from under me with my special instructions."

Asher was the middle child, but the only one of us who still worked in the family business Carlson Corp, which was responsible for most of the major tourism efforts in Trickle Creek. Years earlier, when the mines shut down, Michael Carlson saw an opportunity to pivot the town's main industry and revived the local ski hill with a stunning lodge, turning it into a vacation destination. Over time, he added a world-class golf course and multiple condominium developments, all of which had turned things around for the town and the people of Trickle Creek.

Asher had taken over the role of CEO and was doing an excellent job of it, but at the last family meeting it was revealed that in order to keep our inheritance in the family, Asher would have to walk away from his job for six months and live in a log cabin in the woods.

"Right," Craig teased. "And you hated it, too, didn't you, Asher?"

We all laughed, including Chase and Charli, who'd also joined us in our father's office for the next phase of the will reading.

"I think it worked out pretty well for you." Charli squeezed Asher's shoulder.

"You know I can't argue with that," Asher said. "I wouldn't have Noa right now if it weren't for all this." He waved his hand to encompass the office, all of us, and the reason we were all there.

"And it's your turn, little sis." Chase winked at me. "Do you think you'll get as lucky as the rest of us?"

"Do you mean, do you think I'll find someone and live happily ever after like the four of you?" It wasn't a secret that I'd been waiting for my turn, and I knew that my brothers and sisters all thought that it was at least in part because the rest of them had all fallen in love. "You know I don't care about that, right?"

Charli gave me a look that told me she didn't believe a word I said, but I only shook my head and focused on the two men at the front of the room behind my father's desk. "Can we get started?"

The lawyer, William Evans, smiled and nodded. "If you're all ready, this will be a short meeting since you all know what to expect."

I barely heard anything that came out of the lawyer's mouth for the first few minutes as he went over how the meeting would work and what it meant. We all knew very well what was happening. Our father, Michael Carlson, had left each of us specific instructions to be carried out over a period of six months before the next section of the will would be read. The next section always involved another child and another set of instructions.

I was last.

It was my turn.

Finally, William looked at me specifically and said, "Kat. I'm sure you know what's coming next?"

I nodded and sat up in my chair, hardly able to breathe as I waited for my orders.

"This time it's a little different," William continued.

"Different?" Chase and Asher both spoke at once. They exchanged glances, but it was Chase who asked, "What do you mean, different?"

William smiled a little and adjusted the stack of papers in front of him before he started reading.

"The fifth and final section of Michael Carlson's will requires that Katherine Carlson complete the enclosed list of tasks in a time period of no longer than six complete calendar months."

"Tasks?"

William Evans nodded and passed an envelope to Steven, who crossed the room and handed it to me.

"May I suggest that you read through the tasks privately?"

"Privately?" I looked to Craig and then turned to meet Charli's gaze before accepting the envelope. "Are the tasks a secret?"

"The terms of the will don't specify if the tasks are to be kept secret or not," William said.

"But there are a few things that might be more personal in nature," Steven added.

"You've looked at the list?"

Steven nodded.

"Steven has been appointed to act as an adjudicator as there might be a situation or two where the completion of a task isn't necessarily straightforward."

"What kind of list are we talking about here?" Asher sat up in his seat. "This sounds a little wishy-washy, if you ask me."

"I have to agree with him," Chase added. "Everyone else had very clear terms they had to meet. This doesn't feel quite so official."

"I'm sure William wouldn't allow this if it weren't completely legal," Charli chimed in.

"It is legal," Craig said. "Isn't it?"

I stared at the envelope in my hand while my siblings argued around me. I knew with complete certainty that it didn't matter what was written on the list; I'd complete

every single last item.
No matter what.

Chapter Thirteen

ANDY

I'D SPENT most of my teenage years at the big house with Craig and the rest of the Carlson clan. I'd felt just as much at home there as at my own house, maybe more some days. It had been years since I'd walked through the doors, but the moment I did, it felt just like old times. Especially because the sound of the Carlson siblings' raised voices coming from the kitchen was the first thing I heard.

I hesitated, but only for a moment before making my way down the hall.

"We need to know what's on the list. That's all there is to it." I heard Asher's voice first.

"No we don't," Charli's calm, controlled voice said. "Whatever's on the list is Kat's business. If she wants to share, she will. And if she doesn't—"

"Then we'll never know if she can complete everything."

Again, I hesitated. They were obviously discussing the outcome of the family meeting, and even though I was just like family... I wasn't family. I turned to sneak away, not wanting to interrupt, but before I could make my getaway, I was spotted.

"Andy? Andy Fisher, is that you?"

Too late.

I turned around to see Annie Darling come around the corner. "Hey." I lifted a hand and greeted her with a hug and a kiss on the cheek. I'd known Annie when we were in school years ago, but I'd seen her more recently as Chase's fiancée.

"Do they know you're here?" She pointed toward the kitchen, and I shook my head.

"I was actually going to come back later," I said. "It sounds like family business, and I—"

"You *are* family." Annie linked her arm through mine. "Besides, you'll be a good distraction. They've been like this since they came out of the office," she said. "Just between you and me, I'll be glad when these meetings are finished with and they can all just move on." She winked. "But I'm not complaining, because they did lead me to Chase."

Before I could add anything, Annie stopped and stared at me. "Oh. Do you think Kat will finally find someone now, too?"

"What do you mean?" I didn't like the flush that raced

through my body at the suggestion that Kat would *find someone*.

"Oh, come on." Annie smacked my arm a little. "You know exactly what I mean. Every time a new part of the will is read, that Carlson sibling ends up not only completing their task, but falling in love. It's Kat's turn now."

I had a strong, almost violent reaction to the idea of Kat falling in love, but I forced myself to swallow and paste a smile on my face. "Symon mentioned that, too." I shrugged. "I guess we'll see."

She gave me a sly look. I wasn't stupid; I knew there was a very good chance Kat had told her at least something about the two of us hooking up. But Annie also knew better than to say anything. Nobody needed the rest of the family finding out.

Together, we walked into the kitchen, arm in arm. "Look who I found in the hall."

Everyone in the room turned to look at us.

"Andy!" Craig was the first to greet me with a hug and a friendly slap on the back.

"Glad to see you're feeling better, man. Sorry to intrude. I can come—"

"Just a twenty-four-hour thing," Craig interrupted me. "And don't you dare think about leaving. This conversation needs to end anyway," he said in my ear before stepping back.

"It's good to see you, Andy." Asher greeted me next, followed by Chase before I gave Charli another hug.

By the time I was done greeting everyone properly, the

tension in the room seemed to have dissipated a little bit. I looked around, one critical person missing from the group. "Where's Kat?"

"She's probably—"

"She went home," Charli said sharply, giving her younger brother a strong look. "To read her letter," she added. "Privately. Which is her right."

Asher looked like he might disagree again, but after a moment, he crossed his arms over his chest and leaned against the counter, silent.

Charli nodded with satisfaction as Symon joined us in the kitchen, along with Noa, Asher's new fiancée.

"Have you told them the good news?" Symon looked pointedly at me, and I shook my head.

"Good news?" Craig raised an eyebrow. "I think we could all use a little of that right about now."

It wasn't how I planned to tell the Carlson family, but there didn't seem to be any reason not to. I shrugged and held my hands out. "Well, it turns out that you're all going to be seeing a lot more of me in the future, because just before I came over here, I officially accepted the position of the head trainer for the national downhill ski team. I'm moving back to Trickle Creek."

My announcement was met with various cheers and whoops of congratulations, followed by more hugs and kisses that filled me with the kind of happiness I hadn't felt in a very long time.

"Thank God you're going to be around more," Craig said as he handed me a beer to toast to the news.

"Why is that? I mean, I know you missed me and all." I laughed and clinked bottles with my friend.

"Things with the shop have really picked up," Craig said. "And now that Lucy and I…well, you know how it is when you couple up."

I didn't. When I didn't say anything, Craig continued. "Well, anyway, we're all so busy with everything that I'm a little worried about Kat right now and the pressure she's under."

"I take it that has to do with the meeting you all just had?"

Craig nodded. "She was given a list of things to do instead of just one thing."

"A list?"

"But the thing is, we don't know what's on it."

The argument I'd walked in on suddenly made a lot more sense.

Craig took a drink from his bottle before he continued. "Anyway, I think it'll be good to have someone else to talk to who isn't one of us. Besides, we're not allowed to help." He shook his head. "Anyway, you're like a brother to Kat. You've always been close."

If only he knew.

I nodded while I drank to avoid making eye contact.

"I know you'll probably have a lot to do, what with moving back and starting a new job, but if you—"

"Consider it done, man." I agreed before I could think better of it. "Don't give it another thought. I'll be there for her." I swallowed hard. "Whatever she needs."

KAT

The moment I walked into my apartment, I knew I'd made the right decision not to open the letter in front of my siblings. The quiet welcomed me, and I went straight to the kitchen to make a cup of tea before I took my envelope into the living room, where I pulled my fluffy knit blanket over my legs and settled in.

The little two-story space over my hair salon wasn't big and it wasn't fancy by any means. But it was mine. And it was peaceful. Free from the bickering and clamor of my siblings, who were no doubt still at the big house debating how they could force me to tell them all what was on the list my father had left me.

I smiled a little to myself with the knowledge that they were probably all going crazy because I'd slipped away.

There was very little doubt in my mind that I was going to share the contents of my letter and the list with the rest of them. But at least for now, I could have the space to process things on my own first.

I turned the manila envelope over in my hands and took a deep breath. "Okay, Dad. What have you got for me?"

I exhaled slowly as I slid my finger under the envelope flap and slid the papers from within. My breath caught in my throat at the sight of my father's handwriting. I'd known it was coming. All my siblings had their personal letter from Michael Carlson; of course I'd have mine, too.

Still.

Holding it in my hand felt different as it all became very, very real.

> *Kat. My baby girl.*
>
> *I'm sorry I had to save you for last. I'm sure the last few months have been hardest on you while you waited your turn.*
>
> *You were never very good at that.*

I shook my head with a laugh. He wasn't wrong.

> *But there was a very good reason for that and I think you'll agree, because this challenge might be the hardest one yet. At least for you, kiddo. First, I want to make sure that you know how proud I am of you.*

My chest tightened, and I pressed a palm against my heart. I knew my father was proud of me, but I couldn't remember ever hearing the words come out of his mouth. I blinked back tears as I continued to read.

> *I never said that enough, did I? Or maybe not at all. And for that, I'm so sorry, kiddo. Because I am immensely proud of your talent and your hard work. You've always been so driven and known exactly what you wanted. And then you've gone after it. What you've created with your shop at such a young*

age is nothing short of incredible and a true testament to all your unrelenting hard work.

A swell of pride rose up inside me. Even from beyond the grave, my father's words impacted me deeply.

You're so much like me in so many ways, kiddo. I'm afraid that not only did you inherit your exceptionally high drive to succeed and ability to focus on a goal from me, but also your workaholic tendencies. It took me a long time to learn that there needs to be a balance in life, and truthfully, I wasn't always good at achieving that balance, especially after your mother died and I threw myself into work as a way to cope with losing her.

But if there is one thing I know for sure, it's that life is so much richer when your work—no matter how much you love it—isn't your only focus. I see you already going down the same path as I did, but only at a much younger age. And that's why I've given you this particular challenge, Kat. I don't want you to waste even one moment of your life by working it away.

I've given you a list of sorts. Some of these things might be familiar to you as something I wished I would have done, or made the time to do. Some might surprise you. But I promise you that each and every task I've given you has been thought out and they are all equally important, so don't dismiss anything out of hand.

I know that everything you do, you do with one hundred percent effort and a full heart, and I know this will be the same, kiddo.

Have fun with it and try to think of me a little bit on the way because I wish I could be right there tackling each of these challenges alongside you. Well, most of them. But you'll know which ones are for you and you alone.

Love always, Dad.

I took a moment to let my father's words sink in before I slid the second piece of paper from the envelope. From the moment William announced that Dad had given me a list of items to complete, I'd suspected I might know what a few of the tasks were, based on some conversations I'd had with him over the years. After a quick scan of the list, my suspicions were confirmed.

— **Learn to paint.**

On more than one occasion, he'd told me how envious he'd always been of people who had true creative talent. That one didn't surprise me. I smiled at the thought of wielding a paintbrush. No doubt it would be an epic disaster, but it was doable.

— **Skydive, bungee jump, or parachute.**

My smile twisted into a frown. That would be a lot harder. I hated heights. When my dad had first told me that he'd once had the opportunity to bungee jump when he was young on a trip to Australia and he'd always regretted not doing it, I'd shaken my head and told him at that time that it was something I'd never do.

Apparently, he'd had other plans. I kept reading.

— **Sing karaoke in public.**

I laughed out loud. I had the worst singing voice in the family, second only to maybe my father.

— **Hike to the top of Pulpit Peak.**

My breath hitched in my throat. We'd talked about doing that hike together one day. It was one of the most infamous hikes in the area, and a badge of honor for many of the locals. I'd never been a big hiker beyond some of the local trails, but on one of our monthly lunch dates, my father had mentioned how he'd always wanted to do it, and I'd agreed to do it with him.

Of course, something always got in the way; we'd both been too busy and he'd died before we got that chance.

And that was the point of the list. I blew out a breath and kept reading, skimming through a few more items.

— **Learn another language.**

That one might be a reach. How was I supposed to learn another language in such a short time?

I shook my head and kept reading.

— **Learn how to salsa dance, and perform in front of an audience.**

My eyes got wide at that one. Dance? The only dancing

I ever did was when I'd had a few drinks and there was live music at Brickhouse. And even then, it could hardly be considered actually dancing.

Still, the list mostly seemed manageable. Although a few of the items were going to be challenging, the final thing on my father's list just served to prove that everything else leading up to it was just the warm-up to the main event.

— **Go on a solo overnight backpacking trip and sleep under the stars.**

I sucked in a breath. My father knew exactly how I felt about being alone in bear country. In fact, he'd been the one who'd hammered home safety in the woods and how they should never go out alone.

I swallowed hard and shook my head, because it didn't matter what crazy things he'd put on his *bucket list*. My father had known, just as I did: no matter what, I'd cross off every single thing.

Chapter Fourteen

ANDY

IT WAS ONLY a short drive from the big house where I left the Carlson family, back to the plaza and Kat's apartment. But by the time I parked my car and picked up my phone, I had at least a dozen messages from Charli's real estate agent friend, Jess, with listings for me to choose from.

I chuckled and was about to turn my phone off to ignore them altogether, when a call came in. I answered with a shake of my head and laughed out loud when the woman on the other end of the line introduced herself.

"I thought it might be easier to just give you a call," Jess said. "I don't mean to be so forward, but Charli—"

"Is pushy." I grinned. I started to walk from the parking lot through the pedestrian-only plaza where Kat's shop was, with her apartment over the top. "I think she's more excited about me moving back to Trickle Creek than I am."

"She did seem pretty enthused," Jess agreed. "I'm sorry if I'm overstepping, Andy. It's just she made it sound like you were pretty serious, and in this market, it's really important to be on top of things."

I stopped under the gazebo and looked up at Kat's apartment. It was still too early in the evening to see any lights on inside, but I knew she was up there. I couldn't help but wonder what she was thinking and how she was feeling about the letter her father had left her. I'd meant it when I told Craig I'd be there for her no matter what she needed, and I was eager to get up there to see how I could help.

"It's fine," I said to Jess. "And you're right, I should probably give it a little bit more thought." I started walking again and let myself in the door that would take me up to the apartment.

"I have a lot to show you. But I think it would be better to get a feel for what exactly it is you're looking for first."

I stopped outside the door. "Sounds good. Why don't we meet for coffee? It'll be nice to put a face to the name."

"Great. I'll send over some options, and we can go from there."

I ended the call and tucked my phone away before turning the door handle and letting myself in. "Kat?"

"In here."

"Hey." I wasn't sure what to expect when I walked into her living room, but I didn't expect Kat to be lying flat on the floor of her living room with her arms and legs outstretched. "Kat?" I stood over her with a tentative smile on my face.

She didn't answer, but opened one eye and then closed it again.

I dropped my car keys on the coffee table before shoving it over to make room for me to lay down next to her.

I stretched out on the hardwood floor and closed my eyes. We stayed that way without speaking for a few minutes before I slowly reached my hand over and threaded my fingers through hers.

I squeezed gently just to let her know I was there for her and wouldn't rush her or pressure her into talking if she wasn't ready. I couldn't even begin to imagine what it would be like to go through the emotional roller coaster that Kat and her brothers and sister had been through with Michael Carlson's death.

It was never easy to lose a parent, but what Kat was going through was next level.

When I heard what sounded like a sniffle, I turned my head and saw a tear slip down her cheek. Still, I waited, and a moment later, her eyes fluttered open.

"You okay, Kitty Kat?"

She pressed her lips together and shook her head.

I tugged her hand and pulled her toward me, until she was lying with her head on my chest. Having her in my arms felt like the most natural thing in the world. She fit perfectly as I wrapped my arm around her back and stroked her hair.

We didn't speak, the only sound Kat's soft sobbing.

"It's going to be fine," I said after a moment. "Whatever

it is, you don't have to do it alone, okay? I'm here for you. No matter what."

Kat lifted her head and looked up at me. My heart clenched at the sight of her tear-streaked face. More than anything, I hated to see Kat sad.

"You'll help me?"

I shifted, so I could sit up, but still keep my arm around her. "You know I'll help you, Kitty Kat. Whatever you need. I've got you."

She opened her mouth to say something, but closed it again. Finally, a sad smile took shape on her lips. "I appreciate that, but I know you have a life to get back to in Vancouver, and I—"

"Don't worry about that." It didn't feel like the right time to tell her my news, but I needed her to know I wasn't going anywhere. Even if I hadn't taken the job, there was no way I could leave her now. Not when she needed me.

"But you—"

I silenced her with a finger to her lips. "I promise you, Kat. I'll be here for you, whatever you need. Don't worry about anything else, okay?"

She nodded. "Thank you."

"Anything for you. You know that."

The surge of love I felt for her in that moment threatened to overwhelm me. It wasn't often that Kat Carlson let down her guard at all, and it was even rarer when she asked or accepted any offer of help.

I reached out and rubbed my thumb gently over her

cheek to dry her tears. She closed her eyes and, in that moment, with all her defenses dropped away, she looked so vulnerable. The bravado she normally wore like armor was gone. It was just Kat.

I leaned forward to close the gap between us and pressed my lips gently to hers in a soft kiss.

KAT

I let myself sink into the kiss.

His lips on mine felt good. It felt safe. *He* felt safe.

And I believed him when he said that everything would be okay.

His presence gave me that. From the moment he'd come in and laid down next to me, I'd felt like everything might be okay.

"You look confused."

Andy reached for me, but I pulled back. As much as I would love to fall into Andy's arms and his kiss and…maybe more, it wasn't the right time.

I shook my head. "It's just a lot to take in." It wasn't a lie. "I'm trying to sort out all of this." I waved my arm around. "My dad gave me a list of things to complete."

"I heard." He shrugged before he explained. "I stopped by the big house before I came back. I have to say, your family is all…well…"

"Wait." I held up a hand with a laugh. "Don't tell me. Asher is freaking out because I left without showing them the list." I bit my bottom lip. "And maybe Chase, too. They're a lot more alike than either of them would care to admit."

Andy laughed, because we all knew it was true.

"Charli and Craig are probably defending my right to have some time alone. But secretly, they're also freaking out because nobody really knows how I'm going to react to all this."

I knew my brothers and sister well.

"You're not wrong, Kat. That's exactly what's happening over there."

"I know." I shook my head and moved into the kitchen. More than anything, I needed a drink.

"For what it's worth, I don't think they have anything to worry about." Andy followed me and pulled two wine glasses out of the cupboard when he saw me go for a bottle of red.

"You don't?" I twisted the top off and poured us each a generous glass before leaning back against the counter.

"Not at all." He took a sip of his wine, and I tried not to look at his lips when he licked a drop from them. "You're a strong, capable woman, Kitty Kat."

I couldn't help but laugh. "I don't sound all that strong *or* capable when you call me that."

He looked directly at me. "Does it bother you?"

I shook my head.

"Good," was all he said.

I took a drink of my wine and let it roll around my mouth for a moment before swallowing. "You really think I'm strong and capable?"

"Absolutely. It doesn't matter what's on that list—you're not going to have any problem knocking it out."

"Did you mean what you said about helping me? Or were you just saying that because it's what I wanted to hear?"

Andy set his wine down and closed the distance between us before grabbing my hand. "I will never say things just because I think it's what you want to hear." He squeezed my hand. "I only say what I mean, Kat. I'll never blow smoke."

"So you're really going to help me out?" I wiggled my eyebrows in an effort to lighten the mood, because what I really needed was to let the heaviness of the afternoon go. "No matter what's on the list?" I forced myself not to think about the final item. I'd focus on the manageable things, like jumping out of airplanes or off bridges.

"No matter what," Andy agreed without hesitation. "I told you I would, and I will. Especially since you're kind of crippled right now."

I narrowed my eyes and resisted the urge to smack him with my cast. "This thing is coming off soon. And you know it."

"So, you don't want my help?"

I shot him a look and moved to the kitchen table. "I want you to agree before I tell you what's on the list."

He retrieved his glass of wine and pulled out the chair across from me. "Done. I agree."

"Just like that?"

He shrugged. "I meant it when I said it, Kitty Kat. I'm here for you. No matter what."

I lifted my wine glass and looked over the rim. "How do you feel about jumping out of an airplane?"

Chapter Fifteen

ANDY

"I CANNOT BELIEVE you talked me into doing this."

The smile Kat flashed me was worth any of the anxiety I was feeling at that moment from standing on the top of the out-of-service rail bridge that spanned the river gorge over a hundred feet in the air. And I *was* feeling a lot of anxiety.

"You agreed to help," she reminded me with a mischievous smile. "No matter what. Besides, it could be worse. We could be in an airplane right now."

She was right. On both counts. I *had* agreed to help her with all the things on her list, and it very well could have been an airplane that she'd chosen. Not that it could have felt any worse than it already did.

"I'm surprised you look so casual about all of this. You hate heights."

It was something we had in common from when we

were young. Craig used to tease us when we were on the chair lift together. Both Kat and I refused to ever look down, and on the few occasions when the chair would be stopped, we would take turns keeping each other occupied, so that neither of us would panic.

"I do." She swallowed hard and tilted her head up to look at the few fluffy white clouds in the otherwise bright-blue sky. The sun would set soon, but for now we had a gorgeous day. "So do you."

I laughed nervously, but there was no way I was going to walk away from the challenge. Not now. I'd given her my word, and I intended to keep it.

"Okay, you two." The woman named Juniper, who looked far too young to be officially in charge of either of our lives, stood from where she'd been crouching in front of us. "You're all strapped in."

I swallowed hard and reached for Kat's good hand. It was clammy, and she clenched mine tightly while we listened to Juniper give us instructions. Not that there were many. It all seemed pretty straightforward.

Step backward.

Fall.

Sure, there was a bungee rope attached to our ankles, but all at once it didn't feel adequate to be the only thing standing between us and the riverbed a hundred feet below.

"Are you sure you want to do this?"

She shook her head. "I *know* I don't want to do this." She squeezed her eyes shut, and when she opened them again, I saw the familiar flash of determination that meant Kat was prepared to do whatever she needed to do.

"Same." I winked, and she laughed.

Juniper gave us each a concerned look. "If you want to back out, I need to—"

"We're not backing out."

"No way."

We spoke at the same time, and Juniper chuckled. "Okay. Since you guys decided to go tandem, you need to hold onto each other in some way."

No problem. I had no intention of letting go of Kat while we plunged through the air.

"You can hold hands if you want." She gestured with her head to our linked hands. "But I'd recommend an embrace. It's a pretty intense experience. I don't know what your relationship is, but it's pretty wicked to experience it with someone else. It's intimate, really."

A shot of desire that I had no business feeling at that moment raced through me.

I turned to face Kat. "I think that's the perfect way to do this, don't you?"

I didn't wait for an answer before I wrapped my arms around her petite body and pulled her close. She responded by reaching around my back and squeezing with her good hand. Her cast rested heavily against me. I tightened my grip. There was no way I was going to let go.

I looked down into her eyes. "Breathe with me, Kitty Kat."

She nodded and fell into rhythm with my deep breaths.

"Perfect," Juniper said. "Now, whenever you're ready, just count to three and step off."

I waited a beat. "Ready?"

Kat nodded, and I counted.

The next thing I knew, we were falling through the air; someone was screaming and the world was rushing past me in a blur as we plunged toward the river.

It took me a moment to realize I was the one screaming, and right when I did, we hit the end of the bungee rope and bounced back up through the air.

My scream turned to hooting and hollering, and Kat joined in, too, as we bounced through the air.

"That was incredible!"

"Holy shit!"

The world around us was still a blur, but I focused on Kat, who came into perfect clarity. Her cheeks were tear-streaked, but she had a grin on her face. She'd never looked sexier.

"That was absolutely——"

I cut her off with a kiss. She moaned into my mouth, and I pulled her even closer while I greedily deepened the kiss, needing so much more in that moment.

When I finally pulled away so we could take a much-needed breath, we were both breathing heavily.

"This is crazy." Kat looked around and laughed. "We're upside down."

"It sure looks different from this angle, doesn't it?"

She laughed even harder. "My hair must be insane."

I didn't take my eyes off her. "You've never looked more fucking gorgeous than you do right now."

The laughter died on her lips as she locked eyes with me again. "She wasn't wrong when she said it was an intimate experience."

Kat sucked on her bottom lip, and I was completely lost to her once more.

"As soon as we get out of here, I'll show you something a hell of a lot more intimate than this, Kitty Kat."

KAT

My body felt like it was going to explode if I didn't have him inside me. Now.

I hardly remembered how we got back to the bridge surface. And I had almost no recollection of the debriefing by Juniper, or walking hand in hand with Andy off the bridge to his parked car.

My blood was running so hot that the only thing I could focus on was getting him naked as quickly as possible. There was literally nothing else that mattered.

The moment he sat in the driver's seat and turned the key, I was already climbing over the armrest to him, but he stopped me with a gentle hand.

"Kat. Let me...ohh." His eyes closed, his mouth open as I ran my palm over his very hard cock that was straining against the zipper of his jeans. "Shit, Kat. Not here."

"Yes. Here."

He groaned and again, his eyes shut as he momentarily gave himself over to the pleasure I was giving him with only the simplest touch. "Let me drive. To somewhere a little more private."

It made sense, and even through my lust-driven fog, I could see the value of not getting arrested for public indecency. "Okay." But just because I'd agreed didn't mean I was going to make it easy for him. Andy put the car in drive, and as deftly as I could with one wrist in a cast, I slipped the button of his jeans free and tugged the zipper free.

Andy moaned when I pushed his underwear down and freed his cock. I took a moment to enjoy the sight of him, but only one before I wrapped my fingers around his hard shaft and squeezed before slowly and methodically working my grip up and down.

"Dammit, Kat. That feels so fucking good."

"Mmm." I licked my lips and shifted in my seat until I could bend easily over his lap and take him into my mouth.

He sucked in a breath.

I smiled to myself and continued with my task. My tongue swirled around his head, tasting the salty precum of his excitement before I slowly licked the length of him and then—sucked.

"Holy shit, Kat."

His body tensed beneath me, but I couldn't have stopped if I'd wanted to. And I certainly didn't want to.

"I'm going to crash the fucking car if you keep that up."

I pulled my mouth from him just enough to look up. "Then park the fucking car."

He growled in response as I refocused on what I was doing. Vaguely, I felt the car speed up briefly, before we turned and finally he applied the brakes and mercifully put the car in park.

His fingers twisted in my hair, and he gently tugged. "I'm going to need you to get your pants off and get over here." He issued his orders in a tightly controlled, low voice that left no room for argument.

Not that he would get one from me. My panties were soaked with need. And he hadn't even touched me yet.

I lifted myself from his lap and looked him straight in the eye as I ran my index finger over my bottom lip before sticking it between my lips.

The growl rumbled deep in his chest, and desire flared in his eyes. "Kitty Kat, you are fucking killing me."

"That's the idea." I winked and before he could ask again, I kicked my sneakers off and with my good hand, tugged my leggings and panties down and over my feet.

Andy had pushed the driver's seat back as far as it would go and had somehow found a condom and sheathed himself by the time I was finished.

"Get over here." He reached for me, and as smoothly as I could, I climbed over the armrest and onto his lap.

My already tightly wired body sparked to life the moment my skin touched his. He held me up, hovering over his hard length.

I sucked in a breath and closed my eyes, but just for a

moment. I'd dreamed about our first time together so many times, I could hardly believe that finally, after a few near misses, it was actually going to happen.

Up until then, we'd always been able to pretend we were only friends. We hadn't technically crossed the line and hit the point of no return. But if we did this, there wouldn't be any coming back from it.

No more pretending that whatever there was between us was only sort of platonic and maybe that was a bad idea. But in that moment, I didn't care.

As if he read my mind, Andy looked straight into my eyes. "We're doing this?"

I bit my bottom lip and nodded. Oh yeah, we were definitely doing this.

In response, Andy wrapped his hand through the strands at the back of my head and pulled my mouth to his.

ANDY

"Say it." I breathed the words against her lips. "I need to hear you say that you want this as much as I do."

I held her in place, our lips and bodies only inches apart. My body ached for her in a way I'd never experienced before.

I couldn't think straight with my need for her racing through my blood. More than anything, I wanted to make my Kitty Kat mine, once and for all, but I needed to know she wanted it just as badly, because it would change every-thing between us forever.

"I do," she murmured. "I want this, Andy. I want *you*."

It was all I needed to hear. I pressed my mouth against hers as I settled my hands over her hips and gently guided her down onto my throbbing dick.

She sucked in a breath, and I froze, forcing myself to move slowly. I took my time exploring her mouth with mine while I let her body adjust to my size. She was so tight, but her body molded easily to me, taking all of me just as I'd imagined she would.

After a moment, Kat moaned and started to rock her hips against mine.

I pulled away from the kiss and looked into her eyes; her pupils were blown, nothing but desire and heat in her gaze.

"You're so fucking perfect, Kitty Kat." I kissed her again as I pulled her tight against my chest. My hands slipped down the smooth skin of her back and circled over her rib cage before moving up to her breasts.

"You are wearing far too many clothes." Without waiting for a response, I pushed her T-shirt up and over her head, and with a quick flick relieved her of her bra, too. "Better." I sat back as much as I could so I could take in the sweet sight of her.

"I could say the same for you." Kat sat back a little, making me groan.

I took the opportunity to reach out and let my hands slide over her perfect tits and creamy skin.

She took a moment to assess my still half-clothed body.

A small, sexy smile played at her lips as she ran a finger along the hem of my shirt before she rolled her hips, which had the very desirable effect of pressing me deeper inside her.

I dropped my head back and moaned. "Dammit, woman. You are absolutely incredible and if you want me naked, I will be more than happy to strip myself bare for you." I held her gaze. "Later." My hands clamped tightly on her hips. "In fact, when we're done here, I will be driving you straight back to your apartment, where I plan on both of us being very, very naked so I can lay you down on your bed and worship that beautiful little body properly. But right now, I'm afraid I don't have that kind of self-control."

Her nostrils flared with desire and again, she rolled her hips, grinding herself against me. I gritted my teeth. Holding back was proving to be an increasingly difficult task.

Kat wrapped her good hand in the hairs at the back of my head and kissed me hard before pulling back and licking her bottom lip. "Fortunately for you, I agree to those terms."

"Hell ya, you do."

Like two horny teenagers, we moved together, furious and fast. I thrust up into her sweet heat while using my tight grip on her hips to move her up and down onto me until I felt her muscles tighten around me, and not a moment too soon as I felt my own climax building to the unstoppable point of no return.

I held her tighter, my arms wrapping around her as we each let our climaxes wash through us. After a moment, she shifted a little on my lap and dropped her head to my shoulder. She pressed a kiss to the sensitive skin on my clavicle before nuzzling into my neck. It was single-handedly the best cuddle I'd ever experienced. And as far as I was concerned, I never wanted it to end.

And maybe it wouldn't have either, but after a few minutes, I felt her shiver, reminding me that it was getting late and the sun was starting to go down. Even in the summer, when the sun slipped behind the clouds, it could get cold, fast.

Never mind the fact that we were still in the car, where anyone could come across us. I'd managed to drive a little way down the mountain service road before I found an old logging road to pull off onto, but it was far from private.

"You're cold, Kitty Kat."

She shook her head against my chest. "I'm fine."

"You're definitely fine." I chuckled. "But you're also cold. Let's get you home."

The promise of what awaited us in the privacy of Kat's apartment made the thought of her moving her perfect naked body off my lap a little more bearable.

I gave her one more kiss on the top of her red head before gently lifting her chin and kissing her lips softly.

She looked up at me and blinked slowly. "Can we stop for celebratory burgers on the way home?"

I couldn't help but laugh. "Are we celebrating that we finally—"

"No!" It was Kat's turn to laugh. She climbed over the console into the passenger seat and tugged her T-shirt over her head. "Did you forget the whole jumping off the bridge thing?"

I scrubbed a hand over my face and shook my head. "Is it bad that I kind of did?"

Kat smacked me gently in the arm.

"I mean," I said, "that was cool and all, but…" I leaned over to give her another kiss. "I really like what came next."

She shoved me lightly with a giggle. "That was fun, too. But we need to celebrate that I crossed the first thing off my 'Dad's Do-It List.'"

"Is that what we're calling it?" I tilted my head and gave her a look.

Kat shrugged in response. "I haven't decided on a name yet." She reached down and tugged her leggings up before grabbing her sneakers. I had tidied up and refastened my jeans by the time Kat was done tying her shoes.

She pulled her hair back into a ponytail and gave me a wink. "So? Burgers at the Shed? I feel like something extra bad for me

Chapter Sixteen

KAT

I DIDN'T REALIZE how hungry I was until I was reclining on the couch with the aftermath of the greasy burger and fries on the coffee table in front of me. I put my hand on my belly and laughed at myself.

"I have to say, Kat. I've never seen a woman put a burger away like you before."

I struggled to sit up and stare at Andy. Maybe I should have been embarrassed by the way I'd inhaled my dinner, and with any other man, I might have been. But this was Andy. It was different with Andy.

And after what we'd done in the car, it was *very* different.

Not that I was complaining.

"What can I say." I winked at him before flopping back onto the cushion. "I worked up an appetite earlier."

"That was pretty crazy. I've never done anything like that."

Was he talking about the bungee jumping or the sex in the car? I was desperate to know, but before I could ask, Andy added, "In case you're wondering, I meant both the jumping off the bridge *and* hooking up in the front seat of my car."

I couldn't help myself; I rolled over so I was facing him and propped my head up on my hand. "So you've hooked up in the *back seat* of your car before?"

"Wouldn't you like to know?" He chuckled.

"Actually, no." I rolled onto my back again so he couldn't see the conflict on my face. "I'm sorry I brought it up."

The couch sagged under Andy's weight as he moved closer to me. "Are we going to talk about it?"

"It?"

"Don't play dumb with me." He reached out and traced a finger down my bare arm, sending shivers through me. "I know you way too well for that. And we do need to talk about it."

"Do we?" I already knew the answer. Of course we did. It was one thing to pretend that there was nothing going on between us *before*. But now that we'd crossed the line, pretending all of a sudden got a whole lot harder.

Especially because I had full intentions on crossing that line again.

And again.

"Okay, fine." I pulled myself up to a sitting position and pulled a throw cushion onto my lap. "We had sex."

"We sure did."

I inhaled deeply. "I enjoyed it."

Andy chuckled. "So did I. Very much."

I blew out my breath and took a chance. "I'd like to do it again."

He was silent for a moment, and I worried maybe he didn't feel the same way. Which shouldn't have been a problem, but for more reasons than I wanted to admit, it mattered. A lot.

It felt like forever before Andy reached for my hand. "So would I." His voice was low, and full of promise. "And I think that's a problem."

He wasn't wrong.

I'd fantasized for so long about what it would be like to be with Andy, but the reality had been so much better than anything I could have ever imagined. And now that I'd had a taste of how it could be with him, I knew with perfect certainty I'd want more.

Andy was right. It was a problem.

"I agree." I held his gaze. "But it's not an insurmount-able one."

He tilted his head in question. "How so? You know as well as I do that your brother will murder me if he found out we…" Andy waved his hand between us. "You know."

I laughed. "I do know. And you're right, Craig would lose his shit if he found out, which is why he can never know."

"Agreed." Andy dropped my hand, and I immediately felt the loss of his touch. "And it's also why we can't do it again."

I sat back sharply, as if I'd been slapped. "That's bullshit."

"Kat, I—"

"No." I pulled away as he tried to reach for me again. "I don't accept that, Andy. We're grown-ups. And yes, Craig would be upset. They probably all would be. But you just told me you wanted to do it again."

"I do."

"So do I." Exasperated, I almost yelled. Instead, I tried to make my point a different way. I reached for him and pulled him toward me so I could kiss him.

He groaned against my mouth the second our lips touched. I knew he felt the same spark I did. How could he not? It was fire between us. And it was so much more than just a quickie in the car.

So. Much. More.

ANDY

I was fucked.

Well and truly fucked.

I scrubbed a hand over my face. I knew I'd been playing with fire when it came to Kat. I never should have agreed to the bungee jumping. I knew better than to put myself in a situation where I'd lose control.

But there was no way I could have done anything else.

Not when it came to Kat. She'd always had some kind of spell over me, and that was before. Now, I was completely bewitched by her. And it went a whole lot deeper than just the amazing sex we'd shared earlier.

How could it not?

This was Kat. She wasn't just any woman.

She was…she was *Kat*.

I moved my kisses to her neck. She tasted sweet and salty and absolutely delicious. "You're right," I said between kisses. "It *is* bullshit. I need more of this." I sucked her delicate skin between my teeth until she moaned. "I need *you*."

She wriggled beneath me and dropped her head to the side, giving me easier access. "You did promise to carry me up to my bed and—"

"That's right." Screw talking. It was overrated. I stood and scooped Kat up into my arms easily. "And that's just what I'm going to do."

Suddenly the idea of having her spread out on her bed, naked for me to feast my eyes and mouth upon, seemed like a much more pressing issue than finishing our conversation. Especially considering neither of us was going to like the outcome of that conversation anyway.

I moved quickly up the stairs, and we each made short work of our clothes, leaving them in piles on the ground. "You're so damn gorgeous." I let my gaze move slowly over every inch of her.

How did I think—even for a moment—that I could deprive myself of this sight?

"You're pretty impressive yourself."

Her eyes lingered on my dick, and when her pink tongue slipped from between her lips before she looked up to lock eyes with me, I thought I might combust.

I closed the distance between us and put my hands on the gentle swell of her hips, splaying my fingers over the curve of her ass. "You know what I think?" I lowered my mouth to her perfect tits, sucking first one nipple and then the other into my mouth.

Kat moaned.

"I think you're right. We're grown-ups and we can do whatever we want as long as no one gets hurt." I bent again and suckled her breasts until she gasped. "Do you agree?"

"Um hum."

I lifted my head. Her eyelids fluttered open, and I caught the hesitation there. "Kat? We don't have to—"

"No." She put a hand flat on my chest. "It's not that. I just…it's probably for the best that this can't go anywhere, right? I mean…with my family and…"

I swallowed hard. More than anything, I wanted to object—to stop her from putting more limits on us. Instead, I let her finish.

"I mean, you live so far away. It could never go anywhere anyway. We're just friends. No one's going to get hurt."

Was she trying to convince herself? Or me?

"What did you say?" I pretended to think about it,

despite the fact that her words had been seared into my mind from the moment she spoke them in my apartment two years earlier. "Happy for right now?" Was it my imagination, or did she flinch when I said that? "This can be temporary. Something fun."

She took a moment to think about it, then a smile curled her lips. "Right." She nodded, and I pretended not to notice the way her breasts jiggled. "You said you'd help me with my list."

I didn't hesitate. "And I meant it. Whatever you need."

"That's perfect. It's kind of a built-in time limit for… well, whatever this is."

What it was, was perfection. But I swallowed hard to keep from interrupting her.

"When my list is done, then we…"

"Go back to being just friends," I finished for her. "No more benefits."

She giggled. "I mean, it kind of makes sense."

Did it? I wasn't convinced. But I wasn't stupid either. And I'd take what I could get when it came to Kat.

"So, six months?"

She nodded. "I mean, I guess whenever you're in town. I know you have a whole life and career and everything in Vancouver. So, I don't expect—"

"I'll be here," I interrupted. "I told you I'd be there for you, and I meant it. You have six months to complete your list, right?"

She nodded.

"So, six months it is." I said it like it was a done deal. And as far as I was concerned, it was. It was also a sharp reminder that I still hadn't told her I was moving back to Trickle Creek and had taken a job locally. But I couldn't tell her now. The only way she was agreeing to this *situationship* was if it had a time limit.

I knew that.

And I also knew that more than anything, I wanted her to agree. I *needed* her to agree.

In that moment, I needed her like I needed oxygen— and I was dangerously close to choking.

"But your job? Your—"

"Don't worry about it." I pulled her close again, unable to stand even the smallest distance between us. "All you need to worry about is the *Dad's Do-It* list."

She laughed. "I don't think that name is going to work out. It sounds creepy."

"You're right." I shook my head and kissed her neck again. "It does," I said between kisses. "You need to come up with a new name. Later."

I slowly lowered myself to my knees as I moved my kisses down her body. Kat wrapped her fingers through my hair and tugged when I dipped my tongue into her belly button. She squealed a little.

"You're going to have to stay here, with me." Her words came in short little gasps as I used my hands to nudge her legs apart.

I glanced up. "I wouldn't stay anywhere else."

I dropped my head to my task and kissed my way up one sweet thigh, then the other, before finally kissing her inviting, wet center.

She was just as delicious as I remembered. My dick throbbed between my legs while I took my time licking and lapping up her sweet nectar. Her thighs quivered beneath my grip; I could feel her edging closer to release—but I wasn't ready for that yet.

She groaned when I got to my feet and gently led her back to the bed, where I pushed her softly onto the fluffy duvet.

"I think this could work out quite well."

"I think you might be right." As long as it meant having Kat in my bed, in my arms, and just like this for the next six months, I couldn't see any flaw in the arrangement.

At least none I was willing to entertain in that moment.

I reached for the condom I'd remembered to bring upstairs and made short work of sheathing myself before I pushed her legs apart and moved between them.

"One more thing." She stopped me moments before I sank into her sweet heat.

With my arms braced, holding myself up, I waited.

"We have to promise…" She bit her bottom lip and tried again. "We can never…well, it can't ever be anything more than this, Andy."

Her words speared straight through my chest, but I swallowed hard.

"Promise?"

I couldn't answer. It was an impossible request—because I already knew it was a promise I couldn't keep.

Instead, I kissed her until she was moaning into my mouth again, and then I buried myself deep inside her.

Exactly where I needed to be.

Chapter Seventeen

ANDY

"I CANNOT GET over how damn good it smells in here." I stopped and inhaled deeply before laughing and walking all the way into the Sugar Shack. "I don't know how you work in this environment and aren't five hundred pounds." I greeted my best friend with a shake and half hug, clapping him on the back.

"We totally should have met at the Bean Bag. At least then it's only the cinnamon buns I'm trying to resist instead of..." I scanned the display case of ice cream flavors before tapping on the glass. "Peanut butter brownie?" I looked up at Craig. "Is that a new flavor?"

"I just brought it out for testing a few days ago. Want to try?"

"You know I do."

Craig chuckled and scooped out a portion into a cup

before joining me on the other side of the counter. "The least I can do is provide you with free ice cream. We all really appreciate you being there for Kat right now."

A flash of guilt flared through me, and I busied myself with a spoonful of the delicious treat so I didn't have to respond. The truth was, I *had* been there for Kat. Every single night since we'd gone bungee jumping together—and most mornings, too.

The chemistry between us had been impossible to ignore. If I thought that our hot and heavy session in the front seat of my car would be enough to finally get her out of my system and go back to just friends, I'd been sadly mistaken.

Or not so sadly—because we'd been having a lot more fun as friends with benefits, or *happy for right now*, or whatever the hell it was we were to each other.

"You're the only reason I'm not beating her door down right now."

I choked on my ice cream. "What?"

Craig shook his head. "Kat's been avoiding us all since the meeting. No one's spoken to her, and she hasn't told any of us about the list or what it says."

That surprised me. Kat and her siblings were close—closer than any other family I knew. Especially since their father died.

"Wait. So you haven't seen the list at all?"

Craig shook his head.

"You have no idea what's on it or what's required of her for the next six months?"

Again, Craig shook his head. "I suppose you do?"

I put my spoon down and pushed my cup away. I *had* seen the list. But not right away.

It had been almost a week since we'd come to an arrangement—or agreement—or whatever the hell we were calling our situationship—and a lot had happened.

Almost none of it that I could tell my best friend.

Still, I *could* be honest with Craig about the list. At least as much as I was at liberty to discuss.

It hadn't been until later that first night—after I'd finished worshipping Kat's body the way it deserved to be worshipped—when we finally came up for air, starving again and ready for a late-night snack.

Kat ordered a pizza for us to eat in bed, and it was after our second slice when she climbed out from under the comforter and left the room without a word. She returned a few minutes later, handed me the folded piece of paper that contained the list her father had written, and climbed back into bed without another word.

I hesitated before unfolding it, knowing the weight of what I was about to read—and how much it meant that she was sharing it with me. I read over the items in silence before gently folding the paper again and placing it on the bedside table.

I reached for her hand and squeezed it until she looked at me.

"So," I'd said. "What are we doing next?"

It had been the right thing to say. The smile that crossed her face lit up her eyes. "Really?"

"I told you I was here for it." I tugged her toward me until she was in my lap, the blanket falling away to reveal the same perfect breasts I'd had my face buried in less than an hour earlier. I traced a finger down the side of her face, to her neck, and finally between her breasts.

"All of it?"

I shrugged. "Well, except for the solo camping trip. Sounds like you might need to do that one alone."

"But what about your job and your apartment and—"

I stopped her with a finger to her lips. "I already told you—don't worry about it. I've got some time off, and it's all just details I can sort out." I waved a hand. "At any rate, it's definitely not something you need to worry about. Have you changed your mind about me helping you out?"

"No way." She laughed—a sound that reached deep inside me. "I think it's going to be nice to have someone share this with me."

"Someone?" I kept my voice light, teasing her. But the truth was, she would never be *just someone* to me.

"You," she confirmed. "It'll be nice to share this with you." She leaned over and kissed me.

Her bare breasts pressed against my chest, instantly making me hard and setting my mind racing with all the dirty things I wanted to do to her next.

"So?"

Craig's voice snapped me back to the present. I blinked hard and scrubbed a hand over my face before looking at him.

"What the hell is wrong with you, man? You look—"

"Sorry," I cut him off quickly. "My mind drifted for a moment." There was no way I was telling him I'd just been replaying exactly what had happened next with his little sister. I needed to remember that no matter what happened, Craig could *never* know. I was dancing on the edge of a cliff, and I damn well knew it.

"So? Do you know what's on Kat's list or not?"

I nodded. "I do."

"And are you—"

"Going to tell you?" I winked. "Not a chance. It's not for me to tell."

Craig slammed his hands down on the table.

"You know Kat." I grabbed a napkin and wiped up a stray drop of ice cream. "She's shit at keeping secrets." I really hoped—for both our sakes—that wasn't entirely true. "She probably just needs time to process everything. I'm sure she'll tell you guys about the list at the next family dinner. But if she doesn't, don't worry too much. I told you I'd be there for her, and I committed to helping Kat with everything—as long as she wants me to."

Craig raised an eyebrow, and I knew I'd stepped close to the line. "Is that why you're still at her place instead of coming to stay with us?"

Something in his voice warned me to tread carefully. "Yeah. That, and you and Lucy are still very much in the newlywed phase." I blew out a breath. "I don't think you need me hanging around until I find my own place."

"You forget we have a kid—privacy is nonexistent. You know it wouldn't be a big deal to have you. But I get it if you want to stay at Kat's. I bet she was happy to hear you were moving back to town."

"Why would she be happy?"

Craig shot me a look. "Because she loves her family—and you know you're family, Andy." He rolled his eyes.

"Right. Of course." I swallowed hard. "But I didn't tell her yet."

"Why not?"

That was a damn good question—and one I couldn't answer honestly. Not without risking a broken jaw.

"I just didn't want to give her anything else to worry about," I said, shrugging and hoping it sounded casual.

"I guess that makes sense." Craig studied me, but if he was bothered by me staying at Kat's, it didn't show. "And really, if you want to stay there, it's good with me. It's probably quieter. Ultimately, you're going to be around a lot more now anyway. Had any luck finding something yet?"

I glanced at the time on my phone. "Actually, Jess is meeting me here in a few minutes to go over some options. Charli hooked me up with her."

"I bet she did." Craig laughed. "Wouldn't be surprised if she's trying to hook you up with more than a place to live. Jess is nice—and super cute, too."

I shook my head. "She seems nice. I'll take your word on cute—I haven't actually met her yet. But I'm not looking to get involved with anyone right now."

Because I'm already involved with your little sister.

"Who said anything about getting involved?" Craig made air quotes. "I know that's never been your style."

"I could've changed."

I'd completely forgotten the bullshit I'd fed him—about never settling down, about preferring to date around. I'd panicked back then, after almost sleeping with Kat, because for the first time I'd let myself believe there *could* be more…

If it weren't for the distance.

And the fact I'd lose my best friend.

"Yeah," Craig said. "You could have. But I doubt it."

The bells over the door chimed, and an attractive brunette walked in with a stack of papers in her arms.

Jess.

"Well, I'll leave you to it." Craig winked and stood, cleaning up the cups and napkins. "Hey, Jess. Nice to see you."

KAT

There were definite drawbacks to living and working in the plaza in the center of town. Most days, I loved the convenience of being only steps away from my business, the shops, restaurants and cafés of Trickle Creek, and of course my brother's ice cream shop and my sister's flower shop.

I loved hanging out with my siblings. Along with Annie Darling, they were all my best friends and were my favorite people to spend time with.

Which was why it was so strange that I'd been actively avoiding them all for the last week. I couldn't remember the last time I'd gone even a day without speaking to one of my brothers or my sister. And it wasn't that I was avoiding them —well, maybe I was, a little bit—but mostly I just needed some time to process...well, everything.

They all must have sensed my need for space, too, because if any of them thought it was strange that I had mostly withdrawn from the family since the last meeting, they hadn't said anything. I knew they were probably going crazy trying to figure out what was on the list our father had left me. Just the way I would have been if I'd been the one left in the dark when it had been their turn.

There was no real reason why I didn't want to tell my brothers and sister about the list, and I would. But for the time being, it was nice to have it all to myself.

Truthfully, I hadn't kept it entirely to myself. It had felt natural to share it with Andy. A lot of things with Andy felt natural. A whole lot of things.

I couldn't let myself go down that trail of thought right now. I needed to focus on the matter at hand: my family. And the fact that it was only a matter of time before they finally banged down my door and demanded to know whether I was okay.

And that was exactly what I was trying to avoid. Especially considering Andy was still staying with me and was no longer sleeping in the guest room.

What I really should do was make the first move and go to one of them. At least that way it would keep them away from my apartment, where they might see something they shouldn't.

"Might as well get it over with," I muttered to myself as I finished reviewing the accounting on my laptop.

Even though I'd canceled or rescheduled most of my regular clients, I still liked to be in the shop, and I'd been working from the front desk of Strands for most of the morning. My little salon had grown fast over the few years I'd been in business and not only with my own clientele: I also had a nail technician and an aesthetician who each rented space and saw regular clients. And more recently, I had gotten over my fear about being a manager of employees and had hired two additional stylists for the shop, which had turned out to be a blessing because Carla and Alison had been able to cover everyone I had to reschedule because of my wrist.

And that was perfect because even though the cast had been replaced by a brace, I had decided to lighten my client load for the next few months so I could focus on getting through everything on my list.

A flash of movement out in the plaza caught my eye. Before I even looked, I knew it would be a member of my family. I shook my head, put a smile on my face, and looked up to see my niece Meri doing a particularly bad job of hiding behind a tree.

I used my good hand to put my thumb to my nose, stick out my tongue, and wiggle my fingers. Meri burst out laughing.

"Alison," I called to the woman who was at the sink, rinsing color off a client. "I'm heading out for today but I updated my availability in the schedule in case anyone calls in."

"No problem, Kat. Have a great day."

I grabbed my phone and belt bag and headed out into the warm sunshine, where I immediately spotted my niece crouched next to a bench.

"I see you over there, kiddo."

Meri popped up and threw her arms up in the air.

I laughed and greeted my niece with a hug. "We're going to have to work on your hiding skills. When I was your age, I was epic at hide-and-seek."

"I wasn't really trying to hide." Meri rolled her eyes. "I wanted to show you the ribbons I got at sports day, but Dad and Lucy told me not to bother you."

"They did?" Guilt squeezed at my heart. It was one thing to be avoiding my siblings, but I never wanted my niece to think she couldn't come to me for anything.

Meri nodded. "They said you were stressed."

"Do you even know what stressed means?" I looked at her sideways and tried not to laugh.

"It means you want to be alone to think about things," Meri answered seriously.

"Well, you're not entirely wrong. But I'm not stressed. And even if I was, that would never mean that you have to leave me alone, okay?"

Meri nodded.

"Now, show me these ribbons. Did you kick some butt?"

Meri giggled at my use of the word butt and proudly thrust her ribbons toward her auntie.

"You got second in the skip rope contest?"

Meri scowled. "I would have gotten first, but Harrison stuck his tongue out at me, and I shouldn't have looked, but I did and then I tripped over the rope so Brittany got first, and she never should have won because I'm better at skipping and everyone knows that and if it wasn't for Harrison, I would have won."

She stuck her hands on her hips and looked so put out that it was absolutely adorable and I had to work hard not to laugh.

"That doesn't sound fair at all," I said instead. "What do you say we get some ice cream? Because you'll always be the best skipper I know."

Meri grabbed my good hand and pulled me toward the Sugar Shack.

I blew out a breath and braced myself. I couldn't avoid my brothers and sister forever. I might as well get it over with.

Besides, there was no reason for any of them to suspect that anything else was going on. And there really wasn't any reason why they should think that my avoidance had anything to do with Andy.

My lips curved into a natural smile the moment he popped into my head. The last week with him staying with me had been...well, to say it had been fun would be a massive understatement. But there was no other word for it, because that's exactly what it had been.

We both knew that what we were doing together was wrong and Craig would lose his mind if he ever found out.

But he wouldn't find out. Because we'd agreed that it was only some temporary fun.

The *fun* we'd gotten up to that morning flashed through my memory, sending all kinds of good feelings through me. But the moment I stepped through the door, the good feelings evaporated when I saw who was sitting at a table in the corner, heads together, deep in an intimate conversation.

ANDY

"There's got to be at least one in here that catches your eye."

I shuffled the papers around the table in front of me. Jess had really come through with a variety of different types of properties for me to look at.

I hadn't given her much to go on as far as criteria, so she'd arrived with everything from family-style homes that were newer builds in some of the more recent communities on the edge of town, to a few older miner houses that needed renovation work. There was an acreage property complete with a barn and outbuildings; that was an easy one to reject because I didn't have any time for land.

Jess had even come through with a studio suite that was situated over the kitchen shop in the plaza. The location was perfect, and that didn't even take into consideration that it was only a few shops away from Kat's place.

Still, none of them appealed.

None of them were Kat's apartment.

I knew that was ridiculous and not at all the way I should be thinking. It's not like we were even in a relationship. We were in a situationship.

I almost laughed out loud at the idea, but caught myself moments before I did.

"Andy? Anything?"

Jess was waiting for an answer. And really, I owed her one.

I exhaled slowly and reached for the paper on the top of the pile. "This one looks pretty good."

Jess took the paper from my hand, looked at it strangely before lifting her gaze up at me and back to the paper. "This one? Really? I didn't really take you for a fixer-up type."

For the first time, I took a peek at the house I'd chosen to see that it was a house built almost one hundred years ago that would require a complete remodel. Jess was right. I was not the remodel type. Between the new job and helping Kat with her list, I wasn't going to have much free time at all.

And even if I did, the last thing I wanted to spend it on was ripping out old flooring and painting walls.

But Jess was watching me expectantly, so I smiled and shrugged as casually as I could. "Well, you never know. I might be up for the challenge."

She laughed and shook her head before choosing a different paper from the pile. "What about this one? When I saw the listing, I thought of you immediately."

I looked at the paper she'd chosen for me and smiled a

little to myself. It was the listing for the apartment in the plaza close to Kat.

Was that a good thing? Or would the proximity turn out to be more temptation than I could handle when things between us finally ran their course?

The smile slipped from my face at the thought.

"No?"

I met the Realtor's concerned eyes.

"I thought the convenience of this one might really suit you and—"

"It does," I interrupted her. "It's just that…" I pretended to examine the paper. "It's not big enough for what I'd like."

It was a lie. The studio was more than big enough for what I needed.

"Well, maybe we could go take a look at this one—"

"Uncle Andy!"

I spun around at the sound of the little girl's voice, ready to greet Craig's little girl Meri, but my eyes locked on someone else instead.

Kat.

Despite seeing her only a few hours earlier, my instinct was to jump up and greet her by pulling her into my arms. Instead, I swallowed hard and focused on the little girl who, in typical Meri style, was running full speed toward me. I stood, caught her easily in my arms, and swung her around before setting her down.

"Hey, kiddo. What are you up to?"

"I found Auntie Kat," Meri said proudly. "She caught me spying on her."

Behind her, still standing close to the doorway, Kat shrugged, but she wasn't smiling. The expression on her face was unreadable.

"Hey, Jess." Kat slowly walked toward us. "I didn't know you two knew each other."

Ah. That's what it was. The expression on Kat's face was *jealousy*.

I couldn't help but grin, but the grin quickly fell away when Jess spoke up. "Andy and I are actually—"

"On a date." I looked quickly at Jess, who had not hid her shock well. She blinked a few times, and must have seen something in my expression that alerted her to the fact that I did not want Kat to see the real estate brochures.

Although, when I turned back to Kat and saw the look on her face, I realized that my backup story was far worse.

"I mean, it's not a *date* date." Even to my own ears, I sounded like an asshole. Could I not have come up with any better excuse? "It's just that your sister really wanted me to…"

Jess stopped me with a hand to my arm. "It was just a coffee." She winked and quickly swept up the papers before Kat could see them. "I'll give you a call." She smiled at Kat. "It was nice to see you, Kat. I'll need to book an appointment with you when your wrist is feeling better."

"For sure. Give the shop a call, and the girls can book you in." Kat lifted her bad hand that was out of the cast and now in a brace. "But I've actually taken some time off to deal with some family things, so if you can't get in to see me, Carla and Alison are great."

"Sounds good. Thanks." Jess gave us each another wave and then she was gone.

"I'm gonna see if Dad will get us ice cream," Meri declared. "Auntie Kat said we could have some."

I tore my gaze away from Kat to look at the little girl. "Well, if Auntie Kat said so, I'm sure he won't be able to say no."

"That's what I think." Meri nodded smugly and took off running for the back room where Craig was working.

I knew we didn't have long before Craig would join us, so I moved quickly to close the space between us. I knew it was risky, but I reached for her cheek and cupped it gently. "It wasn't a date, Kat."

"It's fine if it was, Andy. We're not together or anything. This is casual, remember? We agreed. Happy for right now." She shook her head free from my touch.

I was really starting to hate those words. Still, she was right.

And I hated it.

Chapter Eighteen

KAT

WE'D BEEN HIKING for hours, and I was starting to think we might not ever get to the peak. Not for the first time, I cursed myself for not training enough. I was an idiot to think I could do such a challenging hike without more training.

I spotted a fallen log and sat heavily on it. "I think I made a mistake, Andy." My shoulders sagged in defeat, and I let my head drop forward. "I can't do this. It's too hard."

"You can."

I heard him move to stand in front of me but refused to look up.

"And it's not."

"It is."

He chuckled. "Whine about it if you need to, but I'm not letting you turn back. No way."

With a sigh of frustration, I lifted my head. "You're very annoying, you know?"

"I know." He laughed again. "And that's why you love me."

My heart skipped with his word choice, but the grin on his face told me that he didn't mean it. Not like that. And that was my own damn fault for insisting that whatever it was we were doing wasn't serious. If I could take back that moment in the Sugar Shack, I would. Especially after the last few weeks we'd spent together with him in my apartment.

But when I'd seen Jess sitting with Andy like that, so cozy and intimate, I'd panicked. And when he said they were on a date… Well, that pretty much sealed it for me. There was no way I was going to be made a fool of. Especially considering it was true. We were never supposed to be anything more than casual. Nothing long-term would ever work.

No matter how much I wanted it to.

"Right," I said with as much sarcasm as I could muster in my currently exhausted state. "I'm beginning to regret having you as my partner in all this chaos."

It was a lie, and we both knew it. I had loved every minute of having Andy help me with the list. After the bungee jumping night, we'd sat and examined everything that was required of me, making a reasonable and totally doable plan for me to accomplish everything. Including knocking some of the tougher things off the list first. Like the hike to Pulpit Peak. At the time, it seemed like a good strategy. But I was very quickly starting to question that decision.

Every single one of my muscles protested when I let Andy pull me up from the log. "Vamos, Andy."

His lips quirked up into a smile. "Muy bien, Gatita." Andy wiggled his eyebrows at the use of my nickname in Spanish.

"I told you I was practicing." Together, we started to walk along the trail again. "I think I'm going to have to ask Steven what qualifies as learning another language. Because at this rate, it'll take me years to be able to speak a complete sentence."

"Well, I don't think he expects you to have a full-on conversation with a native Spanish speaker. Besides, we've only been using the app for a few days."

"Are you using it, too?"

After seeing that I needed to learn how to speak another language, Andy immediately jumped into action and found an app that I could install on my phone that promised to help teach me another language in only a few short minutes a day. True, they didn't specify how many days it would take, but at least it was a start.

"Of course I am," Andy said. "I told you I was going to help you with your list, and I meant it. Whatever it takes, Kat. You don't have to do it alone."

My heart did that thing where it squeezed a little bit and made me think of things that could never be, so I quickly shook my head and reminded myself that whatever it was that was going on with Andy, it was temporary.

"And anyway," he was saying. "It's going to take longer than just a few days of practicing another language. You have to give it time." Andy chuckled. "Not that you were ever very patient, though. Were you?"

I spun to face him and pushed a finger against his chest. "What's that supposed to mean?"

He caught my finger in his hand and held it. "Kitty Kat, from the moment I met you, you've been chomping at the bit for whatever's coming next. You are not a patient person. Not even close."

"That's not true."

He tilted his head but said nothing else. He didn't need to. The smirk on his face said it all.

"It's not." I pulled my hand away and started to walk again.

We walked in silence for a few minutes before I dropped my hands and groaned, "Seriously, how much longer is this hike?"

The moment the words were out of my mouth, I realized what I'd just said, but Andy was already laughing.

"Case in point, my little impatient kitten."

He had me there. Still, I shot him a glare and then picked up my pace. The only way to get through this was to get to the top.

ANDY

"Just a little bit more. You got this, Kat. We're almost there."

I hoped like hell I wasn't lying because, truthfully, it was starting to feel as if we might never reach the top of the mountain.

There was a reason this was a bucket list hike.

I'd lost track of time since we'd left the packed trail behind and started the scramble through the loose rocks and scree to the very top of the peak. The climbing was rough, and it was a lot more challenging, to be sure, but it wasn't anything we couldn't handle. I was confident of that.

Next to me, Kat was using climbing poles to steadily climb. Her wrist was still in a brace, and I knew it still gave her trouble, so I stayed close in case she needed assistance. Kat's lips were pressed together in a line, her face set in a mask of pure determination as she worked her way to the top.

A wave of pride and emotion washed through me.

I held back a little as we approached the peak. It was a big moment, and I wanted her to have it for herself.

A few more steps, and she was there.

Kat raised her arms in the air, pointing her hiking poles straight up as she threw her head back as she yelled out a whoop of excitement. "I did it! I did it! Dad, this one's for you."

I stood and watched her from where I'd stopped, a few feet below her, and let her have a minute to process what had happened.

As soon as she lowered her arms and her head dropped down to her chest, and I realized her cries of excitement had turned into tears of emotion, I resumed climbing and joined her at the top.

"You're amazing, Kat." I pulled her into my arms and held her close. "You are absolutely incredible. Your dad would be so freakin' proud of you."

She sobbed against my chest, and I just held her, letting her work through her emotions. The act of completing such a challenging hike was emotional in itself. But the reason we were there in the first place added a whole different element, and I knew it was hitting her hard.

After a few minutes, Kat looked up at me with her tear-streaked face and smiled a little. "We did it." She squeezed her eyes shut and shook her head a little. "I'm not going to lie. There were a few times I wasn't sure we were going to make it."

I used my thumb to wipe a tear from her cheek, and her eyes fluttered open again. "I never doubted you for a second, Kitty Kat."

I'd held myself back long enough. There wasn't a chance I could hold out any longer. I lowered my face to hers and kissed her deeply.

The moment my lips touched hers, my whole world spun the way it always did when we connected. But this time it was different. This time, as I lost myself in the taste of her and the feel of her lips on mine, I felt myself falling in an entirely different way. Maybe it was the thrill of the accomplishment, or the sheer exhaustion in my body, or that we were standing on the top of a mountain with the most amazing view all around us—but whatever it was, kissing Kat and holding her in my arms felt like forever.

And that was going to be a real problem.

KAT

The trip back down the mountain only took about half the time going up did, and a whole lot less effort. Which was a good thing, because I had nothing left in me.

And not just physically. Emotionally, I was also completely wrung out.

Getting to the peak of the mountain had been a lot more emotional than I'd expected it to be. Maybe because the bungee jumping, although exhilarating, hadn't given me the same feeling. Something about being on the top of a mountain that my father had always wanted to climb, but didn't have a chance to, hit me differently.

The moment I stepped onto the top and threw my hands up in the air, the emotions crashed through me. Dad should have been there with me. We should have been able to accomplish that feat together the way we'd planned.

The reality that I would never be able to do something so special with my father ever again slammed into me.

Thankfully Andy had been there to catch me and let me cry. Just the way he had been for the last few weeks.

He'd been a constant presence in my life, and I knew, logically, it couldn't last—for so many reasons. Not the least of which was that he wasn't even supposed to be in Trickle Creek. He was only there temporarily, to help me with the list. And maybe it was that temporary status that had given us the false sense of security that had let us slip so easily into a…whatever it was we were doing.

I stopped and watched Andy for a moment while he deftly jumped from rock to rock in order to keep his boots dry while he crossed the last stream before we reached our parked vehicle.

When he was across, Andy turned and caught me watching him. "What are you looking at?"

"You."

"Oh yeah?" He smiled and crossed his strong arms over his chest. "And you like what you see?"

He was teasing and trying to keep things between us light, because wasn't that exactly what we did? Nothing between us was real or serious. I was responsible for that.

I blew out a breath and forced a lightness into my voice. "I mean, I was just thinking that you looked a little old."

"Old?"

I laughed. "Well, you are older than me. I'd say you're kind of an old man."

"Is that right?"

Even with the creek between us, I could see the flash in his eyes. Before I knew it, he was splashing through the creek, headed straight for me.

"Would an old man be able to do this?"

I squealed and tried to run, but I was too late. Andy scooped me up easily and tossed me over his shoulder as if

I weighed nothing. He held me in place with his big hands and I wiggled against his grip, but didn't try in any real way to get free. Because not only was Andy holding me, but I was getting a free ride across the stream, and given that my legs were about to give out on me after the strenuous hike, I was definitely not in a position to turn that down.

When Andy finally put me down in front of the car a few minutes later, I gave him a sassy grin. "Thanks for the ride."

"Anytime, Kitty Kat."

It didn't matter how many times he used my pet name, it did something to me. And like a secret password, it was all I needed to hear to ignore any of the negative thoughts that continually tried to creep in.

I stood on my tippy-toes and pressed my lips to his. Andy responded by pushing me gently up against the side of the car and deepening our kiss with a groan that held the promise of a whole lot more to come.

But first, I needed a shower. Badly.

I broke our connection first. "I don't know about you, but I'm starving."

His eyes flashed with a completely different kind of hunger. But, when a second later, his stomach growled, we both laughed and started to pack up our gear into the back of the car.

"If I wasn't so hungry, I'd be looking for another reason to bail on family dinner."

"Really? It's not like you to miss any."

"True." I shot him a look. "But nothing is normal right now. But…it's just that they feel like a lot right now."

He winked in my direction. "You know they love you and just want to make sure you're okay. Besides, I'll be there. I got your back."

"Thank you," I said as we started the drive down the mountain road and back into town. "Not just for that, but for everything. I feel like I'm saying that a lot lately, but I can't thank you enough for everything you're doing for me. I know it means you've been taking so much time out of your own life."

"You don't need to thank me, Kat. I'm enjoying every single moment of it and honestly…" He kept his eyes on the rough gravel road but reached over to take my hand. "I think I might be enjoying our time together a little more than I probably should."

My stomach flipped. "What does that mean?" I hoped I knew what it meant. Would it be any easier to feel the things I was feeling about Andy if I knew he was feeling the same things? Of course it would. Together, we could deal with any of the challenges that being together for real would bring. Together, we could do—

Before he could answer, the notifications on his phone started playing through the car's speaker system.

"We must be back in service." He pulled his hand away and reached for his phone, just as it started to ring. "I'll turn it—"

"Call from Jess." The car's Bluetooth system announced the caller who'd unknowingly intruded on our moment.

"Jess, huh?" After running into the two of them at the Sugar Shack over a week ago, I'd wanted to believe Andy when he told me that they weren't on a date. And even if they were, I had no business feeling jealous about it at all.

I'd done my best to pretend it was nothing and put it out of my head.

Still.

I never had been a good actress.

"I thought you weren't dating?"

"We're not." Andy reached forward and pressed the button to ignore the call. "She's actually—"

"It doesn't matter." I forced a smile to my face. "You know what matters right now? Family dinner. Are you sure you want to subject yourself to that after today?"

As far as segues went, it wasn't a good one. But the last thing I wanted to talk about after the day we'd shared together was Andy's dating life. He didn't owe me anything, and we'd never actually set any boundaries for our situation-ship, so it wasn't like I could say anything without sounding like a crazy person.

Besides, it was probably a good thing that Jess's call had interrupted us before either of us said something we couldn't take back. The last thing I needed right now was anything else making life more complicated than it already was.

Chapter Nineteen

ANDY

AFTER A QUICK SHOWER AND CHANGE, Kat and I walked into the big house. If it weren't for the promise of barbecued ribs with corn on the cob and all the fixings, I might have found an excuse to beg off the dinner. And judging by how exhausted Kat looked, too, I wasn't the only one, which was the real reason I was there. Kat needed support, and as long as she did, I'd give it to her.

I gave her an encouraging smile and swallowed back the urge to squeeze her ass as we walked through the foyer into the bustling kitchen, where we were greeted with hugs from the women.

"I didn't think we were going to see you two today," Charli said. Without asking, she handed us each a glass of water while Lucy put a bowl of chips out for us. "You must be exhausted."

"I've heard about that hike," Noa, Asher's new fiancée, said with a shake of her head. "You two must have trained for a long time."

"Not so much," Kat said with a mouthful of chips.

"But we did it." I reached for some chips. "And you killed it, Kat. Really, that scramble at the end is no joke."

"Thanks, Andy. I couldn't have done it without you."

We locked eyes, and I held her gaze for a moment longer than I probably should have.

It was Annie who cleared her throat and pulled my attention away.

I shook my head and chuckled. "I think I'm half asleep." I looked around at the women, who all watched me with various expressions on their faces. I silently cursed myself for letting my guard down when it came to Kat. I needed to remember that we were just friends. Especially where her family was concerned.

I pushed myself up from the chair. "Where are all the guys? Out at the smoker?"

"You know it," Lucy said. "I swear, I've never seen men so excited for meat."

I laughed. "Obviously you haven't spent enough time around smoked food. I, for one, am very excited about dinner. But I am going to go in search of a beer."

I knew none of them would object, and as much as I wanted to check on Kat before I left, I didn't dare risk a glance in her direction.

I found the men just where I'd expected they'd be: gathered on the deck, watching the smoker. "It smells amazing out here." I grabbed a nearby chair and collapsed into it before Symon handed me a beer. "Thanks. This is either going to wake me up or put me to sleep."

"I heard you were hiking Pulpit Peak today." Asher pulled up a chair and joined me. "Was that—"

"I know what you're going to ask." I stopped him. "And before you do, please direct any and all questions to your sister."

"Pulpit Peak, huh?" Chase said. "That was on her list?"

"I told you—"

"I'm not asking," Chase interrupted. "Just guessing." He nodded, satisfied with his own explanation. "That's a hard hike."

"Dad did talk about it," Craig joined in. "I actually remember him and Kat talking about doing it together one day. That was years ago, but it makes sense if it was on the list."

They all nodded in agreement.

"Good for you for doing it with her," Symon said. "I don't think I would be up to a climb like that right now. Not without training all summer."

"Interesting." I shot him a look. "Maybe I should put that in the training protocol for the team?" Just as quickly as I said it, I shook my head, dismissing the idea. "Except we can't risk anybody getting hurt in that scramble." I looked at Symon. "But if you're ever up for it…"

"Oh yeah? You'd do it again?"

"Hell no." I laughed. "I was going to suggest you take

one of these guys. They all look like they could use the challenge."

The conversation quickly devolved into challenges about who was in better shape than who, and I relaxed into the evening. Being around the Carlsons was good for my soul. These guys were all like brothers to me. I'd do anything for them.

Apparently that also included pushing the feelings that were growing stronger and more dangerous with each passing moment, further down. But if that's what it took to keep my family, I'd do it.

KAT

Dinner was delicious, and I ate way too much. But then again, I'd more than earned it.

"More ribs, Kat?"

I reached for the platter Charli held out before snatching my hand back and shaking my head. "I want to. They were delicious. But I may explode if I do."

Charli laughed. "I can't remember the last time I've seen you eat so much. And I mean that in the best possible way."

"She earned it," Andy said from across the table as he took the platter from Charli. "And so did I." He wiggled his eyebrows and heaped more meat on his plate.

"Speaking of the hike…" Asher refilled Noa's wine glass

before topping up his own. "We've already kind of guessed that climbing Pulpit Peak was on your list."

"You did, did you?" I crossed my arms and leaned back. I probably shouldn't take so much joy in it, but I couldn't seem to help myself. I knew Asher especially was likely going crazy not knowing what was on my list. "Good guess."

"Come on, Kat." It was Craig who finally lost his patience. "Are you really not going to tell us what Dad asked you to do? Really?"

I took my time and looked at each of my siblings in turn, as well as all their significant others. The family dinners really were getting bigger. Each of my siblings had not only completed their specific tasks assigned by our deceased father, but they'd also done so while finding love.

I had to force myself not to look at Andy, because love wouldn't be in the cards for us. The thought made me suddenly very sad, but it was probably just the exhaustion.

It was also the exhaustion that led to me finally relenting.

"Okay," I said after a minute. "I'll tell you."

Almost everyone spoke at once.

"Really?"

"Finally!"

But it was one voice that pulled my attention. I finally blinked and looked at Andy, who watched me with a look of such genuine concern that I almost changed my mind.

"You're sure, Kat?" he asked again.

"Why wouldn't she be sure?" It was Chase who spun on Andy. "We're family."

"Besides," Craig added. "You already know."

All heads turned to look at Andy then.

"You know?" Asher looked between Andy and then me. "You told him?"

I really was far too tired to deal with this. Especially if my brothers were going to get all territorial about it.

"Yes, I told him," I said with a deep sigh. "I told Andy because he offered to help me out with everything." I held up a hand to stop any objections. "I'm not allowed to have any family help, but as much as we all think otherwise, technically Andy isn't family." I made the mistake of looking at my friend Annie, who had a wry grin on her face.

I looked away. "So yes, Andy knows what's on the list but it's not a big secret. Not really. I just needed some time to absorb it all." It had to be because I was so tired, but still it annoyed me that I felt tears threatening.

"It's okay, Kat." Charli reached across the table and took my hand. "There's no right way to handle this kind of thing."

That was true. But yet, each of them had already handled their turns and survived. And for the last few years, while I was watching Chase, Charli, Craig, and Asher, selfishly, I'd hardly even thought about how hard it might all be for them. I'd been so focused on when it would be my turn.

And here I was, completely overwhelmed by it all. Still, that didn't mean I should keep them all in the dark. They had a right to know.

"There are a few things on the list. And with Andy's help,

I've already taken care of two of them. I think I wanted to get the scary ones out of the way first." There was one scarier thing, but I didn't feel like sharing that particular detail right away.

"So we know you climbed Pulpit," Craig said. "I still can't actually believe you did that one without more training." He shook his head. "Especially with a bad wrist."

"I hiked with my feet, Craig." I rolled my eyes, and Lucy laughed.

Craig shot his fiancée a look before blowing her a kiss.

"But yes, that was a scary one, and I'm willing to bet that Dad didn't think I'd tackle that one right away either. But I'm glad I did." I locked eyes with Andy. There was no way I would have been able to conquer such a feat without him.

He gave me a slight nod of acknowledgment.

"You said you'd done two." Asher was impatient. "So what else did you do?"

With my eyes still locked on Andy, I let myself remember the night we'd jumped off the bridge together, and everything that happened afterward, but only for a moment before I forced myself to look away.

"We jumped off a bridge."

"What the—"

"Cool!"

"Kat!"

"That's crazy!"

My head bounced around the table, as everyone reacted to my confession. But ultimately, my gaze landed on the single most excited person in the room: Grady, Annie's nephew was staring at me with wide eyes.

"Cool," he said again, and I laughed.

"It was kinda cool."

I could say that now, especially considering the kiss I'd shared with Andy as we'd bounced around in the air—not that I planned to share that particular bit of information.

"You did not jump off a bridge." Charli put her glass down with such a thump that the baby she was holding in her arms stirred and started to fuss. With her voice lower, she added, "Tell me you didn't do that, Kat?"

In response, I merely shrugged. "It was either that or jump out of a plane."

It was the wrong thing to say. The room erupted in chaos, with my siblings all roaring in displeasure. The baby started to cry, and Grady jumped from his chair, little Meri close behind, and they used the opportunity to slip from the room to escape any after-dinner chores.

Somehow, through the chaotic noise, I made eye contact with Andy, who lifted his hands and shrugged. I shook my head, and then, with too many emotions rolling through me, I pressed my lips together and inhaled into my cheeks, puffing them up before squeezing my eyes shut.

ANDY

Uh oh.

I knew that look. Kat was about to crack, and I knew her well enough to know that it would be a full meltdown. Especially given how exhausted she was.

I moved quickly around the table and crouched next to Kat's chair. I put my hand on her thigh and squeezed. "It's okay, Kat."

She didn't open her eyes but shook her head in response.

"They're just surprised. And you're tired. There's nothing here to get upset about." I spoke softly, but quickly, directly into her ear so only she could hear. "Wait until they hear you say something in Spanish."

It was the right thing to say. Kat blew out a breath that turned into a laugh. She opened her eyes and looked at me as she gave in to the laughter.

Around us, the others had settled down a little, possibly even realizing that their sensitive little sister might be on the verge of an epic breakdown. Not that I was going to stop to check on any of them. My only concern was Kat. It was always Kat.

"Hola, mi amiga," I whispered into her ear, and she burst out into a fresh round of hysterics. This time I joined in.

The two of us were so caught up in our private joke that it took us a moment to notice that the room had grown silent, and all eyes were on us.

I worked hard to swallow my laughter. I cleared my throat and waited for Kat to do the same. When we were both under control, it was Craig who spoke first.

"I'm glad you both think it's hysterical that you risked

your life by jumping off a bridge." He crossed his arms over his chest and glared at me as if it were my fault that Kat jumped off a bridge.

Before I could defend myself, Kat spoke up. "Don't get your panties in a twist, brother. It was totally safe."

It had been safe. But also terrifying. I didn't think it was going to help matters to say that out loud, so I kept my mouth shut.

"It's not like we tied a random bungee cord around our legs and jumped off a bridge without any safety equipment." Kat rolled her eyes and reached for her glass of water. "We went to the professionals. It was all totally legit. We were really lucky that they got us in so quickly, too. Because we just kind of made the—"

"We?" Chase looked past Kat, directly at me. He also crossed his arms over his chest and glared.

Again, before I could say anything, Kat spoke up. "Yes, *we*. I told you, Andy is helping me out with my list. And thank goodness he did, too. Because you guys are all acting ridiculous about this. It's not like bungee jumping isn't safe. People do it every day and don't die." Charli started to speak up, but Kat cut her off. "Besides, I didn't have a choice. It's on the list. Would you rather I didn't do it at all and forfeited?"

That shut them all up. I faked a cough to hide my smile, but Craig still shot me a look as I stood from my position crouching next to Kat and took the chair Meri had vacated. "Can I just say something really quickly?"

All eyes, including Kat's, turned in my direction. "I think

you all know me well enough to know how much I care about Kat." I didn't risk looking in her direction. "I care about all of you as if you were my own family," I added quickly.

"You *are* family, Andy." Asher tipped his head, and the others all murmured their agreement.

"So please trust me when I tell you all that I will never let anything happen to Kat. She was never in danger, and she never will be. I'll be sure of it."

Next to me, Kat laughed. "Which is easy to say because we're done with all the dangerous things now."

"So does that mean you're going to tell us the rest?" Charli, who'd handed baby Poppy off to Symon, leaned her elbows on the table and stared at her sister. "Finally?"

Kat took a deep breath and looked at me.

I gave her a smile of encouragement. I didn't fully understand her hesitation to tell them about the list, but I did know that Kat's relationship with Michael Carlson had been special, and I could appreciate that once she shared the list with them all, it would no longer be completely hers and hers alone.

"I'll clear the table." I gave Kat's shoulder a quick squeeze as I stood. "Give you all a few minutes."

KAT

"I was being silly, wasn't I?"

I was draped across Andy's naked chest while his fingers traced patterns on my bare back after having just given me an incredible orgasm.

After the physical exertion of the hike, followed by an even more emotionally exhausting conversation with my family, I had been sure I would fall asleep the moment my head hit the pillow.

And I probably would have, if it wasn't for the way Andy had kissed me goodnight. Something about the way his lips felt on mine, never mind his hands on my skin, had woken me up. And I was not complaining.

"When? A few minutes ago? I would not call that reaction silly."

"No. Not that." I pushed up so I could look in his eyes and see the sparkle of mischief there, letting me know he was teasing. "There was definitely nothing silly about that." I bit my lower lip, and he groaned before pulling me back down to him.

I let him stroke my hair and twist his fingers through the strands before I spoke again. "I meant about the list. Was I being silly keeping it to myself?"

"Do you feel like it was silly?"

I hesitated, but only for a moment. "No."

"Then that's the only answer you need."

I shifted so our mouths were only inches apart.

"You have to trust your instincts, Kitty Kat. This is your journey. And you get to do it however you want. If you want to tackle everything on your list right away and get it all done, you can. But if you want to take your time and give yourself the whole six months, that's okay, too. And the same goes for who you tell about it. It's up to you. No one has any right to tell you how to deal with it. Not even your brothers and Charli."

I nodded slowly. Andy was right. Still, I'd seen how happy they were to finally know what was on the bucket list. And even happier to know that the dangerous items had already been crossed off. It felt good to know that I'd relieved some of their worry. At least a little bit.

In fact, their response to learning that I only had a few minor or easy things to cross off had been almost dismissive.

But I hadn't been completely truthful with them. Although I'd told them about the karaoke, the cooking lessons, the art lessons and the second language, I'd kept the last thing to myself and hadn't mentioned the overnight backpacking trip.

"Thank you for saying that." I kissed his cheek. "It's kind of funny really, because on one hand, I waited for so long for it to be my turn, that I feel like I should just hurry and be done with it."

"And on the other hand?"

I let my lips curl up into a sly smile. "On the other hand, I really want it to last."

Andy let his hands slid down to rest on my hips, his fingers splayed over my naked ass.

"That makes two of us, Kitty Kat."

Andy lifted his head and kissed me softly before rolling us both over until he was wrapped around me. He held me close against him and whispered in my ear. "Rest now. It was a big day."

I let my eyes drift closed. Warmed by Andy's body holding me tight, I knew it wouldn't be long before I gave in to the sleep that threatened. But before I did, I tried to freeze the moment in my mind and my heart.

He'd told me to trust myself, but that was the whole problem. I wasn't sure I could. Because my mind was screaming at me to push Andy away before I got hurt, and my heart knew it was already too late.

I didn't want my six months to end, because as long as my list wasn't complete, I could pretend that what Andy and I were doing together was real.

Chapter Twenty

KAT

IT HAD BEEN JUST over three weeks since I had crossed anything off my list. If my siblings had noticed, they hadn't said anything. A fact that I was grateful for. They were giving me all the space I needed to do things in my own time, even though there was no doubt that at least half of them probably couldn't understand what was taking me so long.

Truthfully, I didn't blame them. If the roles were reversed, I knew I wouldn't be able to be so patient.

But I was the youngest, and I was fully aware that gave me certain privileges. I might as well take advantage of some of the perks.

I tilted my head back and so the summer sun warmed my cheeks, and let myself enjoy every single second of the moment. When was the last time I'd simply sat in the quiet of the lake's edge and taken in everything?

Months? Years? Maybe never?

But my painting class instructor, Denise, had told me and the other three students who took her Wednesday night class, that part of painting was to sit in stillness and absorb the world around us before we tried to capture it in art.

For a workaholic like me, the first few times I'd tried doing nothing, I'd struggled more than I'd expected to. But my brain just wouldn't shut off. What about my clients? Or the books? Had I ordered all the product I needed for the shop? Andy.

Just. Andy.

It took a little bit of time, but after a little while I got it. Mostly.

I inhaled deeply, letting the fresh lake air fill my lungs before exhaling and opening my eyes to the scene before me.

The lake was quiet for a late July afternoon. I could make out a rowboat with a fishing line cast over the side, off in the distance, and a few ducks swimming along the shore. But beyond that, the water was flat, and the mountains reflected beautifully in the still water.

Capturing the reflection was the hardest part, and I'd been taking my time working to get it just right so I could get some feedback from Denise at the next class.

I dabbed my brush in the paint, touched it to the canvas and repeated that a few times before sitting back and letting my vision scan the horizon again.

After a moment, I blew out a sigh and put the brush

down on the easel before standing up and stretching out the kinks in my spine.

I was procrastinating, and I knew it. On the painting, on the day, on…well, everything.

But only because before I'd driven up to the lake, I made the decision—and then worse, told Andy—that I was going to start looking into the logistics of my overnight solo camping trip.

It shouldn't be a big deal.

But it was.

The idea of hiking alone in the woods with all the bears, mountain lions, and all sorts of other critters was enough to scare me. But camp? Overnight? By myself?

Oh, hell no.

I'd never been a camper, much to my father's disappointment. Although all the other kids liked to pack up and trek out into the woods, I almost always chose to stay home with our mother—who also wasn't a camper.

It wasn't until after my mother died that I would reluctantly allow myself to be dragged along. But that was only because there was no other option.

I hated every moment of it, and I wasn't afraid to let everyone know about it. It didn't take long before my dad started to arrange sleepovers for me with a friend, so the rest of them wouldn't have to be subjected to my constant complaining.

Looking back, maybe I should have tried harder. But it wasn't just that I didn't like to camp. That would have been something I could deal with. But I was actually terrified of it. Huddling in a sleeping bag with only a thin piece of nylon between me and whatever was out there in the dark shadows kept me up all night when I was young. I'd toss and turn and drive myself crazy with an overactive imagination of what might happen to me if I so much as moved the wrong way.

I never told anyone how scared I was, certain they'd all make fun of me. After all, I was born and raised in the mountains. It was ridiculous that I was afraid of them. But then, as we got older and the camping trips naturally stopped on their own, there was never a need to tell them the truth.

Until now.

Of course, only Andy knew that a solo camping trip was on my list, and I planned to keep it that way. At least until it was done and I could put it all behind me. Telling the others would only ratchet up my anxiety. No doubt they'd have questions, and they would absolutely have concerns. It was best to keep it to myself until it was done and over with.

But it was never going to be over with if I didn't get over myself and at least start looking into what equipment I needed. As far as first steps went, it was a small one. But it would have to do for now.

"I can't put it off forever." I spoke to a robin who'd found a snack in the grass nearby. The bird looked at me, snatched up the worm it was working on, and flew away.

"Okay." I laughed. "I can take a hint."

Twenty minutes later, I was walking through the doors of Summit Style. Run by Kane and Krysta, a brother and sister, the shop was the hub for all things outdoor activities, which meant that in a town like Trickle Creek, it was a very popular place.

"Hey there!" I was greeted by Kane, almost immediately. "I heard about your bike crash." He looked at my wrist. "All better?"

I held up my arm and wiggled my wrist. "Good as new."

"Glad to hear it." He flashed his handsome smile at me. "Then there's no reason for you not to join us for our weekly trail rides. Rumor has it you're not working nearly as much these days."

I shook my head. Kane had been trying to get me out on the weekly bike rides for years, but there had never been enough time in my schedule with the shop and...well, the shop. The ride with Andy where I hurt myself had been the first time I'd been on my bike in ages and besides the whole injury thing, it had been fun.

For all kinds of reasons.

"We'll see. I'll try to make it." I knew I was blushing a little, and I didn't want to give Kane the wrong idea. Not when he'd been flirting mercilessly with me for years. So I cleared my throat and smoothly changed the subject. "But that's not why I'm here today. I was hoping you could help me out with some camping gear."

ANDY

"That was one hell of a workout today, man."

I looked to my left to see Symon, dripping in sweat, lean against the wall next to me and drop his head back.

"You didn't have to join in." I couldn't help but laugh at my friend. I handed him a bottle of water and shook my head. "You are the coach, right? You don't have to do the athlete workouts."

"The fuck I don't." Symon stood and stared at me. "I've only been retired for a few months...I'm not washed up yet."

I finished tucking my things back in my duffel and pulled the strap over my shoulder. "You are far from washed up, my friend. You killed it out there." Together, we started walking through the training facility where the Canadian ski team now trained. And where I officially worked.

A detail I still hadn't shared with Kat, but the secret was getting harder and harder to keep. Especially with the training camp in Switzerland coming up soon. I hated lying to her and the longer it went on, the harder it got to come clean.

But I wasn't stupid. If I didn't tell her, she was going to find out another way. And I knew her well enough to know she'd be pissed if it didn't come from me.

"How's the house hunt coming?"

Symon's question pulled me from my thoughts and reminded me of an entirely different issue. Not only did I need to tell Kat about the job and the fact that I wasn't leaving Trickle Creek anytime soon, but I also needed to tell her that I was house-hunting.

Which meant I would be moving out of her place.

And wasn't that the real reason I hadn't said anything?

If it wasn't the whole thing, it was definitely part of it. A big part.

More than anything, I didn't want to do something that would jeopardize what I had going on with Kat. Quite the opposite. I never wanted it to end.

And maybe that was the very reason it *should* end.

I was getting too close to her in a way that was not familial at all. No matter what lies I told myself.

It was getting far too easy to pretend that I could ever have a chance at anything real with Kat.

"You know what?" I turned to Symon. "I've been putting it on the back burner, but I think I should probably make time to look at some of the properties Jess keeps sending me."

"Oh yeah?" We walked out into the bright sunlight of the summer day and each of us slid our sunglasses on. "Time to get out of Kat's place? I was beginning to wonder how long you were going to stay there."

I was grateful for the sunglasses hiding my eyes. I turned away, toward my car. "To be honest, I hadn't thought much about it." It was a lie. I thought about it all the time. "There's been a lot going on and since I'm helping her out and..."

"That's pretty cool of you." We reached our parked cars, and Symon popped the back of his SUV open. "I know that Charli really appreciates you stepping in the way you have."

I tried not to feel guilty about why exactly I'd stepped in.

"With the new baby, plus the flower shop and me working more, I know Charli wishes she could be there for Kat more than she is. It weighs on her."

I could believe that. Charli was the caretaker of the family, for sure. Even if there was nothing she could personally do for Kat in this situation, it wouldn't stop Charli from worrying about it.

"I'm happy to help," I said without looking at my friend. "But truthfully, there's not much I can do to help right now. Kat's taking an art class, and she's actually getting really good. Not that I'm surprised. I think she's just naturally—what?" I turned to see Symon had taken his sunglasses off and was giving me a very suspicious look before sliding them back onto his face.

"What's the look for?" I asked again.

"You sound like a proud boyfriend or—"

"Or a good friend?" I hoped like hell I sounded more confident than I felt. "Because I am proud of her."

"Right." Symon crossed his arms and sat back on the edge of his trunk. "As a friend."

"Yes."

"Are you sure that's all it is?"

I inhaled deeply and turned, my hand on the roof of my truck. "What are you saying, Symon? Because I'm too exhausted to pretend I have any idea."

Another lie, and we both knew it.

I waited a beat and when Symon's only answer was a

raised eyebrow and a sharp shake of his head, I blew out the breath.

"We're just friends, Sy. That's all—"

"Who's just friends?"

Neither of us had seen Craig arrive. I almost choked over my words, coughing dramatically as I tried to quickly recover from the fact that my best friend almost overheard something he really wouldn't understand.

"Me and Jess." I said as smoothly as I could. "I was just telling Symon that she's great, and I know Charli was hoping it would be a love match, but…" I shrugged as casually as I could and looked at Symon who, thankfully, had his sunglasses on again—because I was sure the other man's eyes were wide in question, wondering what the hell was up with me.

I hoped like hell Sy was smart enough to put two and two together and that if he said anything out loud, they'd be looking for a new trainer for the ski team because Craig would kill him on the spot.

"Jess, huh?" Craig took a moment to digest what I said. "She's great. But not your type at all."

"Wait." I shot him a look. "How is she not my type?"

Jess was gorgeous, successful, funny, and a genuinely nice person. The insinuation that she wasn't my type rubbed me the wrong way, and for a moment I forgot that the whole point of bringing Jess's name into the conversation was to keep the focus off the real situation.

"Sorry," Craig said with a laugh. "I should say that

you're not really *her* type. After all, you're more the love 'em and leave 'em type, right?"

I was really starting to regret telling Craig that stupid lie. Add it to the list of lies. They were really starting to build up.

I swallowed back my guilt.

"Who? Andy?" Symon didn't even bother trying to hide his surprise. "No way." He dismissed the idea with a wave of a hand. "I don't see it at all."

Spotting my chance, I seized it. "I went through a bit of a phase," I started to explain. "It was my player phase, I guess." I turned to Craig. "But it's totally over now. I'm not at all like that now."

Fuck.

"Is that right?" Symon asked. "So you're looking for a relationship then?"

I hoped like hell the man would just keep his mouth shut.

"I don't know why we're talking about this anyway." I turned to Craig. "What the hell are you doing out here at the training center, anyway? Don't you have a business to run?"

Craig laughed. "I was actually on my way home from the city and thought I'd pop in. I haven't been here since the team moved in. Show me around?" He directed the question at Symon, who hopped up and closed the back of his vehicle again.

"Sure thing."

We turned to head toward the building, but before we

did, Craig looked at me. "If it's true that you're looking for a relationship, Andy, you better get the hell out of my sister's place."

I froze. I turned slowly, hardly daring to breathe as I faced my friend. There was no way he knew.

He couldn't know.

"Why is that?"

Craig laughed, the serious expression on his face melting into one of humor. "Are you seriously going to bring women home to Kat's apartment? I can't even imagine the hard time she'd give you."

I blew out the breath I was holding. "Right." I forced a laugh. "That probably wouldn't go over very well."

No probably about it, I thought as I drove away. It wouldn't go over well at all. But I had no intention of dating another woman. And that was the real problem, because there was only one woman who occupied my thoughts.

I was in trouble.

Chapter Twenty-One

KAT

I SOMEHOW MANAGED to wrestle all my new gear through the plaza and up the steep steps to my apartment. Kane had been more than happy to supply me with everything I would need for my trip, including—and probably most importantly—his excellent advice.

He'd pulled out a map and shown me a few trails that would be good for my skill level and done his best to reassure me that I was more than capable of hiking in everything I'd need for a night or two on my own. He even tried to convince me that I would enjoy it.

He wasn't successful in his efforts, but if nothing else, I felt slightly more prepared. At least when it came to the appropriate gear.

As for emotionally prepared, well, I didn't think I'd ever be ready for it.

The door was unlocked and Andy's shoes were at the front door, which meant he was home from his workout. I felt the familiar thrill race through me knowing he was already home.

"Hey," I called out, unable to see past the pile of things I was carrying. "Guess what I did today? Look what I—"

"Hey, Kat. We have company."

"Company?" The question was no sooner out of my mouth than Andy had relieved me of my packages and I had a clear line to the visitor sitting at my kitchen table.

"Jess."

The beautiful brunette looked up and gave me a warm smile, which only made me feel like an even bigger bitch because dammit, Jess was a lovely woman and I knew that logically. Still, there was nothing logical about the jealousy that instantly consumed me.

"Hi, Kat. I was just—"

"On a date with Andy?" Oh God, I could hear the cattiness in my voice, but I was totally unable to stop myself. "In my house. Yeah. I can see that." I nodded and without a glance in his direction, I left Andy holding my things.

"Kat, that's—"

"Inappropriate?" I shot the word like a dagger in his direction and marched straight through the kitchen to the staircase. "It really is."

It wasn't until I got upstairs and shut my bedroom door —with a little too much force—that I released the breath I'd been holding.

I leaned back against the door and dropped my head in

my hands. I'd been a first-class bitch to a woman who did not deserve it.

Andy didn't belong to me. He could date if he wanted to. Besides, I already knew that he was interested in Jess. Not that it made it any easier to see with my own eyes. Somehow I'd managed to push the thought of them together completely out of my head. And that only made it all so much worse when I'd walked in, because not only did I feel like an idiot, but it also became crystal clear to me that despite all the lies I'd been telling myself for way too long, Andy meant a lot more to me than just a happy for right now situationship, friends with benefits, or whatever stupid label I'd tried to put on it.

Tears pricked at the back of my eyes, but I refused to cry because I was the only person responsible for all of this. I'd done—

"Kat?"

The knock on the door startled me.

"Can I come in?"

"No."

I heard him sigh. "Well, I am."

There was a trace of humor in his voice that shifted my mood in a flash from one of feeling sorry for myself to full-on rage. I spun and flung the door open.

"You think it's funny? You bring your date into my house after…well…when we are…gah!" Frustrated, I moved to slam the door in his face, but Andy caught it and stepped forward, making it impossible for me to close the door.

"When we're what?" He looked straight into my eyes.

I narrowed them, letting him feel the full force of my glare. "Go back to your date."

"She left," he said simply. "And she wasn't my date."

"Yeah, right." I tried to turn away but a hand on my arm stopped me. "What else would you call it then? Oh God." I slapped a hand to my forehead as it all became clear. "She's just a friend with benefits, too, isn't she? And you brought her—"

"Enough."

Andy stepped forward and grabbed my other hand in his as he pushed me up against the wall, my hands over my head, so I couldn't get away. Anger, mixed with hurt and passion and too many things for me to sort through, pulsed through my veins. I struggled to wrench free from his grasp, but he held me tight.

Andy dodged my knee smoothly, before pressing his hips to mine, holding me in place and rendering me unable to kick out. "Kat. Stop." He stared directly into my eyes. "Will you give me a minute to explain what—"

"There's nothing you can say."

"That's not true." His lips twitched up into a little smile that he was only barely containing. "I can say that Jess and I are only friends. I can say that she's not my type at all."

I stopped fighting against him, but I couldn't look at him. I squeezed my eyes shut and turned to the side while Andy kept talking.

"I can tell you that I'm not into tall, willowy brunettes."

There was the slightest trace of laughter in his voice again, but it was gone a moment later when he said, "Fiery redheads with a completely unreasonable temper are more my type."

ANDY

I watched her suck in a breath.

She still wouldn't look at me, but I knew she was listening to me now.

"I can say that there's no one else, Kat. Not even close. There hasn't been for a long time, because as much as I know it's a bad idea..." I inhaled deeply. "No," I said on an exhale. "It's a terrible fucking idea. But it doesn't matter, Kat. I can't stop thinking about you. You are in every one of my thoughts. It doesn't matter what time of day it is. Or what I'm doing. It's you. It's always you."

She opened her eyes and turned slowly to face me.

There were tears in her eyes, but I couldn't stop. "I know this is supposed to be temporary or some situationship or whatever else it is that you keep saying, but I don't want that and I can't pretend anymore that I do."

"Andy, I—"

"Kat." I stopped her. I wasn't ready to hear her tell me all the reasons we couldn't be together. Why we didn't make sense and how her family would never be okay with it. I knew it was coming. But I needed just a few more minutes of pretending.

Without releasing my grip on her, I shifted both her arms into one hand, being careful of her still-healing injured wrist. I used my newly free hand to cup her cheek and keep her face turned up to me. "Kat, I'm done with all this bullshit of happy for right now. I want to be happy. With you." I shook my head and tried again. "No. I am happy with you. And I think you are too, Kat. Tell me I'm wrong."

She didn't answer right away. As the moments passed, I started to question whether I'd read everything wrong. Every kiss, every hug, every single fucking moment that we'd had together. Had she really bought into her own bullshit?

"Andy, you don't even live here." When she finally spoke, her voice shook. "You live eight hours away. Even if I wanted this for real, how could it even—"

"If I did? Does that mean—"

"Andy, I can't let myself get hurt. Not right now, not with everything going on. This isn't real, Andy."

"Fuck that." I dropped her arms and used both my hands to hold her face. "This is very real, and you know it, too." I kissed her to prove just how real it was between us. The moment our lips met and she melted into my kiss, I knew I hadn't read anything wrong. Kat felt exactly the same way I did.

I pulled away from her enough to say, "And, I do live here, Kat. I didn't want to tell you right away, but I took the job working for the ski team. That's why Jess was here. She's helping me find a—"

She shoved me back so sharply and suddenly, I almost tripped over my feet, but I caught myself before I fell on my ass. "What the fuck, Andy?"

Kat had her hands on her hips, the tears on her cheeks now dry. She stared at me, open-mouthed. "You mean, all this time you've been lying to me?"

I put my hands out and stepped cautiously toward her. "Not lying so much as not wanting to add to your stress. And selfishly, I didn't want you to put an end to things if you thought I was staying. Don't be mad."

"I'm not mad. I'm just—" She dropped her arms. "You're staying?" The anger had drained out of her voice. She looked up at me and shook her head. "Really?"

I pulled her into my arms and kissed her again. "Really. Jess was helping me find a place, but I've been putting that off, too, because, dammit, I really like being here with you, Kat. And I know I can't stay here forever. It doesn't make sense, so I am going to get my own place, but that doesn't mean I want this to end."

"You don't?"

"Woman." I laughed and scooped her up so she could wrap her legs around me. "You have got to know by now that I don't want this to end. Turns out I like you, Kitty Kat."

She trailed kisses on my neck. "I like you, too."

I needed her naked. Two strides across the room, and I tossed her back onto her bed. "Oh, I know you do."

I reached down, tugged her leggings off, and tossed

them to the side. "You like it when I do this." I dropped down on the bed between her legs and pressed her thighs apart, to give me access to her sweet center.

She moaned with anticipation. "You know I like that."

I had no self-control. I dipped my head and dove straight into my task. She shrieked and writhed immediately, but I held her still with one arm as I alternated between licking and sucking in just the way I knew would drive her crazy.

It didn't take long for her body to tense. "Andy, I'm going to—"

"Fuck yes, you are, Kitty Kat."

The moment I slipped a finger into her wet heat, she clenched around me as her orgasm took hold.

Hearing Kat cry out in pleasure was the sweetest sound in the world. I waited until her body relaxed under my touch before climbing up to pull her into my arms and kiss her. "That is the sexiest thing in the whole world."

She slipped her hand between us and squeezed my hard length, making me groan. "Oh, I don't know about that. I can think of something else that's pretty freakin' hot."

KAT

Fully satiated, my body limp and exhausted from our *make-up* session, all I wanted to do was stay in bed and let Andy hold me. But he had other ideas and insisted that we get dressed and head downstairs so I could show him what I'd bought earlier.

My trip to the store to pick up camping supplies felt like a lifetime ago, so much had happened. Hiking alone in the woods was the last thing I wanted to think about, but Andy was relentless. And when he promised to make me a quesadilla at the same time, I gave in.

After all, a girl needed to eat.

"It looks like you've got everything you need." Andy stood with his hands on his hips and assessed the equipment I'd laid out on the living room floor. "Sleeping bag, tent, stove, backpack."

"Don't forget these delicious-looking dehydrated food packs." I held up the pouches. "Kane said these ones weren't half bad."

I gave them a side eye and tossed them back on the pile.

"So when are you going?"

That was the question I'd been trying to avoid. "We still need to do the dance." We'd taken a few lessons in salsa dancing from a local dance instructor. And although we weren't completely hopeless, we still needed a lot of practice before we performed in any way.

"I didn't think you had to do the items in order." Andy returned to the stovetop to flip the quesadilla he was cook-ing. "You don't really have much left now, do you?"

I didn't. Not technically.

My painting was coming along nicely and more than that, I'd found a new hobby because I was actually enjoying the painting more than I thought I would. Learning Spanish was going to be an ongoing endeavor, for sure. But any language would be. That one would be up to Steven's discretion, whether he felt I learned enough or not. Either way, I was having a lot more fun learning Spanish than I expected. But that probably had a lot more to do with my partner in learning than anything else.

I shrugged. "I guess not." I grabbed a stuff sack and started to jam the sleeping bag into it. Kane had assured me that it would not only fit in the tiny bag but that I'd be able to squish it down to make it even smaller.

It was doubtful. Still, it was a good distraction from thinking about the actual hike.

"Would you like me to go on a trial trip with you before you do the solo trip?"

I looked up to see Andy standing at the stove with a flipper in his hand, watching me.

"It could be fun," he continued. "You and me, cozy in a tent? I mean, I think we'd be able to think of a few ways to stay warm."

I couldn't help but laugh. "I'm sure we could."

The idea of a trial run was tempting, but that would mean I'd have to go out into the woods twice. Besides, there was something about this last thing on my list that felt different from the others. I had to do it all on my own. From start to finish.

"But I think it's best if I just rip off the Band-Aid on this one." I finished stuffing the sleeping bag in the tiny bag, rolled the top of it and clipped the sides up the way Kane had shown me. And to my complete astonishment, the bag sucked down to an impossibly small size. I held it up triumphantly. "Look!"

Andy laughed at me before leaving the stove to kiss me on the forehead. "You're very cute, you know?"

I brushed him away and stood, leaving the pile of items on the floor to deal with later. "Remember, you can't tell anyone about the hike. I don't want to tell them until after."

"After…"

"After I get back," I said. "Or maybe after the whole will thing is done. I don't know." I shrugged. It was impossible to explain how I really felt about everything, and I was too exhausted to even try. "Just don't tell, okay?"

Andy made the sign of zippering his lips shut, locking them and throwing away the key. "I'll add it to the things I can't tell anyone about."

Before I could look at his expression and see whether he was kidding or not, Andy turned back to the stovetop and flipped the quesadilla out of the pan and onto a plate. "Dinner is served."

I grabbed a few napkins along with the cutlery and set it up quickly on the table while Andy brought the plates over.

I waited until after we'd had a few bites before I said anything. "You know why we can't say anything about…" I waved my fork between us. "Craig will lose his mind and—"

"I know, Kat." He sounded sad, but he stuffed another bite in his mouth and chewed before speaking again. When he did, there was a lightness in his voice. "He'll unalive me. And I like being alive."

With a little smile on my lips, I slipped from my chair and straddled Andy's lap. I kissed him and his body responded almost immediately, despite our earlier bedroom session.

"So, we won't say anything." I pulled back, catching his bottom lip between my teeth. "Because I like you alive, too."

Chapter Twenty-Two

KAT

"PURPLE. DEFINITELY GO WITH PURPLE."

"No way." Annie shook her head and plucked a Gerber daisy from a bucket. "Yellow. How can you not go with yellow?" She waved the flower in my direction.

"Because these are way too pretty." I grabbed a few iris stems from the bucket I was standing next to and wielded them as if they were weapons. "Purple for sure."

From the back of the storeroom, Charli groaned. "You two aren't really helping, you know."

I locked eyes with Annie across the rows of flowers that were ready to be turned into beautiful bouquets and laughed. "I don't know. I think we're being very helpful."

Annie crossed the distance and put her daisy next to mine. "Maybe yellow and purple?" She turned to Charli, but my sister wasn't paying any attention to us, so she looked at me with a grin. "Maybe we aren't being very helpful?"

"Nonsense." I grabbed the flowers and dropped them into a nearby bucket of water. "We are *always* super helpful." Together we walked through the storeroom until we found Charli, who was surrounded by different types of roses that she was carefully removing from their shipping boxes.

"I'll be the judge of that," she said with a shake of her head. "And right now, you'd be a lot more help if you could keep Poppy from putting anything else in her mouth." She gestured with her head to the baby, who was sitting up on a blanket, surrounded by plush toys.

"Anything else?" I grimaced and mouthed the words to Annie, who laughed, but I didn't ask for clarification, because it was probably best not to know what Poppy had gotten into.

"This little angel is never any trouble." I bent and scooped up my niece. "Are you, sweetheart?" The baby reached for my nose, and I laughed as I pulled away. "See? Charli, I don't know what you're even saying. She's perfect."

"She *is* perfect." Charli shook her head. "She's also a menace when she wants to be. Kind of like her auntie."

Behind her, Annie burst out laughing.

I turned and glared at her. "What are you laughing at?"

"Ohh…nothing."

I turned away but not before I saw the wink Annie gave my sister.

Charli busied herself with a box of white rosebuds. "You'll understand one day when you're a mother."

The thought stopped me and wiped the smile from my face. "What makes you think I'm ever going to be a mother?"

Annie reached out and took a bundle of roses that Charli offered her. She put them in a bucket of water and moved them to the side before handing Charli an empty one.

"Of course you're going to be a mother." My sister wiped her hands on the apron she was wearing. "You're going to find someone who makes you want things you never knew you wanted before, and everything will change so quickly your head will spin."

It was a good thing Charli was preoccupied because I was pretty sure that everything I was feeling was written all over my face. Visions of walking through the plaza hand in hand with Andy as we pushed a baby stroller flashed through my mind. But just as quickly, I pushed it away.

I'd never let myself think about such a future before. But then again, I'd never let myself think about anything beyond fooling around with Andy.

It was different now.

Wasn't it?

I inhaled deeply and closed my eyes.

Yes. It was different. Mostly.

After our fight, for lack of a better word, when Andy confessed that he was moving back to Trickle Creek permanently, things had felt very different between us, like we might actually be able to have something real. Maybe we could be a real couple.

But that was still a very big maybe.

"Ouch!" I snapped my eyes open to see my niece with a fistful of my red hair. "No, no, no, kiddo. We don't pull Auntie's hair."

Charli laughed. "See? A menace. Besides, she was just trying to get you to pay attention."

"To what?" I looked at my sister and best friend, who stared at me expectantly. "What was I supposed to be paying attention to?" There was no point denying I'd been daydreaming when I'd clearly been caught out.

"I was just wondering out loud what it would take for you to fall for someone who made you want things you never wanted before." Annie grinned at me and wiggled her eyebrows.

I had to resist the urge to murder my best friend.

Thankfully, Poppy once more reached out and tried for my hair.

"No way, kiddo." I held the baby out from me and distracted her by pretending to fly her through the back-room toward the exit. "You know what, I think maybe Annie and I should take Poppy for a little walk and give you a chance to get some flowers sorted."

ANDY

As far as I could tell, there was nothing wrong with the apartment. It was an open-concept studio style, but big enough for everything I needed. I didn't have much stuff, and what I did have would work well in the space.

It was bright and recently updated with new appliances, a light finish hardwood floor and neutral paint. The location was ideal as far as being in the middle of everything in the plaza. It was walkable to most of the shops, and had off-street parking.

Jess told me over and over how lucky I was that the apartment hadn't already been snapped up by someone. In fact, it already had, but the deal had fallen through, which was the only reason why I stood in it now.

"It won't last long," Jess told me again. "I'm personally showing it to three other interested parties later today. If you're even remotely interested in this place, you need to make an offer today."

"Today, huh?" I walked to the window that looked out over the plaza. Just across the way, and a little to the right, was Kat's living room window. I let my eyes drift up to the tiny third story, where the bedrooms were. Including the bedroom I'd been very happily sleeping in, with Kat in my arms.

The studio apartment was nice, but it wasn't nearly as nice as the feel of Kat's naked body pressed up next to mine.

Not even close.

"Even if your offer is accepted, the earliest move-in we could guarantee you wouldn't be for two months."

I turned to look at Jess, who had no doubt noticed where I was looking. "Two months?"

"There's currently a tenant in here," she said, not bothering to hide her smile. "Two months is generally the accepted amount of notice to give. As long as it's okay for you to stay at Kat's for two more months?" She wiggled her eyebrows, and I shook my head with a laugh.

"I know the other day you—"

"I didn't see anything." Jess held up her hands. "Nothing that is any of my business, anyway." She winked. "But I can see you're still a little hesitant about this space." She moved back into professional mode. "Is it the apartment or something else?"

Yes, I wanted to yell. I was hesitant about signing the paperwork on a new place when the only place I wanted to be was with Kat. But it wasn't as if I could say that. Not to Jess. Or anyone else.

"Two months you say?"

A lot could happen in two months. It could be enough time to figure out a way forward with Kat that didn't involve sneaking around like teenagers.

"Two months for this tenant, yes. And there's always an option to use the space for an investment property as well," Jess added. "I know Craig Carlson was using the space above the Sugar Shack as a short-term rental before his new chocolatier moved in."

I nodded and turned away from the window. "That's right. So that's always an option?"

Jess smiled knowingly. "Absolutely. In fact, if your

personal situation changes," she spoke carefully, "this would be an excellent investment property. I really don't think you can go wrong here, Andy."

"Okay." I clapped my hands together. "Let's put in an offer and make it official."

Jess immediately started talking numbers and details, but I was no longer listening. My attention was pulled by the flash of red hair in the plaza below.

Kat and Annie were coming out of Charli's flower shop. Kat's long red hair had been pulled up into a messy knot on the back of her head. Instantly, my memory flashed to earlier that morning, when her hair had been splayed out over the pillow when I looked up from between her legs and she screamed my name while she came apart all over my tongue.

That was a memory I would happily replay over and over.

A few minutes later, after agreeing to pretty much everything Jess suggested when it came to the offer, she'd headed back to her office and I was jogging over to Kat and Annie, who'd stopped in front of the Bean Bag coffee shop.

KAT

Charli was more than happy for the break and a few minutes later, Poppy was safely strapped into the stroller as we headed out into the plaza.

The moment we were alone, I spun on my best friend. "What are you thinking?"

Annie shrugged. "I'm thinking that I want the best for you."

"And having my family go ballistic would be the best?"

Annie laughed. "They wouldn't go *ballistic* if they found out you were sleeping with Andy."

"Annie! You can't say that out loud." I stopped abruptly and grabbed my friend's arm. "Besides, how do you know we're," I lowered my voice, "sleeping together?"

It was true that I generally told my best friend everything, which was exactly why she knew and had always known about my crush on Andy since we were kids. Annie also knew details about our hookup on my trip to Vancouver. But that was before. Now that Andy was staying with me, it was so much riskier. Not to mention the fact that Annie and my oldest brother were happily shacked up and madly in love.

Best friend or not, I couldn't risk Annie telling my secrets to Chase. Not if I didn't want everything to blow up in my face.

"Ha!" Annie pointed at me triumphantly. "I knew it!"

Shit.

"I didn't admit to anything."

Annie laughed. "You didn't have to, Kat. You forget that I know you. Like, know you know you. I can see it all over your face. Never mind the way the two of you look at each other."

"We do not." I froze with a moment of panic as I

quickly tried to dissect how the two of us behaved when we were around other people. "Do we?"

Annie was about to answer when a familiar voice sent a thrill through my body.

"Hey there, you two."

When I turned around to see Andy behind us, I couldn't help the full-body response I had at the sight of him.

"Hey, Andy. What are you doing here?"

"See?" Annie practically shouted the word and clapped triumphantly.

"See, what?" Andy looked between us, confusion on his face. "What are you two talking about?"

I glared at my friend before answering Andy. "Annie is just being—"

"Annie is trying to save your ass," my friend interrupted, the glee gone from her voice now.

Again, Andy shook his head, but before I could try to explain, Annie jumped in.

"I'm not trying to get involved with whatever is going on between the two of you, but I do think it's fair to tell you both that you're terrible liars and if you don't want anyone else figuring out what is going on here," Annie waved a finger between the two of us, "I strongly suggest that you sort out how to fix your facial expressions when you're around each other."

Andy looked at me with raised eyebrows.

"Yes," Annie continued. "Obviously I know. And so will everyone else if you don't stop looking at her like you can't wait to strip her clothes off and do dirty things to her."

"Annie!"

My face flamed with embarrassment, but Andy laughed.

He scrubbed a hand over his own face and shook his head. "Well, you're not wrong," he said, causing my blush to intensify. "But you do have a point." Then to me, he said, "She has a point. Maybe we need to be a little more discreet?"

"Well, it looks like you're both going to have the opportunity to practice that discretion right now." Annie waved at someone over my shoulder. "Hey, guys." She held out her arm and a moment later, my big brother Chase joined us, kissing Annie by way of a greeting.

"What are you all doing here?" Craig asked, as he too joined the group. "And you have the baby." He knelt and tickled Poppy until she giggled.

"We're giving Charli a break," I said. "She had a huge shipment come in, and it turns out we're more help with the baby than we are with the flowers."

Andy chuckled, but cognizant of what Annie had just said about practicing discretion, I made a point not to look at him.

"Don't tell me you're helping babysit, too?" Chase asked Andy.

"I can't take any credit for helping out," Andy said. "I was actually just with Jess."

A shot of completely unreasonable jealousy shot through me at the mention of the other woman, despite the fact that I knew nothing was going on with her and Andy. A moment later, the feeling of jealousy was replaced completely with a brand-new emotion when Andy said, "I'm putting in an offer on the apartment over the kitchen shop."

"What?"

Annie elbowed me sharply in the ribs.

I worked to keep my expression as neutral as possible. "You're buying an apartment?"

"He can't live in your tiny place forever," Craig said with a laugh.

"It looks like it will be a little bit longer though."

I still refused to look at Andy, despite the fact that he was clearly speaking directly to me.

"I mean, my offer still needs to get accepted. But there's a renter in there, so I have to give two months' notice."

Two months.

The thought of him moving out at all made me want to cry, but there was no way I could let that happen. Not now. Not in front of my brothers.

"What?" I shrugged and rolled my eyes. "I have to put up with you for two more months?"

I risked a glance at him then but quickly looked away when I saw the longing in his eyes.

"You can always move in with us," Chase said. "We have lots of room at the big house, and I'm sure Kat would like to have a little bit of space with everything that she's got going on right now."

My mouth fell open as I turned to stare at my brother and my friend. Annie gave me a look, and I quickly shut my mouth and busied myself with the baby, who'd thrown a toy out of her stroller.

"I mean, I don't think it's too much of a big deal," Andy said. "But if—"

"I kind of like you staying at Kat's place, actually."

I froze, the plush giraffe in my hand when I heard Craig. He liked that Andy was staying with *me*?

"Why is that?" Annie asked for me.

"If she's got a roommate, it's harder for any assholes to come along and take advantage of her." Craig spoke as if I wasn't right there. "Especially now with all this stuff with the will winding down. I think it's more important than ever for us to make sure that some dude doesn't mess with Kat."

Poppy let out a screech of protest and tried to lunge for the giraffe, reminding me that I was holding the baby toy hostage. I gave it back to my niece and rose to standing.

"What on earth are you talking about?" I asked my brother with a shake of my head. "Do you think I'm some helpless woman who will fall for some douchebag dude who only wants to date me for some family money that they think I might be getting?" I stared at Craig in disbelief. There was no way he was serious.

"It's actually not a bad thought," Chase added. "I mean, you're our baby sister, Kat. It makes sense that we should be protective of you."

"Protective, sure." I shot a look at Chase. "But not all caveman."

Chase shook his head, dismissing me. "No. I think Craig has a good point. As long as Andy's around, he can vet any jerks who might come around."

"Because *my* own personal judgment isn't enough?" I could truly not believe what I was hearing.

Andy had apparently chosen that moment to stay quiet, so it was Annie who stepped in. "So, you're not worried about Andy and Kat?"

If looks could kill, I would have been looking for a new best friend after the look I shot Annie. So much for flying under the radar.

But my brothers were way too focused on my personal lack of judgment to notice anything else. Craig laughed, and Chase made a snorting noise at Annie's suggestion.

"Yeah, no," Chase said. "Andy's one of us. He's our brother."

Annie raised her eyebrows.

"Besides," Craig spoke up. "Andy already knows how I feel about anyone like him going anywhere near Kat."

"Anyone like *him*?" I raised my brow in question. "And what is that exactly?"

"He's a total player, with more women than he can keep track of." Craig rolled his eyes. "Andy's made it perfectly clear that he's never going to settle down, and just keeps women around for—"

"Whoa." Andy raised his hand. "First of all, I already told you," he said first to Craig before looking at me, "I am not a player."

"If a leopard has spots," Craig muttered under his breath.

Andy shook his head and ignored his friend, focusing

instead on me. "People change," he said softly, his gaze locked on mine. "Things change."

He looked like he was about to say more, but Annie cleared her throat loudly. "It's not like any of this matters, anyway." She stepped between me and Andy, forcing us to look away from each other. "First of all, Kat is her own woman, and I think we can all trust her judgment. Wouldn't you agree?" When Craig and Chase didn't respond immediately, Annie nudged them. "Right, guys?"

"Yeah."

"Sure."

"Okay." Annie grinned. "Now, I think we should get this sweet little girl back to her mama for a nap. Come on, Kat."

With a sigh of relief, I steered the stroller around and together, Annie and I started walking. We'd only gone a few steps when Craig called out.

"Wait. What was the second thing?" he asked. "You said first of all. What was the other thing?"

Annie reached for my hand and gave it a reassuring squeeze before she turned to Craig. "There is no other thing. We can trust Kat's judgment. Period."

And then, before anyone else could respond, we walked away, and I couldn't help but wonder what I'd done to get such an amazing best friend.

Chapter Twenty-Three

KAT

A TRICKLE of sweat slipped down my spine. I plucked at my dress. It was hot. Way too hot. There was no breeze to speak of and even with the sun down, the heat of the day lingered.

I flipped open my green satin fan that was fringed with what only could be described as *fluff* and used it for what it was intended. But the breeze generated by the prop was hardly enough to bring me any relief.

"Damn, woman. You look—"

"Do not say a word." I pointed my fan at Andy as he joined me backstage. "I know I look ridiculous."

"You look far from ridiculous." Andy's eyes widened, and he took in the length of me with what even I could recognize as an appreciative gaze. And judging by the bulge in his very tight pants, it was obvious that he meant what he said. "You look positively sinful, Kitty Kat." He closed the distance between us and pressed me up against the makeshift walls that had been erected on the portable stage.

As much as I would have preferred to make out with Andy for the rest of the night, especially considering what the alternative was, it was way too risky. We stood on the edge of a stage with only a few thin curtains between us and most of the town.

Including my entire family, who were all eagerly waiting to bear witness to me and Andy dance the salsa in public.

I stepped away from Andy's arms and once more used my fan, this time needing to cool off for a different reason. "It's way too hot to do this," I said. "Maybe we should postpone?"

"You know we're not doing that." There was the slightest trace of laughter in Andy's voice. "We've been working too hard and you look too damn sexy to waste this outfit." The humor in his words was gone, replaced by a hunger that my body responded to. "I'm really glad we let Simone talk us into dressing the part."

Secretly, despite the bout of stage fright I was experiencing, I was glad we'd gone all out with the costumes. We'd practiced so hard with Simone and for hours every week in the living room of my apartment until both Andy and I agreed with our teacher that we were ready. And we were. When Simone suggested we perform on stage at Summer-Fest, Trickle Creek's annual summer festival, it felt like the perfect way to satisfy the requirements. We might as well look the part if we were going to go all out.

My dress was a rich emerald green with a plunging

neckline. The fabric that hugged my body was covered in a long fringe that I knew, from practicing in my bedroom earlier, spun and shook beautifully when I moved.

It truly was perfect.

"Hopefully the fringe distracts from my lack of skills."

He reached for me and whispered close to my lips. "Kitty Kat, I happen to know for a fact that you have—"

"Are you two ready to go?" Simone's head appeared between the curtains. "I'm going to announce you."

"Announce us?" I shook my head and turned to walk off, but Andy's hand clamped around mine.

"Go ahead," he said. "We're ready."

The moment the other woman's head disappeared, I shook my head. "I don't—"

"We're ready," Andy said again. "Just pretend it's the two of us in the living room." He led us to the center of the stage as Simone's voice boomed over the loudspeaker.

I didn't hear what she said or how we were introduced.

Instead, I focused on the strong presence of Andy behind me; he rested one hand lightly on my hip, and the other hand guided my arm, up behind me to his face.

"We got this, Kitty Kat," he whispered. "Let's just have fun, okay?"

"Okay." I squeezed my eyes shut for a moment. *Okay, Dad. Salsa seems like an odd choice. But this one's for you.*

Then the curtain opened, the lights flashed on, the music started and, with a well-rehearsed touch, Andy traced his hand down the side of my body until his hand was in mine and with a flick of his wrist, he spun me out on the floor, an arm's length away.

And just like that, we were dancing the salsa on a stage, in front of everyone in town hooting and hollering their appreciation.

ANDY

It was over almost before I realized it had begun. The moment I realized she was nervous, I swallowed any of the nerves I'd been experiencing and pretended I was way more confident than I was.

In the end, we'd pulled it off perfectly.

The crowd roared with delight as I spun Kat one more time. Shaking and shimmering in her green dress, she was without a doubt the sexiest woman on the planet. And her ear-to-ear smile as she performed absolutely lit her up.

With a final flourish, I pulled her in tight against me as the music ended.

The crowd went wild.

Sweating and breathing hard, her breasts rose and fell against me as she looked up at me with a look of pure delight. "We did it."

I bent and spoke into her ear. "You are fucking amazing, Kitty Kat."

Before I lost control and kissed her in front of the entire

town, I straightened up and took her hand, so we could take our bow.

The crowd chanted for an encore as we walked off stage, but we were let off the hook with the announcement of the next performer, local favorite, the Stoke Fires.

"I can't believe we did that." Kat jumped up and down the second we were safely off stage. "Can you believe it? We didn't screw up. Not once."

"Of course we didn't." I laughed and caught her face in my hands. "You're so fucking incredible." I bent to kiss her, but Kat spun away from me.

"You're crazy. We can't do that here." She chastised me, but there was a flirty grin on her face. "Remember what my brothers said...I need to stay away from men with ill intent."

I shook my head with a laugh. After Craig and Chase more or less insisted that I stay at Kat's house to protect her from basically all men, it had become one of our favorite jokes. "Oh, I definitely have some intent," I growled. "But it'll have to wait."

"It will." She reached for my hand and tugged me toward the stage stairs.

"Promise me you won't change out of that dress."

She shook her ass, sending her fringe flying and giving me a very nice view of the top of her thighs.

She winked and blew me a kiss, and I almost lost control again.

There was no time to entertain thoughts of what I'd like to do when I got her alone because a moment later, we were swallowed up by a crowd of well-wishers congratulating us on our performance as we made our way together to where the Carlson clan was waiting for us.

"Wow."

"Holy shit!"

"Incredible."

The women all crowded around Kat and heaped her with well-deserved compliments.

"Dude!" It was Craig who clapped me on the back and pulled me away from the women. "Who knew you had moves like that?"

I laughed. "Truthfully?" I gratefully accepted the beer that Craig put in my hand. "Not me. Thankfully, I had a good partner."

"I didn't think Kat had a rhythmic bone in her body." Chase and Asher joined the conversation.

"She was more of a tomboy than a dancer growing up," Asher said.

I swallowed back a retort about exactly how much rhythm Kat had when it came to certain activities, choosing instead to take a drink of the cold beer.

"So that's one more thing off the list then?" Craig looked at me expectantly.

I had a flash of guilt for knowing something more about the family matters. But I'd promised Kat I wouldn't say a word, and I intended to keep that promise.

It was just one more thing I was keeping from my best friend, and I hated it. But there wasn't much choice.

"You know that isn't for me to say." I lifted my beer in a

sort of salute but my friend just shook his head and turned to find his sister.

"Kat!"

She lifted her head from the group of women who were still fawning over her, as they should. What Kat had just pulled off had been nothing short of incredible.

"Hey." I grabbed my friend's arm and pulled him around. "Let her have her moment," I said when Craig looked at me. "It's been a big night and she's worked hard. She was so nervous to perform in front of everyone. Just give her tonight."

"I agree." Chase backed me up. "The list isn't going anywhere. Let's just relax and have a little fun tonight."

I gave him an appreciative look.

It took a moment, but Craig nodded in agreement as well. "You're right."

"I know." I laughed as I drank deeply from my beer in an effort to quench the thirst I'd just worked up. I was going to need to switch to water if I didn't want to catch a buzz. "What is this SummerFest, anyway? I mean, I'm not the most observant person, but I don't think I remember this festival when we were kids."

"It's something the businesses in town came up with as a way to celebrate tourism and summer," Asher volunteered. "The local chamber of commerce is in full support."

"Besides," Chase said. "Who doesn't love a little summer fun?"

I couldn't disagree with that. Maybe next year, I'd be

able to partake in a bit more of that fun. With the dance performance looming over our heads, Kat and I had been squeezing in some last-minute rehearsal time in her apartment—not to mention a little stress release in the bedroom—and had missed most of the festivities during the day.

"Looks like a huge turnout anyway." I scanned the crowd, my gaze ending up on Kat. Always Kat. She was the star of the show and, surrounded by her friends and family, she was positively glowing.

She was so damn radiant and sexy as hell. I couldn't take my eyes off her. As if she sensed me watching her, she turned and locked eyes with me. I was rewarded with a smile and a quick wink meant just for me before she was once more swallowed up by the group.

KAT

"Careful," Annie whispered in my ear. "Your feelings are written all over your face, and I can't be the only one who sees it."

I pulled back and stared at my best friend. "My feelings?"

"Sorry," Annie corrected herself. "I should say your *lust*."

My eyes widened, and I purposely turned away from Andy. We'd been so careful; there was no way. I shook my head and dismissed her concerns. "You're crazy. It's just because of the dance."

"Which was so hot." Noa jumped into the conversation. She fanned herself dramatically. "If I didn't know better, I would think the two of you were a couple."

"We're not!"

"They're not!"

I looked at Annie and nodded my appreciation before turning to my brother's new fiancée. "Andy and I have been friends forever," I explained. "He's like a brother." The lie burned on my tongue, but it wasn't the time nor the place to get into anything more.

"Andy's been hanging around forever," Charli said. "It's so nice that he's helping Kat out with everything."

"He's been a good sport." I nodded and tried to move the conversation safely onto a different topic. "Did anyone—"

"But you two totally looked like a couple out there." My sister narrowed her eyes, as if she were thinking about something. "I mean, I know it was a dance. But there was something different about the way you both looked at—"

"Hey! There's Kane."

I had never been so grateful for Annie and her mad skills when it came to distraction.

"Kane!" Annie raised her hand and waved to the man over the crowd.

I copied her, turning my back on my sister as I did so. "Hey, Kane." I greeted him with a hug. "What are you doing here?"

He laughed. It was a deep, throaty sound that rumbled through me. There was a time I'd been a little bit attracted to Kane, and it wasn't a secret that he'd been interested in me. But that's as far as it went. Just a mutual attraction and interest between two people who didn't have time in their lives for anything more. And who wasn't secretly in love with their brother's best friend.

After a while, we'd settled into an easy friendship, but it wasn't hard to see that Kane would be an incredible catch to a woman who was more available.

"I think the whole town is here." He grinned. "Besides, I wouldn't have missed your performance. You were incredible."

"Thank you. I had a good partner." Annie's warning fresh in my mind, I resisted the urge to look in Andy's direction.

"From where I was standing, you were the star up there." Kane flashed me another devastating smile. "I know you're kind of a big deal salsa dancer now," he said. "But do you think you could do me the honor of a regular dance? It does look like a lot of fun out there."

It did.

After Andy and I left the stage, the band had immediately fired up the crowd with a series of upbeat tunes and the dance floor in front of the stage was packed.

Next to me, Annie jabbed an elbow into my side, and it was the only reminder I needed that it was probably a good idea for me to look even a little bit interested in anyone besides Andy.

"Sounds good." I took Kane's proffered hand and without a glance back, let him lead me onto the busy dance floor and into his arms.

Chapter Twenty-Four

ANDY

I DOWNED the rest of my beer and crunched the can in my hand. My teeth clenched, my body tense as I watched Kane leading my woman onto the dance floor.

She didn't even look back. Not once.

Jealousy flared through me, and there wasn't a damn thing I could do about it.

If I went and cut in, everyone would talk about it. Especially when I pulled Kat into my arms and kissed her in front of her entire family. Because that's exactly what I'd do. More than anything, I wanted to claim her as mine for everyone to know. Even her family.

Fuck the consequences.

"Whoa, tiger." Symon, who'd appeared next to me, holding his baby girl in his arms, spoke just loud enough for only me to hear. "You might want to give that can a break before anyone else puts two and two together."

I looked down at the crushed can in my hands and quickly tossed it in a nearby bin. I shook my head and looked up at my friend. "There's nothing to put together."

Symon put his hands loosely over Poppy's ears. "The fuck there isn't." He dropped his hands and kissed the baby on the top of her head. "Right now, I think I'm the only one who sees it." He shrugged. "That and the conversation we had the other day…it didn't take much to figure it out."

"I told you, there's nothing to figure out." I tried to look away, but I couldn't take my eyes off Kane, who had his hands on Kat.

"Right. You keep telling yourself that." Symon chuckled. "But don't worry, it's not for me to tell. I'm not going to say anything."

"Say anything about what?" Asher joined us. He offered me another beer, but I shook my head. "Oh." Asher pointed over the crowd. "About that?"

I didn't have to look to see that he was pointing at Kat and Kane.

"That's not a match I saw coming," Chase said, joining in the conversation.

"I don't like it." Craig shook his head. "Nothing against Kane, but—"

"He's not good enough for her." I swallowed back a possessive growl.

"Exactly." Craig pointed at me. "He's a good guy, but he's not right for Kat."

"I don't know," Asher said. "He owns a business."

"With his sister."

Asher shrugged. "We have a family business."

"It's different," Craig insisted. "Besides, I thought we decided to keep men away from her."

"We did." Damn it. I really needed to just shut up and stay out of it. But I couldn't help myself. "Besides, I agree with Craig. He's not good enough."

"So, who is good enough for Kat, Andy?"

If Symon hadn't been holding his baby, I would have punched him square in the jaw. I clenched my fists and gritted my teeth when Symon stirred the pot even harder.

"You?"

I didn't have a chance to reply, because it was Craig who spoke up first. "Yeah, right. You know I love you, man. But there's no way I'd let you anywhere near Kat. It's a good damn thing you're like a brother to her."

Right. A brother.

I glared in Symon's direction and swallowed hard before nodding once. "Good thing." I turned and caught a flash of green as Kane spun Kat out of his arms before catching her and holding her close.

My blood boiled through my veins. There was no way I could stand there and watch them for another moment. Not without doing something I would regret.

"You'll have to excuse me, guys. I need to find a bathroom and a bottle of water."

I didn't wait for a response and didn't risk another

glance in the direction of the dance floor before pushing my way through the crowd in the opposite direction.

KAT

I tried to stay in the moment with Kane, especially considering Annie had already pointed out how obvious my connection with Andy was. But I couldn't help but sneak a glance over in Andy's direction on my last spin.

He was watching me and even from the distance, I could see he didn't look happy. Surely he knew Kane was just a friend? Still. I knew how I felt when I saw Andy with Jess.

I twirled out to the end of Kane's arm before he spun me quickly back to him.

"Your dress is incredible," he said with a smile as his hand once more found my back.

"It is made for spinning." I smiled but didn't meet his eyes. I hoped I wasn't giving Kane mixed signals. It was just a dance.

We moved together with the music until the band wrapped up the song. The moment it was over, I took a step to the side, putting distance between us, and clapped and cheered for the musicians on stage.

"How about—"

"Thanks for the dance." We spoke at the same time.

Over Kane's shoulder, I looked to where Andy had been standing with my brothers. He was gone. I quickly scanned the crowd and caught the flash of his green shirt that matched my dress sneaking to the end of the plaza toward the river. "Sorry." I gave Kane an apologetic smile. "There's something…" I shook my head. "I have to go. Thanks, Kane."

Without waiting for his response, I slipped through the crowd. I avoided the section where my family was sitting and moved straight to where I'd seen Andy go.

There were fewer people at the far end of the plaza. "Andy!" My voice was mostly swallowed up by the band, who'd resumed playing.

I saw another flash of movement and moved through the darkness between two buildings that led to a back alley.

"Andy?"

I heard the crunch of gravel and spun around. "Andy. What the hell are you—"

The question was lost as he caught my mouth in a hungry kiss.

A moan slipped from my throat, and I melted into his touch.

Andy's hands were all over me. My own hands tugged at his shirt and pulled it from his tight dancing pants so I could slip them under the fabric and feel the heat of his skin.

"You drive me fucking crazy, woman." His hands moved up my legs, under my dress, and his fingers dug into my ass, lifting me up.

I responded by wrapping my legs around his waist and crushing my lips onto his again. I was starving for him.

Andy backed me up until my back hit the brick wall of

the building behind me. "I need you so bad." His voice was rough in my ear. "Watching you dance with…I fuckin' hated it, Kitty Kat. You're *mine*."

Pleasure shot through me at his words and straight between my legs, where I was already so wet for him.

"I'm yours, Andy. Always."

He growled and nipped at my lip. One hand held me in place while the other searched between my legs and found the scrap of panties I'd opted to wear instead of the sheer pantyhose that had been part of the costume because it was far too hot of a night.

If only I'd known just how hot my night was going to get.

I tore my mouth from his so I could focus on the task of undoing Andy's pants and shoving them down to release his hard cock.

My hands fisted his length, and he moaned. "You're killing me."

"The feeling is so mutual."

I lifted my hips, and Andy guided himself to my entrance but stopped. "This is crazy."

I nodded. "It is."

"Anyone could see us."

"Then we better be fast."

He groaned and dropped his forehead to mine. "There's no way I can walk away from you right now. I need you so bad."

"Not as bad as I need you, Andy." I gripped his ass cheeks with my fingers and urged him on. It was risky.

Beyond risky. My entire family was only steps away. Not to mention the rest of the town. The odds of being found out were ridiculously high. And as much as I hated hiding our relationship, it wasn't the right time to say anything.

Still.

I couldn't have stopped myself for anything in the world. And I was pretty sure Andy felt the same way. We needed each other with an intensity that was beyond anything either of us had ever felt.

Andy thrust deep into my heat, and at the same time caught my mouth in a kiss to swallow any noise I would make.

He filled me completely and he felt so good inside me, it only took moments before I felt the start of my orgasm building within me.

Andy's thrusts came hard and fast. His hand protected my back from slamming into the brick wall. Not that it would have mattered. The only thing I could feel was the pure ecstasy of having my man claim me in such a way.

Soon, my orgasm crashed through me at the same time Andy took his own release.

It was fast, furious, and the hottest thing I had ever experienced.

"Holy shit, woman." Andy cupped my cheek in his hand.

"My thoughts exactly." I giggled as he slowly lowered me to the ground. "I can't believe we just did that." I straightened my dress while Andy put himself back together. "I mean, my apartment is right there."

"No way." Andy tucked a hair behind my ears and shook his head. "I wouldn't have made it." I started to giggle but he looked so serious my laughter died on my lips. "I want to be with you, Kat."

"You just were, silly." Once again, I tried to giggle. I took a step toward the plaza. We would need to get back soon before we were missed. "Isn't that—"

He stopped me by grabbing my hand and pulling me back into his arms. "No. I mean, I want to *be* with you. Let's tell them."

More than anything, I wanted that too. But it was too risky. My brothers…my sister…they would freak out. There was already so much going on. So much change. And they'd be so mad. Craig would *hate* Andy if he found out. I'd lose him. And I couldn't risk that.

I shook my head.

"Kat. I—"

"No." I refused to look at him. "I told you. We can't say anything. Not now. Not with everything…I can't."

"Why not? Why can't we? You're an adult. And it's not like I'm some random guy. I'm—"

"I can't lose you, Andy."

"You wouldn't."

"But I could. Don't you get that?"

I could see it on his face. He didn't understand.

"Craig could…and they'd be so mad." I shook my head so hard, my whole body moved, causing my fringe to fly around. "I can't deal with it right now. Not with everything else. We've been through so much as a family. What if they aren't okay with it? What if they freak out and cut you out?"

He opened his mouth but he couldn't speak, because he knew it was a possibility. A very real possibility. It wasn't a secret that all my brothers had some sort of ridiculous protectiveness over me. And it had only gotten worse after our father died. As if they personally were responsible for my future.

"You know they could."

He swallowed hard and reached for me again. "That's a risk I'm willing to take."

I looked at him, the silence between us growing until finally I whispered, "But I'm not."

"Where did you go?" Charli descended upon me the moment she saw me. "I've been searching—are you..." My sister's gaze scanned me up and down, finally locking onto my face. "Are you okay?"

I thought I'd done a good job putting myself back together, but there was probably no hiding the myriad emotions slamming through me. "I'm fine. Just tired." It wasn't a total lie. I was exhausted from pretending I was totally okay with denying anything real with Andy.

I was tired of all of it. Especially the look on his face when I told him no again.

Maybe I should just do it? Rip off the Band-Aid and tell my family I was sleeping with Andy and that we were—

"Kat?"

Steven, my father's trusted employee and executor of the will, appeared through the crowd.

"Steven? Hi. What are you doing here?"

He laughed, and the sound soothed me the way a comfortable blanket would. Something about Steven reminded me so much of my father and made me feel, even for the tiniest bit, that he was still there.

"Are you kidding, Kat? I wouldn't have missed this for anything." His smile was warm. "You were fantastic."

Something about Steven giving me accolades made me blush. I ducked my head and shrugged a little. "It wasn't a big—"

"It was a very big deal." He stopped me. "That's why it was on the list. Everything on the list is—"

"Private." I lifted my eyebrows and gestured to my sister, who was still in earshot.

Fortunately, Steven was sharp, and he picked up on it right away. "I understand. That's actually another reason why I wanted to see you. There's one more thing I need to discuss with you."

My stomach flipped. Was there another list? Or something more that I didn't know about? Secretly, I already kind of thought I'd gotten off easy compared to some of my siblings. But maybe I'd been too hasty?

I let Steven lead me to a quieter spot.

"Don't panic," he said. "It's not bad, I promise."

"I'm not worried."

"Okay." He chuckled. "But it does have to do with the last item on your list."

"So you mean, my Spanish is good enough?"

He chuckled. "There wasn't really an end goal where that was concerned. But yes. You've made pretty good progress with your Spanish lessons. And I think your father would have agreed with that. Your painting, too. The landscape you dropped off at the office last week is gorgeous. I'm having it framed for my living room."

"You are not." My mouth fell open.

"I am, too. It's very good. You have a lot of talent, Kat."

Instead of protesting again, I simply smiled. "Thank you, Steven. That means a lot, coming from you."

"It's exactly what your dad would say, too."

Hot tears pricked at the back of my eyes, but I wouldn't allow myself to cry. Not there.

"So the only thing left on the list is…"

He nodded. "The campout."

"I'm hoping you came here to tell me it was a mistake and I don't need to do it at all." Just thinking about the backpacking trip sent my pulse racing. It was far more terrifying than anything I'd done already—and that included jumping off the bridge and dancing a sexy salsa in front of the crowd combined.

"Sorry, Kat. But I did come here to give you this." He handed me a small bag. "The package isn't to be opened until the first night."

"Wait." My head jerked up. "The *first* night? I thought I only needed to do one night." I wanted to yell, but I kept my voice low. I really couldn't deal with my siblings knowing about the backpacking trip. Not tonight, of all nights. It was far easier to keep it to myself.

His smile was kind. "That is the requirement, yes. But your father did hope you might stay out for a bit longer."

Automatically, I shook my head. "Oh, there's no—"

"Don't make a decision now." He stopped me with a gentle touch on my arm. "You can wait and decide later. Maybe even once you're there. Remember, it's not meant to be opened until you're there. Whenever that is."

I looked down at the bag and back at him. "I don't know when…I haven't really decided…"

"You don't need to tell me anything."

We were quiet for a moment, neither of us speaking while the festival wound down around us. The band was finishing up their set, which meant soon, the lights would come on, and everyone would head home.

After a moment, Steven's smile dipped a little. "Are you okay, Kat?"

The question was so unexpected coming from him, that I almost laughed until I saw his serious expression. I swallowed hard. "Of course. I'm fine."

"With all of this, I mean," he said. "You're handling it okay? I know that…well, I can't help but notice you haven't been to your father's grave lately."

Automatically, I took a step back. "How…how did you know?"

"It was a guess, mostly." Again, his smile was kind, if not

a little sad. "I visit myself, and I know you usually leave fresh flowers when you go."

It was true. I had made it a point to visit my father's grave on the second Friday of every month, the same day that I would have gone for our father-daughter lunch date.

"I've been..." Dammit. The tears that were threatening earlier slipped out. I swiped at my eyes. "I've been busy. It's been a lot." I shook my head and took a deep breath before looking at Steven again. "I'm fine." I stepped back, the conversation over as far as I was concerned. "Thank you for this." I lifted the bag containing the mystery package. "Is that everything?"

The older man nodded slowly. "Just try to remember that your relationship with him was as unique as this list is. He had a reason for everything. And if you take time to let yourself, you'll see what those reasons are."

Chapter Twenty-Five

KAT

FOR THE WEEK FOLLOWING SUMMERFEST, I did a champion job of ignoring everything I didn't want to deal with, including the fact that Andy was sleeping in the spare room instead of my bed. He said it was because he needed sleep in the week leading up to him leaving with the ski team for a training camp in Switzerland, but given the fact that he hardly touched me and wouldn't look me in the eye, I knew it was because of our fight in the alley.

It wasn't so much of a fight as a disagreement. Not that the semantics of it mattered. Not when it was evidence that the two of us were on very different pages.

At least Andy thought we were.

I just needed him to leave well enough alone until I could get through my list and put my father's death behind me once and for all.

Then maybe I'd have the capacity to deal with the inevitable fallout from my family.

Still, when I looked across the backyard at the big house where we'd all gathered for the weekly family dinner, the last one before Symon and Andy would leave for training camp in a few days, I couldn't think of a world where my family—Craig specifically—would be okay with me dating Andy.

I sighed and tipped my head back to the afternoon sun and tuned out the hustle and bustle of the family around me as some of them prepared dinner on the grill, and others set the large patio table so we could enjoy the beautiful late summer day and eat outside.

It was August already, which meant the days were starting to get shorter. Soon, the nights would get cool. Especially up in the mountains. And that meant, if I was going to complete my list, I needed to get moving.

I had done a good job pushing thoughts of the backpacking trip out of my head ever since acquiring my gear. And the mystery package Steven had given me. That was still sitting on the hall table, where I was reminded every day of the challenge ahead of me. All I had to do was tie up my hiking boots and choose one of the trails Kane had suggested.

"Kane! Come sit over here."

Kane?

My eyes flew open, and I lifted my head to see Kane Nelson walk into the backyard. He held a bottle of wine in one hand, and a bouquet of flowers in the other.

What the actual—

"Kat." Craig waved me over. "Kane's here. Come say hi."

I quickly scanned the yard. All my siblings and their partners were beaming, as if they were in on some kind of joke.

More like a setup.

My gaze landed on Andy, who wasn't even bothering to hide the scowl on his face. He glanced in my direction, raised his eyebrows, and with a shake of his head, disappeared inside.

It was totally a setup.

And there was nothing to be done about it except be social. And hopefully, make it clear I wasn't interested. So much for relaxing. With a groan, I stood from my lounge chair and made my way around the pool to where Kane was currently surrounded by my family as if he were my date coming to pick me up for prom.

"Hey. What are you doing here?"

"Your family invited me." He flashed me his handsome grin. "I hope that's okay?"

I shrugged noncommittally. "The more the merrier. Knowing this group, there's plenty of food."

Lucy giggled.

Oh yes. They were definitely in on this together.

"These are for you." Kane handed me the bouquet. "And I brought wine."

"Why don't I open that and bring you both a glass?" Asher swept in and snatched the bottle out of Kane's hands.

It took everything I had not to roll my eyes.

I shook my head. Might as well get dinner over with. "Why don't we sit down? I'm sure dinner will be ready soon."

And then the focus will be off me, and whatever this is, I wanted to add. Instead, I pasted a smile on my face that I hoped looked friendly and in no way encouraging of what was obviously a hookup, and led him to the table.

"The burgers are delicious," Kane said a few minutes later after we were all served and had settled into what I hoped would be a boring family dinner. "Thanks for including me."

"Of course." Asher sounded way too friendly and over-the-top.

I shot him a look but my brother wouldn't look in my direction.

"We're happy to have you."

"Hey, you know what we haven't talked about in the last few months?" Craig sat up in his chair.

He was working hard to pretend he'd just come up with an idea, but I wasn't fooled. Something was going on.

"What would that be?" I narrowed my eyes and looked at each of my siblings in turn. Only Charli would meet my gaze. She smiled encouragingly at me. "What's going on?" I asked her.

It was Chase who spoke up. "We were all talking about the love bonus."

"Love bonus?"

"All of us found love when it was our turn to carry out Dad's requirement," Chase continued, as if I hadn't spoken.

"And here we are a few months into your turn, Kat, and you—"

"Oh no." I held up my hands as if I could stop the freight train that was already in motion.

"Love bonus?" Kane looked confused.

I might have spared a moment to feel bad for the man if I wasn't so busy trying to control the rage toward my siblings.

"It's nothing official," Asher said. "But first was Chase and Annie." He pointed in their direction. "And then Charli and Symon finally decided to face their feelings. And now look. They have Poppy."

"Right, but they already knew—"

"And Craig and Lucy." Asher cut me off. "The two of them found each other because Craig was required to hire a nanny."

Craig draped his arm around Lucy, who dropped her head to his shoulder.

"And of course, I got lucky when Dad made it so that I couldn't work anymore and the love of my life jumped into my truck." Asher kissed Noa on the cheek.

Under any other circumstances, I might have found the whole scene sweet.

But there was nothing sweet about my entire family planning an elaborate setup with a man who I had no romantic interest in while the man I actually had feelings for sat directly across from me at the table. Especially considering that man was currently upset with me for not telling my family about us.

Everything was such a mess.

"So you all thought that maybe I would get this love bonus," I used air quotes, "if you helped it along?"

Charli opened her mouth to agree, but she must have sensed that I was only barely containing my anger, because she quickly closed it again.

"Because you all think I need help when it comes to dating?" My voice rose. "Or maybe you thought that if you chose who I dated that you could make sure he was good enough for me?" I glared at my brothers, who'd done nothing but chase men away my entire life because they didn't measure up to some ridiculous standard they'd made up in their heads. "Did it ever occur to you that I am perfectly capable of handling my own love life?" I swallowed hard and purposely avoided looking at Andy, who no doubt had a very different opinion on whether or not I was handling my love life or not.

My appetite gone, I threw the napkin on my plate and stood. "Can I talk to you for a minute, Kane?" I held out my hand to my shell-shocked friend, who nodded and followed me inside.

"Umm." Kane glanced behind him the moment we were safely inside. "I think I might have walked into something."

"I'm sorry." I sagged against the kitchen counter. "You didn't deserve to be caught up in that. My family is...well, they are full-on crazy is what they are."

"Don't worry about it." Kane laughed. "But it might be

partly my fault. I did kind of tell Asher I was interested in you."

I opened my mouth to set him straight, but he beat me to it. "Don't worry. I know you don't feel the same way."

"I think you're a great friend, Kane."

He stepped closer to me and took my hand. "And I think you're a great friend. I hope that hasn't changed?"

"Not as far as I'm concerned."

"Friends then?" He held out his arms for a hug.

"Definitely." I moved into his embrace. "Friends."

It would be so much easier, so much less complicated if it was Kane I had feelings for.

I blew out a breath and was about to step out of his arms when an angry voice said, "Am I interrupting something?"

ANDY

I'd never been a jealous man. But I'd had just about enough of Kane Nelson putting his hands on *my* woman.

I worked to relax my jaw and unclench my fists. It wouldn't do any good if I got into a goddamn fistfight in the Carlsons' house.

"Andy?" Kat stepped away from Kane, but the other man must have sensed my anger and put himself between us. "What are you—"

"You know why I'm here, Kat." I stepped closer. "I

came to make sure you were okay after…" I waved my hand behind me. "After that ambush."

"She's fine."

A sound dangerously close to a growl slipped from my throat. Maybe a fistfight was exactly what I needed after all.

"Kane." Kat put a hand on the other man's arm. "It's fine. Andy and I…well, it's fine."

I took a step back and forced myself to relax. It wasn't Kane I was upset with. Not really. It was the situation. None of this would be happening if we could just be public with our relationship.

"You and Andy are…"

Kat answered the question with a sharp nod of her head. "Maybe you should go."

Kane looked between the two of us, carefully assessing the situation before finally turning to Kat. "Maybe I should. Let me know if you need anything, Kat."

"Of course." She smiled as Kane finally left us alone, but the moment he was gone, she spun on me. "What the hell was that? Were you going to come in here and—"

"Fight for you?" In two strides, I closed the distance between us. "Fucking right I was." I couldn't keep my hands off her any longer. Consequences be damned. I pressed her up against the counter and held her face between my hands. "Do you know how hard it was to sit there and watch everyone push you two together? And then to see his hands on you…" I swallowed hard. "Dammit, Kat."

I kissed her hard and fast as if we needed the other to breathe. Our hands were everywhere.

"We can't." Kat pulled her mouth away in a gasp. "Not here." But in the next moment, she crushed her lips to mine again.

She was right. It was reckless and crazy to be doing this in the kitchen with her entire family outside, but I no longer cared.

"I'm tired of pretending that this isn't a thing," I said between kisses. "You're mine, Kat." I nipped at her neck, causing her to tilt her head and groan. "You've always been mine."

"Yes."

Again, I sucked and nibbled the sensitive spot, making her writhe against me. "Say it," I commanded. "Say that you're mine. And you're ready for the fucking world to know it."

Her breath was ragged in my ear, her voice hardly more than a whisper when she said, "I'm yours."

Hell yeah.

"And you—"

"What the actual fuck is going on here?"

A hand grabbed my shoulder and tore me away from Kat so abruptly I didn't have time to process that she wasn't in my arms anymore until I saw Asher's angry face inches from mine.

"I'll fucking kill you, Fisher."

"Asher!" Kat squeezed between us before Asher could follow through on his threat. "Stop." She pressed both hands against her brother's chest and shoved, forcing him to take a step back.

"Somebody better explain what's going on here."

Asher was no longer in my face, but I had no doubt he'd swing at me if given half the chance.

"Because it looked like…" Asher rubbed a hand over his face. "I don't even want to say what it *looked* like." He muttered something under his breath and turned away. "What if it had been Craig who walked in? Are you two out of your mind? He will lose his shit."

I tried to reach for Kat, but she stepped just out of my reach as she went to her brother.

"Asher, it's not what you—"

"Yes, it is." I stopped her. "It's exactly what you think it is."

Asher spun on his heel and shot me a look. "You really do need to shut up, man."

I was smart enough to know when to shut my mouth, despite my instincts to grab Kat and proclaim my feelings for her right there. It wasn't the right time. This wasn't what she wanted.

Not like this.

Still, I might keep my mouth shut, but that didn't mean I wasn't going to make sure Kat knew we were in this together. I stepped up and pulled her back into my arms. She didn't resist but sank into my embrace. Asher looked ready to murder me, but everyone in the room knew it was nothing compared to how Craig would have reacted.

"You're playing with fire, man." Asher shook his head and ran a hand through his hair. "Craig is going to—"

"What's Craig going to do?"

All three of us froze when Craig surprised us by slipping in the side door. He held an empty bread basket in his hands.

"What's going on in here?" Craig grinned as he looked around the room. "Where did Kane go and why—"

His eyes focused on me and my arms that were still wrapped possessively around Kat.

I knew without looking that our clothes were disheveled and both of our lips were swollen from kissing, never mind the marks I'd no doubt left on her neck.

I watched the expression on my best friend's face change as he connected the dots. In only a matter of seconds, the smile slipped to confusion, and then to realization before settling into the hard line of fury.

"I'm going to fucking kill you."

Asher caught him as he flew toward me. At the same time, I stepped back and used one arm to push Kat behind me and out of danger of getting caught in the middle of the inevitable fight.

Asher tightened his arms through the back of Craig's and held him firm. "Cut it out."

"Fuck that, Asher." Craig thrashed in his arms. "I will kill him."

I didn't doubt it. Craig's face was unrecognizable. He was normally so relaxed and calm. Our entire life, I'd never seen him so angry. And all that anger was aimed at me.

"Craig." I held up a hand. "Hear me out."

"Fuck you, Andy. She's my *sister*."

I took a step closer. "It's not what you think."

Craig's face started to turn a dangerous shade of purple, and it was quickly becoming clear that Asher wasn't going to be able to hold him back much longer. But I wasn't worried. Craig would understand when he had a chance to explain how I really felt about Kat. They all would. I was sure of it.

"Andy?" Kat tugged on my arm.

I turned to see the worry and sadness in her eyes.

"Maybe you should go? This is all such a mess."

Her brothers momentarily forgotten, I cupped her face in my hands. "It'll be okay, Kitty Kat. I'll—"

"Get your hands off her." Craig spat out the words and jerked hard out of Asher's arms.

"It's not like you think," I said again. I took a step toward her. "Craig, I really—"

The solid connection of Craig's fist in my jaw absorbed whatever I'd been about to say, and I staggered backward with the blow.

My hand went to my jaw. My eyes flew open to see my best friend coming at me again, his fist raised.

"I will kill you, Andy."

KAT

"Stop!"

I'd had just about enough of the bullshit overprotective brother act. And whatever it was Andy was doing. Did he have a death wish? I'd never seen Craig so angry. My normally happy-go-lucky, easy-going brother looked as if he would actually make good on his threats and kill his best friend.

I put myself between them and shoved Craig with both hands.

Hard.

Asher caught him and once more yanked his arms behind his back.

"Enough." I was barely containing my own anger. As the only redhead in the family, I was supposed to be the one with an uncontrollable temper. Seeing Craig so mad was completely new territory.

Of course, he'd never found out that his best friend was sleeping with his baby sister before. That was new, too.

With Craig momentarily restrained, I turned to Andy and crouched down on the floor where he'd landed. "Are you okay?"

"I'm fine." He touched his fingers to his bloody lip. "It's nothing."

"It's not nothing. You're bleeding." I spun and looked at my brother over my shoulder. "He's bleeding, Craig."

"Good." He struggled against Asher's hold. "And I'll do it again. Get up, Fisher."

"Would you just stop already?" I cried. "Can you get him out of here?" I appealed to Asher. But I'd underestimated my other brother's anger, too. He might be holding Craig back, but he was just as pissed.

"I think it's best if Andy leaves." Asher spun Craig around and shoved him toward the door to the backyard before pushing him outside. "I don't know what you two were thinking with this." He waved his finger between us. "But I think it's clear you weren't. Seriously. What did you think would happen?"

Andy struggled to his feet.

Behind us, the door opened and some of the others piled inside. But I didn't turn to see who it was. It didn't matter.

"We treated you like family, man." Asher shook his head. "We *trusted* you."

I opened my mouth to object, but Andy spoke first.

"So, it's like that?"

Asher's fists were clenched at his sides.

I stood in the middle of the room—Andy on one side, my family on the other.

"I think you should go, Andy." Chase stepped forward. His face was riddled with confusion and he was obviously missing most of the details, but it didn't take much to read between the lines of the situation.

"You don't have to—"

"Maybe it's for the best, Kat." Charli put a hand on my arm and pulled me back, leaving Andy alone on one side of the room. "Just let everyone cool off. We can all talk later."

"To hell we can." Craig had reentered the room. "Get out."

Andy looked in my direction and held out his hand. "Come with me, Kat." It was an impossible ask, and he knew it.

A frustrated scream rose up inside me, and I swallowed

it down. The exact thing that I didn't want to happen was playing out. I knew Craig wouldn't understand. I knew it would all implode. And now I was going to lose someone I cared about. Andy was going to walk out and as much as I hated it, I was going to have to let him.

I took a breath and looked down, away from his extended hand, unable to meet his eyes. "I'm sorry, Andy." I took a step away.

My family came first. They had to.

Chapter Twenty-Six

KAT

AFTER THE DISASTROUS dinner when Andy left and like a coward I hadn't gone after him, I'd stayed to face my family's barrage of questions.

Thankfully, Annie stepped in when it became clear that I didn't have the capacity to answer any of them. They knew enough.

And they'd already all formed their opinions about it. It didn't matter what I said about it. They were angry. Especially Craig and Asher. They felt betrayed, and I couldn't blame them.

They *had* been betrayed.

By both of us.

I'd slipped away from the big house as soon as I could. I expected that Andy would be waiting in my apartment. But there was no indication that he'd been there at all.

I texted and left messages on his phone that went unanswered. I waited up as long as I could but finally succumbed to sleep shortly after midnight; the events of the evening had exhausted me.

I woke just after four in the morning and reached over to Andy's side of the bed, but it was empty.

Slipping out of bed, I crossed the hall to the guest room where he'd only slept that last week while we'd been fighting. But the bed hadn't been slept in.

We'd been fighting because I was afraid to tell my family about us. "See?" I said to the empty room. "This is why I didn't want to tell them."

But wasn't it inevitable that it would happen eventually anyway? I'd always known that we could never be together. We'd only been delaying the inevitable.

I retrieved my phone from the bedside table but there were no messages. I tried calling him again, but my call went straight to voicemail.

There was no way I could go back to sleep, but it was too early to do much more. I made my way downstairs and stopped in front of the hall table where the package from my father still sat waiting.

I picked it up and held it. "What do you have for me now, Dad? What more do you need from me?"

I blew out my breath and put the package down again. I was being unfair. My father had never demanded much of me. As the baby in the family, I'd always gotten away with more than the others. My dad always let me off the hook if there was something I didn't want to do.

Except for this.

I stared at the package and my ready pack that was propped up against the wall next to the table.

"Okay, Dad. You win. Let's go hiking."

It had to be better than sitting around, waiting for another fight.

Or worse, having to admit that I screwed it all up and had lost Andy for good.

ANDY

"Thanks for letting me crash here."

The kitchen in Symon and Charli's house was bright and welcoming, full of plants. A tabby cat hopped off the counter when I walked in and threaded herself through my legs. I bent and scratched the cat's ears.

"I know that probably didn't make you very popular with the rest of the family," I said to Charli when I looked up.

"Don't worry about them." She handed me a cup of coffee, which I accepted gratefully. "They'll calm down."

I noticed she didn't say that they'd get over it, or come to accept my relationship with Kat.

"I hope so." I sipped at the coffee and sank into a chair at the table as Symon walked in with the baby on his hip.

"Did you get any sleep, man?"

With nowhere to go after leaving the big house the night

before, I'd been beyond grateful when Symon followed me outside and offered me a bed for the night. I could have gone back to the apartment; everything inside me wanted to, but there was a time to push the issue and time for a little space. I was smart enough to know that a little time for everyone to cool off, me and Kat included, was probably a good idea. Besides, she'd made her choice clear.

I shook my head. "Not much." I watched while Symon strapped the baby into her highchair next to me and tossed a handful of tiny fish-shaped crackers on the tray. She was such a happy baby, it was hard not to smile just watching her. "Someone looks like she got a good night's sleep."

"Ha." Charli laughed from the counter where she was whipping up a bowl full of eggs. "I swear, that child gets by on only fifteen minutes a night. I'm exhausted. It's my natural state by now."

I leaned over and handed Poppy a cracker that was just out of her reach. "If I'd known, I could have sat up with her. I don't think I slept more than fifteen minutes myself. But I probably wasn't very good company."

I sat back in my chair and lifted my mug of coffee.

"So." That was all Symon said as he sat across from me at the table.

"So."

"I had an inkling that's what was going on."

"You knew?" Charli appeared and smacked him with a tea towel. "How could know about this and not say anything?"

"Whoa." Symon held his hands up. "I said I had an inkling. That's like barely even a guess." He raised his eyebrows in my direction, but I wasn't going to be much help. "Nothing was confirmed." He winked at me, and I only shook my head and looked back at my coffee.

Would it have been better if I'd confided in Symon when I had the chance? Maybe I could have softened the blow? The rest of the family didn't seem as protective over Charli and her choice of partner.

"Why is that?" I said out loud. "Why didn't your brothers freak out when you and Symon started dating?" I elaborated before either of them could ask what I was talking about. "Why did they all go straight-up ballistic when it came to Kat, but they're totally cool with you?" I pointed a finger at Symon.

"I am pretty awesome." Symon shrugged.

"Seriously, though?"

Charli rolled her eyes at her husband. "Seriously," she said. "It's because Kat's the baby, Andy. You know that. Craig and Asher have always been super protective of her. And Chase...well, that's different because he was gone so much when we were young, but I think even he recognizes that Kat's, well..." She shrugged. "She's Kat."

I shook my head. I knew all that. I'd seen their protectiveness firsthand growing up. But I never could have envisioned the level of rage I'd witnessed from either of them. "That can't be it. It doesn't make sense that it's just big brother protectiveness."

Charli blew out a breath and took a seat next to Symon. "Honestly, I think it only got worse after Dad died. It's as if they just thought it was their job to look after her."

"And you?"

She laughed. "I never needed looking after."

"But neither did Kat." The way I saw her was a strong, independent woman who had her life together. She owned a successful business and handled her life without a problem. What was I missing?

"That's how you see her." Charli gave me a knowing smile. "But that's because you see her as a woman." She stopped short of wiggling her eyebrows, a detail I was grateful for. "But the guys see her as a little girl. A little girl our dad always coddled a little bit. Definitely more than the rest of us. I think when he died, they just subconsciously kept caring for her like that. But I agree with you, Andy."

"You do?"

She laughed. "Of course I do. My little sister is badass. Are you kidding? She started a successful business and made her own way in the world almost before any of the rest of us. She works her ass off and she's never asked for help. Which is a different issue." Charli nodded. "I have that problem, too." She winked at her husband. "But I do agree with you that she doesn't need to be taken care of, and she definitely doesn't need her big brothers playing gatekeeper on her personal life. Especially not when she's clearly chosen a good one."

I let her words soak in. "Wait. You think I'm a good one?"

"You don't?" She looked at me pointedly. "Because I will retract every single thing I just said if you—"

"No. No." I held up a hand and laughed. "Obviously, I'm a good one. But it means a lot to hear you say that you think that when clearly you're the only one."

I dropped my head and stared into the depths of my coffee cup. I hadn't wanted to admit it earlier, but with everything that went down the evening before, it wasn't the punch to the face that hurt the most. It wasn't even that Kat had chosen to side with her family—I knew she was in an impossible situation. It was that the men I considered brothers hadn't thought I was good enough for their little sister. The way Craig, Asher, and even Chase had looked at me with so much anger and disgust had been the biggest blow I could have sustained.

"Andy. Look at me." Charli used her *mom* voice, so I had no choice but to comply. "I'm going to ask you a question that I'm pretty sure I already know the answer to. And really, it probably should be one of the guys to ask, but since my brothers are clearly too stubborn to pull their heads out of their asses, I'll be the one to do it."

I waited while she sat back in her chair and took a deep breath.

"But before I ask it, I need to apologize on their behalf. You didn't deserve that reaction yesterday." She shook her head as I moved to protest. "No. It doesn't matter if you sprung it on them, or if you held their hand through every moment. It doesn't matter how they found out about you and Kat—the guys never should have reacted that way and you didn't deserve it.

"And you definitely didn't deserve to be punched in the face." She looked pointedly at my swollen lip. "How does it feel?"

I nodded. "I'll live."

"You're a good man, Andy Fisher. We love you like family. All of us," she added. "Even if they're mad right now. They still love you, and they'll get over this, too. Just as soon as the shock wears off, they're going to see what was right in front of all our faces." She laughed and looked at Symon, who shrugged. "Yeah, yeah. You had an inkling."

"I was pretty sure." He winked, and she shook her head.

"So," Charli focused on me again, "the only question left is..."

I inhaled deeply, pretty sure I knew what she was going to ask.

Charli leaned over the table and looked straight into my eyes. "Do you love her? And if the answer is what I think it's going to be, what exactly are you going to do about it?"

"And whatever it is you're going to do," Symon added, "you better do it soon. We leave for Switzerland tomorrow morning."

Fuck.

"I need to tell her," I said, more to myself than anyone else.

Charli smiled knowingly. "But what are you going to tell her?"

"I think Kat deserves to be the first person to hear that, don't you?"

"Good answer." She winked. "Have you heard from her this morning?"

I shook my head. "I lost my phone somewhere last night. Probably on the kitchen floor after..." I touched my jaw tentatively. "It doesn't matter." Only one thing mattered now. Kat. "I've gotta go."

Chapter Twenty-Seven

ANDY

THANKFULLY, it was early enough that the roads were mostly empty as I broke all kinds of laws racing from Charli and Symon's house on the edge of town to the plaza parking lot.

I ran through the empty plaza and straight up the stairs to Kat's apartment. I slipped my key in the lock and moved straight up to the bedroom.

"Kat?" I knocked softly on the door and pushed it open, not wanting to startle her. But as I stepped into the room, I realized there'd been no need to worry.

She wasn't there.

"Kat?"

I went to the bathroom, but it too was empty. A quick search of the house revealed what I feared. She was gone.

Reflexively, I reached for my phone. But came up empty.

"Dammit." I had a few different choice words for Craig at the moment but I swallowed them back. The focus had to be on finding Kat. But where the hell would she go so early? It was only just past seven in the morning and unless she was—

The hike.

I sprinted down the stairs and stopped short by the hall table. The pack was gone from where it had sat for the last few weeks. And the package Steven had given her to take was gone, too.

"Dammit, Kat." I rubbed my hand through my hair and tugged at the roots. "Now? You choose to do this now?"

There couldn't have been a worse time. I paced the hallway like a caged animal, trying to figure out what to do next. There was no way I could go to Switzerland now. Not with her up in the woods by herself.

Her family didn't even know there was a hike. Let alone where she'd be going. I had a very slight advantage in that I knew about it, but Kat hadn't told me where she was going to go. And even if I did know, she was supposed to do it alone. I couldn't charge through the woods and ruin it for her just because I wanted to talk to her. That wasn't fair.

Still, I couldn't sit around and do nothing.

At least if I knew *where* she'd gone, that would be something. And it was only for one night. I'd be waiting for her when she came back.

There was only one person who might know something. And considering how I'd treated him the night before, I wasn't looking forward to that particular conversation. Hopefully, Kane didn't hold a grudge for grade-A assholes.

But first, I was going to need to get my phone back.

KAT

I had no concept of how long I'd been hiking, but with the heavy pack on my back, it felt as if I'd been walking all day. Out of the two options Kane had shown me for the trip, they both involved huge elevation gains, which was to be expected in the mountains, but one was slightly longer, and to my surprise, that was the hike I'd chosen because Kane said it had a small but beautiful glacier-fed lake at the end.

The idea of setting my tent up next to a lake felt right, and so I'd made the last-minute decision to hike to White Swan Lake despite a few extra kilometers needed to reach it.

I'd been so caught up in my thoughts and feelings from the night before, it had been easy to forget my fears of hiking alone in the woods. For the most part.

But several hours had passed, and the flood of emotions that had fueled me at the start of my walk had begun to wear off.

Now it was just me and the woods.

And all the creatures that might be hiding in the trees, ready to attack.

"Hello, Mr. Bear!" I called out the way my dad had taught me when I was a child.

Make noise on the trail, Kat. You never want to startle an animal.

I could hear his voice as if he were there with me. "Okay, Dad. I'm doing it. I'm here." I sucked in a breath and kept walking. "I still don't understand this one, but I guess that doesn't matter at this point, does it?"

The birds chirping and flitting through the treetops were the only answer I got. Not that I expected much more.

"It's just a hike," I said aloud, embracing the idea of talking to myself. "I like to hike. Maybe I would do more hikes if I wasn't so busy with the shop."

Not that I'd been very busy lately. Cutting back on my clients over the last few months had been a welcome break that I never would have expected.

I lifted my head from the trail and looked around at the forest and the mountains that peeked through the branches. I inhaled deeply and let the clean air fill my lungs.

"Maybe I should hike more often?" I laughed at myself and quickly added, "But maybe not alone." I lifted my shoulders back. "Maybe Andy would like to—nope." I cut myself off. "We're not going to think about him today." Or how I screwed everything up. The hurt look on his face before he turned and walked away from me was seared into my brain.

I shook my head to clear the image.

"Today I hike," I affirmed aloud.

And with any luck, I'll be too exhausted to think of anything else.

Like how I screwed up what could have been something

real with the only man I'd ever had feelings for because I was too scared to choose him over my family.

I couldn't let my thoughts go there.

Not yet. I owed it to my family to finish this once and for all. It was up to me now. As soon as I finished up my list, it was over and we'd all be able to move on.

Finally.

———

ANDY

I got lucky when I got to the big house and Annie answered the door instead of Chase. There was a time, less than twenty-four hours earlier, when I would have knocked on the door and walked in. But a lot had changed in a very short time, and I was pretty sure I wasn't welcome there at all.

"Hey, Andy." Annie stepped onto the porch and shut the door behind her as she did so. "I assume you're looking for this?" She handed me my phone.

I glanced at the screen, but the battery was dead so I tucked it in my back pocket. "Thanks, Annie. I wasn't sure what to expect over here this morning."

She sucked in a breath and shrugged her shoulders to her ears. "It's better than yesterday, but..." She glanced toward the closed door. "I think there are still some raw feelings."

I didn't expect much more. "Have you heard from Kat?"

She was the only one who mattered. The rest of them could be as angry as they needed to be. It was Kat I was concerned about.

"Not since last night." Annie shook her head. "She was pretty upset when she finally went home." She bit her bottom lip and looked like she wanted to say more. I knew Kat and Annie were best friends, but Annie was also engaged to Chase. It put her in an awkward position.

"It's okay, Annie. I know it's not the easiest spot for you to be in with…well, all of this. I just want to make sure she's okay." It was a stupid thing to say because of course she wasn't okay. I'd seen it on her face the night before. I'd seen the hurt and worry and pain all over her beautiful features because I'd asked her to do the impossible and choose between me and her family.

If I could take it back, I would. I would never put her in that situation. And not just because I knew I could never win, but because I'd do anything to never see that look on her face again.

I'd got what I came for, and with nothing more to say, I turned to leave.

By the time I returned to the plaza, there were plenty of people—a mixture of tourists and locals—wandering between the café, ice cream shop, and various other stores. I bypassed the Sugar Shack, moving quickly in case Craig happened to be inside and saw me walking past. The last thing I needed was another fight, and something told me Craig hadn't calmed down enough to have an actual conversation with me.

I hesitated outside Alpenglow, Charli's shop. There was no point in telling her yet that Kat was gone on an overnight hike. Not when I still didn't have any more details. Besides, there was no reason to panic, and Kat had her reasons for not wanting her siblings to know about it.

I would honor her desire for discretion. At least for now.

The shop's doors were open to the warm summer morning. A handful of customers browsed the sale rack outside, but there weren't too many people inside from what I could see.

Kane and his sister, Krysta, both stood at the front counter, their heads bent over something they were discussing. Sensing my presence, they both looked up as I neared.

"Oh no." Kane shook his head and held out his hand. "I told you last night, I do not want to get involved with—"

"It's not that." I held up my hands in peace. "I swear I'm not looking for a fight, Kane, and I'm so sorry for everything last night. That wasn't fair to you."

"It sure as hell wasn't." He crossed his huge arms over his chest.

It wasn't lost on me that if I *had* been looking for a fight with Kane, I would have lost. Badly. The man was massive, his muscles built from a life outside on the mountain.

"I know," I said. "And I really am sorry. Things kind of spun out of control last night, and that's why I'm here."

Kane dropped his arms and considered me. "What do you mean?"

Krysta looked between us. "Is everything okay?"

"I'm not sure," I answered honestly, and took a step forward, confident Kane would at least hear me out before kicking me out of his shop.

"It's Kat. I think she went on her overnight hike, but I have no idea where she might have gone. I need your help."

His sister shot him a look, but Kane ignored it. "You don't know where she went?"

I shook my head. "I'm hoping you do."

He nodded and pulled out a map book from below the counter. "I suggested two different spots that would be good for a solo overnight."

"A solo overnight?" Krysta's mouth fell open. "Kat? She went on a campout?" She chuckled and shook her head. "No way. Kat hates camping. I tried to get her to go with me a few years ago and—"

She trailed off when she realized Kane and I weren't laughing.

"Oh shit." She nodded. "She really went?"

"Yes," I said. "At least I think she did. Her bag was gone this morning and...well, last night was a bit of a..." I looked at Kane. "Let's just say it only got worse after you left."

Kane let out a low whistle and returned his attention to the book in front of him. "Here." He pointed to a spot on the map. "This is the first spot. Farmer's Ridge. It's only about six kilometers in and it has a gorgeous view of the valley. And this..." His finger trailed across the page. "Is the second spot I suggested. White Swan Lake. It's a bit of a longer hike in at eight kilometers, but the lake is super pretty and tranquil."

"Oh, White Swan is gorgeous," Krysta said. "I'd go there."

"I agree." Kane nodded. "I don't think she was very excited about the extra distance," he said. "But Kat did seem to like the idea of camping next to a lake if she had to do it."

"And she did have to do it," I muttered under my breath.

"Are you going to join her?"

I looked up from the map. More than anything, that's what I wanted to do. I'd run the entire eight kilometers if that's what it took to get to her. But I couldn't. I shook my head.

"No," I said after a moment. "That's not an option. Besides, she'll only be gone for one night. So maybe I'll go to the trailhead."

"Well, that's good, because she has all the gear she needs, but the storm that's coming in will be a doozy."

In my head, I was already working out the logistics of canceling my flight to Switzerland and staying an extra few days. I'd have to talk to Symon and—

"Wait. What did you say?"

Kane shook his head. "I said she has all the gear she should need and—"

"No." I stopped him. "About the weather. What did you say about a storm?"

Kane pulled his phone out and opened the weather app.

"There's a huge storm forecasted." He turned it to face me. "But it's not rolling in until tomorrow night, so in plenty of time for her to pack up and get back down the trail before it hits."

I scanned the weather report myself and finally nodded. "Okay, that's good. She'll be back in lots of time."

"As long as she doesn't love it and decide to stay an extra night." Krysta laughed, as if the very idea were ludicrous. Which it was.

"Yeah. I don't think we have to worry about that," I said. "One night, and she'll be back."

KAT

The equipment Kane had sold me was easy to use, and it didn't take long once I made it to White Swan Lake to get my tent set up and my sleeping bag unrolled.

I even went for a little walk and found the stream that fed into the lake to fill up my water bottles. I dropped the water purification tablets in the way Kane had shown me and let it sit the required amount of time before drinking.

It was late afternoon before I got hungry and pulled out the little stove with a fuel canister that Kane assured me would heat up water in less than a minute to rehydrate my not-so delicious-looking camp meal. It was yet another thing he'd been right about. After I had a full belly and had settled in on a large rock overlooking the peaceful lake, I couldn't help but admit that maybe a backpacking trip wasn't so bad after all.

I would have guessed that the quiet and solitude would become oppressive and overwhelming. I was so used to being surrounded by people, or the constant connection of my phone and all the distractions of modern life. When was the last time I took the time to just *be*?

With my eyes closed, I inhaled deeply and took my time blowing out my breath before opening them. "Okay," I spoke aloud. "I guess I can't put it off much longer." The sun would be setting soon, and I wanted to be sure I opened the special package that Steven had given me in the daylight.

I reached around to pick up the little package but didn't open it right away.

Something about the package felt final.

"Here goes nothing."

Carefully, I unwound the paper to reveal a letter that had been wrapped around a small bottle of whiskey.

"Whiskey, Dad? Really?"

I laughed and put the bottle aside to open the letter.

My dearest baby girl,
If you're reading this, it means you've done it. You've conquered my life list and your fears. Yes, I knew you'd save the camping trip for last.

I chuckled a little, but it wasn't enough to keep the tears from burning my eyes. Only one line into the letter and already I was a mess. I blinked hard and kept reading.

I hope by now you've spent some time thinking about everything I asked you to do and hopefully you understand why I wanted this for you. You're my youngest, Kat. And that means no matter what happened, I didn't get enough time with you. You see, there could never be enough time for a father to teach his little girl everything about life that he would like, or to tell her everything she needs to hear from him. I hope I've done enough and said enough for you to know how much I love you and how proud I am of you.

In my last letter, I told you how proud I am of you for your hard work, but there's so much more about you that fills me with pride.

You are truly the best parts of both your mother and me. Thankfully, there's a bit more of her in you than me.

I swiped at my cheeks. There was no way I could keep the tears at bay any longer.

I bet you're wondering about what I put on the list.

I laughed because he was right.

Hiking up the peak was something I wished we could have done together. I can't believe I lived in Trickle Creek all those years, and never got around to it. There are a lot of things I never got around to. I hope you thought of me when you got to the top, baby girl, because I was there with you.

I swallowed hard and tipped my head up to the sky in an effort to pull myself together before I continued.

The painting lessons and learning another language were two things I should have done when I was younger. I was always envious of creative people, and learning another language is never a bad idea. As for the karaoke and the salsa dancing, those were two things to push you into the spotlight. You deserve to shine, and I'm willing to bet that's exactly what you did. And I hope you had fun in the process.

Oh, I'd had fun. Memories of that dance would stay with me for a very long time. I kept reading.

I wonder whether you decided to bungee jump or skydive. Either way, I'm sure you cursed me for putting such a thing on the list and honestly, I wasn't so sure at first. After all, those are both very dangerous things and my job as a father is to protect you, not push you out of planes.

But you and I both know that you don't need

protection. I raised you to be strong and capable, and that's exactly what you are. It's important to remember that. Just like it's important to push yourself.

"Okay, Dad. I get it." I put the letter down and gazed out over the lake. It had been months since I'd visited Dad's gravesite and just sat and talked, but the words came easily…and strangely, I felt closer to him than ever. "You want me to push myself and live a full life. I'm trying." I laughed out loud. "Hell, I'm here. That's a pretty big push."

I sat for another moment and let the tears dry on my cheeks before picking up the paper to finish the letter.

One last thing, Kat. Do you remember when you were little and you'd climb up on my lap when I got home from the office? You insisted on sitting with me and having a drink, just like me. Your mother gave you apple juice instead of my whiskey of course, but you always wanted to try it and I never let you. So here you go.

I reached down and picked up the bottle he'd included.

It's my favorite whiskey. So when you look up at the stars tonight, think of me and know I'm always with you.

The one thing I know for sure is that this life is shorter than you expect it to be. Promise me you'll live the best way you know how. Always make time for the unexpected. Push yourself to try new things, embrace your creative side, and never shy away from the spot-light—because you deserve to shine. But most impor-tantly, love hard and without regrets.

Love always,
Dad

Chapter Twenty-Eight

KAT

SLEEPING under the stars was nothing short of magical. Never in my life had I seen so many stars. Even living out in the mountains where there wasn't a lot of ambient light to interfere with the view, it was still nothing compared to being on top of a mountain with no light at all except for the moon. The stars were like a blanket over me as I lay out in my sleeping bag.

The whiskey had made me a little tipsy, so I'd only had a few sips. I surprised myself by getting as comfortable as I had in the wilderness alone, but I still wanted to be sure I had a clear head in case of emergency.

Or wild animals.

Although I'd tried my best not to think of that at all. And soon, I didn't.

Instead, I spent my evening talking to my dad as if he sat

right next to me, and it was all the companionship I needed. Anyone else would have thought I'd completely lost my mind, but I couldn't remember the last time I felt so close to him.

I lay in my sleeping bag, cuddled up against the cool summer evening, and told him all about Andy and how I'd always had a crush on him—but that crush had become a full-fledged love affair over the last few months. I shed a few tears as I told him how Andy had fought with Craig and how mad the others had been. And then how I stood there and let him walk away from me even though my heart was breaking the entire time.

Right as I was drifting off to sleep, I could have sworn I heard my dad tell me it was okay. To follow my heart. Because life was too short to do anything else. And my dad was right—it was important to love hard, with no regrets.

When I opened my eyes again, the sky was the milky gray of predawn and my sleeping bag was covered in dew. I carefully slipped from it and moved into my tent to get a few more hours of sleep before I faced the day.

When I woke again, the sun was high in the sky. My phone—although it had no service—told me it was already nine. I'd slept far later than I'd planned.

But then again, I had nowhere to be.

I stretched my arms over my head as far as I could in the tiny tent and relished the feeling of freedom.

I didn't have any clients. No appointments. No one expecting me. No emails or phone calls to answer. And best of all, none of my siblings were there to give me the third degree about my relationship choices.

Maybe unplugging and going camping was okay after all.

I laughed at myself and reluctantly pulled myself out of my sleeping bag. My plan had been to wake up, pack up, and get the hell out of there as quickly as I could.

But that had been before.

I unzipped my tent, tugged my boots on, and went to stand on the lakeshore.

Before I realized just how purely spiritual it was out there.

I turned and slowly took in my surroundings. The lake was so still that the surrounding mountains gave off a perfect mirror reflection on its surface. Birds chirped all around me; the sky was a beautiful shade of blue, with only a handful of fluffy clouds. There would have been no one more surprised than me that I didn't want to go home.

Steven *had* mentioned that my dad hoped I'd stay for two nights.

My eyes fell to the more than half-full mini bottle of whiskey I'd dropped the night before. "I *do* have enough whiskey for one more night."

I did a quick count of the food rations I had and discovered I had more than enough. Kane had given me a variety of dehydrated meals to choose from, and instead of picking, I'd stuffed them all into my bag.

"I guess there's no reason *not* to stay."

ANDY

I'd done my best to keep busy.

After informing Symon—who fortunately was much more understanding than I'd expected—that I would not be getting on the flight to Switzerland in the morning with the rest of the team, I drove the backroads until I knew exactly which hiking trail Kat had taken.

I found her car parked at the trailhead for White Swan Lake and was secretly very proud of her for choosing the longer hike. She'd either been very determined to take on the challenge or just that willing to get as far away from me and her family as possible.

I spent the rest of the day and night in her apartment, pacing and trying to sleep when I wasn't repeatedly listening to the voicemails she'd left when I didn't have my phone.

KAT:

Andy? Call me.

Where are you? Why aren't you answering?

You're mad. But it wasn't fair, Andy. Don't be mad.

Okay, fine. Be mad at me if you want. But I'm mad at you!

Could you just call me?

She sounded sad the last time she called, the anger from the previous message gone. More than anything, I wished I could pick up the phone and call her back the way she wanted. But I knew that even if she had her phone with her, there was no cell service up in the trails. And I had no intention of leaving a message. Not when talking to her face-to-face would be so much better.

Time moved painfully slowly. I did the math in my head. If she woke up with the sun and had a simple breakfast before packing up, she should be on the trail around nine at the latest.

According to Kane, with a lighter pack it should only take a few hours to make her way back down the trail, which meant that even if she got a late start, Kat should be back to her vehicle by around two o'clock at the latest.

Which was a good thing because the storm was forecasted to start blowing in around five. We should be down the mountain and with any luck, wrapped up in each other's arms and cozy in bed by then.

Just in case she moved faster than I expected, I was waiting at the trailhead by noon. But by two, when there was still no sign of Kat coming down the trail, I started to worry.

Overhead, the clouds were starting to close in and the wind was picking up.

By reflex, I started to hike up the trail but stopped myself. I was wearing running shoes and I didn't have so much as a sweater with me. Even if Kat was hurt on the trail somewhere, I wouldn't be any good to her if I wasn't even a little bit prepared.

But I couldn't sit around and do nothing. A decision

made, I drove as fast as I safely could on the gravel mountain roads as I raced back to the town and ran through the plaza to get to Kane's shop moments before the man was locking up for the day.

"We close at—"

"She's not back."

"What?"

I shook my head. "She's not back. She should be back by now." I pointed to the sky. "The storm."

Without another word, Kane reopened the store and went inside.

I followed him. "I need shoes. Size twelve. A pack and a first-aid kit. And maybe a rain jacket."

Kane shook his head. "You can't go up there."

"The hell I can't."

"Not now. It's not safe. Not with the storm. I'll get Search and Rescue—"

"Give me the shoes, Kane." I held the other man's gaze until finally, Kane looked away.

"Fine. But I'm still calling in S&R. You're not equipped, Andy. It's going to turn into a two-man rescue."

"It's not. I'll get her."

Kane moved quickly and helped me with shoes, a jacket, and a pack that included a handful of food rations, a first-aid kit, and even a change of clothes.

"I owe you."

"You sure as hell do."

"For the record, I know it's not a good idea." I lifted the pack. "But I can't not go, Kane. I need to go."

"I get it, man." Kane nodded and handed me a small device. "This is an emergency locator and communicator. It works on satellite signals. I should have insisted Kat take one." He shook his head. "You can communicate with text just like a phone, and that button there is a direct line to Search and Rescue. If you push that, they'll know exactly where to find you, okay? And if I don't hear from you by nine, I'll call them myself."

"Thank you." I nodded my appreciation and tucked the device safely away before taking off.

I needed to get to my woman.

KAT

I spent my day exploring the shoreline, careful not to stray too far from my campsite. I'd grown bolder, for sure, but I still wasn't completely comfortable out there alone. The sun was out and it turned into a gorgeous, hot summer day. With no one around, I stripped my clothes off and danced around the shore naked before diving into the glacier-fed water to cool off.

My *swim* only lasted seconds before I ran out of the water, laughing and shrieking, having vastly underestimated just how cold it would be. It didn't take long for the hot sun to warm me again and lull me into an afternoon nap.

A cold breeze woke me hours later. I didn't know how long I'd been sleeping, but long enough for the weather to have changed completely. The wind was howling and the once completely still lake had whipped up into whitecaps across the surface.

Overhead, the sun was obscured by dark clouds and the previously bright, sunny summer sky had turned gray and angry.

It was cold—and getting colder. And it was way too late to pack up and head down the mountain. I'd only be stuck in the storm in a worse spot than I was now.

At least if I stayed put, I'd have shelter. My tent was whipping from side to side in the increasing wind, but it was holding strong.

I quickly checked the stakes and ties I'd used to pin the tent down and made one last trip to the stream for fresh water before taking cover inside, just as a crash of thunder sounded overhead.

Chapter Twenty-Nine

ANDY

I WAS SOMEWHERE on the trail when the first clap of thunder sounded.

It was so loud that at first I was sure a tree had been struck by lightning. I quickly scanned what I could see, but all the trees were intact.

The rain had started in the last few minutes, and the wind was getting stronger, pelting my exposed skin like bullets.

I tucked my head down and hiked faster. I'd been making good time until the storm unleashed, but it was a lot slower going now as I avoided fallen branches and tried not to slip on rocks, roots, or mud puddles. It wouldn't do anyone any good if I hurt myself before I got to Kat.

I'd expected to run into her halfway down the trail. Maybe she'd been delayed leaving, or—worst case—had twisted an ankle or something. But the longer I hiked without seeing her, the more worried I became.

What if something serious had happened to her? A wild animal? Or worse, a questionable human hiding out in the forest who happened to come across a young woman alone and—

No. I couldn't let my imagination go there. She was fine. She had to be.

So focused on getting to her as quickly as I could, I hardly felt the driving rain as I powered up the trail. According to the GPS unit Kane had given me, I was almost there. When I was less than a kilometer away, I broke into a light jog.

The moment I left the shelter of the trees and stepped out by the lake, I realized just how bad the storm really was. The wind howled straight off the mountains, across the lake, and slammed into the opposite shore—right where Kat was camped.

My eyes landed on the bright green of her tent, vivid even through the darkness of the storm.

"Kat!" I picked my way through downed branches and mud puddles toward her campsite. "Kat! Are you there?"

Finally—after what felt like an eternity—a light flickered on inside the tent.

"Andy?"

"Oh, thank God." I choked back a sob and shouted, "I'm coming! Stay there!"

KAT

"Andy?"

I fumbled in the dark of my tent, found my flashlight, and clicked it on.

"I'm coming! Stay there!"

It *was* Andy.

I wiggled out of my sleeping bag and unzipped the tent enough to stick my head and the flashlight out into the storm.

When I saw his figure moving toward me in the dark, my heart leapt into my throat. *What was he doing out in the storm?* It was too dangerous.

"Andy." I reached out into the rain as he got close. "Oh, my goodness. Get in here."

The moment I zipped the tent behind him, he pulled me into a big, and very wet, hug.

"Thank God you're okay, Kat. When you didn't come down today, I was so worried and then the storm and—"

"I decided to stay an extra night." My voice was muffled in his shoulder. "But, wait." I pulled back a little. "How did you know I was up here?"

He grinned, and I laughed. Of course he would figure it out.

"But you stayed? I thought you'd be down as soon as you could."

"Me too." I shrugged. "Turns out I kind of like it up

here." The wind chose that moment to pick up, and the tent rocked in the gust. "I mean, I mostly like it up here. By the time I noticed the storm coming in, I thought it was probably safer to stay here than try to hike out. But you—"

"Don't worry about me. I'm just glad you're safe."

"You need to get out of these wet clothes before we both freeze to death."

Andy nodded and handed me his pack before he started to peel his coat off. "There should be a change of clothes in there, and pull out the communication device. We need to send Kane a message and let him know we're safe."

I did as requested while Andy tugged his wet clothes off and put them out of the tent. I listened while he explained about the emergency communication device and together, we decided a rescue wasn't necessary. Andy sent a message to Kane through the satellite device to let him know that we'd be able to ride out the rest of the storm in the tent. Together.

"You're freezing." I brushed Andy's chest as I handed him his extra shirt. I pressed my warm hands on his cool skin. "Maybe you should get in the sleeping bag and warm up?"

He pulled the shirt over his head and reached for me. "Maybe you can help warm me up?"

Happily, I snuggled into his embrace. So much had happened in such a short time, I wasn't even sure I'd ever feel his arms around me again.

The sleeping bag wasn't big enough for both of us, so together we shifted until we were lying down with the bag unzipped and covering both of us. We didn't speak for a while but simply held each other as the storm raged on outside.

Finally, Andy blew out a breath and in a shaky voice, he said, "I was so worried, Kat." His hand came up and stroked my hair. "I don't think I could handle it if anything happened to you. I—"

"I'm so sorry, Andy." I couldn't stop the tears from streaking down my cheeks.

"You don't need to be sorry."

"I do." I laughed a little. "I mean, I'm sorry you were worried, but that's not what I meant."

I pulled back a little so I could look him in the eye. "I'm sorry I ever tried to hide you. Or us. Or what we are…I mean, what we were. It was wrong. And I didn't mean to hurt you."

My words felt so thin and inadequate to how I actually felt and what I really wanted to say.

"I'm not going to say I wasn't hurt, Kitty Kat. I was. But it wasn't just on you. And anyway, it doesn't matter."

"But it—"

"Kat." Andy sat up and pulled me up so I was facing him. "I love you." His words resonated deep in my chest. "And I don't mean like a sister, in case that wasn't clear."

I laughed.

"I should have told you a long time ago how I felt. But just like you, I was scared."

I nodded, unable to speak.

"It was always so much more than for *right now* or a *situa-*

tionship or whatever other stupid labels we tried to put on it to keep from facing what it really was. I've loved you for so long, I can hardly remember a time when it wasn't you. It's always been you, Kitty Kat." He cupped my cheek and rubbed a thumb in slow circles on my skin. "And I think I know how you feel, too. But I need you to know that I won't hide anymore. I want the whole world to know how I feel about you and how much I love you. If your brothers have a problem with that…" He exhaled slowly. "Well, they're just going to have to—"

"Deal with it," I finished for him as a smile I could no longer contain took over my face. "Because I love you, too, Andy. It's always been you."

He kissed me then. And even with the wind shaking the tent around us and the rain lashing the thin nylon, it was the best kiss I'd ever had.

"I thought I lost you, Andy. When I…I…" I dropped my head to his chest and sucked in a breath, filling my senses with his scent. "I can't lose you, too. I just can't."

He tipped my head up gently. "You won't lose me."

"My dad…I…" All at once, it was too much, and the emotions of the last few days poured out. "He's gone, Andy. He's really gone now."

His only response was to tighten his grip on me and rub my back while I cried.

After a few minutes, my sobs subsided, and I lifted my head. "You must think I'm crazy."

"No more than usual." He grinned. "Kidding." His smile faltered, and he gazed down at me with such tenderness I almost started to cry again. "You're grieving, Kat. And that's okay, because grief isn't a straight line. You lost your dad and that's incredibly hard. There's no right or wrong way to deal with that. Add onto that all these extra challenges that you've all had to go through, and of course there are all kinds of strong feelings. It's okay."

He kissed me on the top of my head and pulled me close again. "Feel whatever you need to feel and just know that I've got you. Through it all. I'm here. Always. I'm not going anywhere, Kat. Never again."

Chapter Thirty

KAT

THE WIND DIED at some point in the night and the rain fell softer, until it, too, stopped completely. By morning, when I unzipped the tent and stuck my head out, the sky was blue again, the birds chirped, and the only indication that there'd been any foul weather at all was a handful of downed branches scattered on the ground. Miraculously, none of them hit our tent, although Andy and I had been so lost in each other, I wasn't entirely sure we would have noticed.

"Can I convince you to come back in here and cuddle a little longer?" Andy tugged at my hips and tried to pull me back down into the little nest we'd made of dry clothes and the one sleeping bag.

I twisted my head around and winked. "I would love to, but my bladder has different ideas. And I'm starving."

On cue, my stomach growled, and we both laughed.

"Okay, okay." He released me and sat up. "I think I'd like to see this place in the daylight anyway."

I turned to look outside again. "You're going to love it. It's magical."

Less than thirty minutes later, we perched on flat rocks along the lakeshore and ate a simple breakfast of the dried oatmeal packets as we shared a mug of peppermint tea.

"It is pretty incredible here."

I nodded without looking away from the reflection in the water. "I can't even believe I'm saying this, but I think I'd like to do it again. But maybe not in a storm."

"And maybe with company next time?"

"Maybe." I winked at him, but a moment later, the playfulness was gone. "Oh no! You're here." I sat up, my breakfast forgotten.

"I am."

"But you're not supposed to be." I turned to stare at him. "I was supposed to do this on my own, remember? The list. It was a solo trip."

My mind spun. Had I just gone through all of that just to screw it all up? If I hadn't just spent the last few days crying, I probably would have burst into tears again. As it was, I was pretty sure I was fresh out of tears altogether.

"Hey." Andy reached over and grabbed my arm, grounding me in the moment. "Don't spiral. There's nothing we can do about it now. Besides, there were extenuating circumstances, Kat. I'm sure it will be fine. Why don't we pack up and go back to town? You can talk to Steven in person and see what he says about it all."

It was the only reasonable solution.

Besides, even if the trip didn't count as far as the will requirements were concerned, it counted in every other way that mattered, and I didn't regret anything.

"I'm glad you're here, Andy."

"Kitty Kat, there's nowhere else I'd rather be."

ANDY

The family meeting was officially called for later that night. I still wasn't convinced I'd be welcome in the big house—or anywhere near the family—but Kat insisted that I come with her.

It hurt, but ultimately, it didn't matter what the rest of them thought about me. I needed to be there for Kat. She was a strong woman—one of the toughest I knew—despite the way her family thought she needed taking care of. But the last few days—hell, the last few months—had taken their toll, and as long as she wanted me, I'd be there for her.

That was all that mattered.

Still, I hesitated before we walked through the front doors of the house that, up until now, had felt very much like home.

"It's fine," Kat said. "You belong here. With me." She kissed me on the lips. "I'm glad you're here."

It was all I needed to hear.

Everyone was already gathered in the living room when

we walked in hand in hand. Steven made it clear that everyone in the family was welcome at the meeting, not just the siblings, as this was meant to be the last one.

All heads turned in our direction. Craig jumped out of his seat, but Symon—who should have been in Switzerland —stood and grabbed his arm.

"Sit down, Craig."

Craig pressed his lips together but did as requested, though he shot a glare in my direction as Kat and I walked across the room and took our seats.

William, the family lawyer, cleared his throat and pulled everyone's attention to the front of the room. "Now that you're all here, we can get started." He gestured to Steven. "Go ahead."

Steven stepped forward and clasped his hands together. "Your father truly had some different ideas when it came to the execution of his will," he said. "And I must tell you, as unorthodox as it's been, it has been one of my great pleasures to see the way all five of you have leaned into the process. I can say with complete certainty that your father would be proud of each and every one of you."

I squeezed Kat's hand a little tighter.

"Does this mean it's done?" Chase asked. "Did Kat finish her list?"

"We still don't know what all was on it," Asher said.

Steven responded with a kind smile and looked in our direction.

"Kat?"

KAT

I always knew I'd tell them about the list when the time was right, and now that I'd completed it, it no longer felt as if it were mine and mine alone. Keeping part of it to myself had been a way of clinging to a piece of my father and our relationship, but I no longer felt like I needed it.

Maybe that had been his plan all along. He knew I would save the camping trip for last and that I would need it the most.

However he'd meant it to work out, the only thing that mattered was that I felt better about it now. As much as I missed him and always would, for the first time, I felt at peace with his death.

That sense of peace carried through me as I explained the last forty-eight hours to my siblings, who all reacted with varying degrees of surprise.

"Wait. So you were in the middle of that storm last night?"

"What were you thinking?"

"You were camping? By yourself?"

"What the hell, Kat? You could have gotten hurt!"

"That was so irresponsible."

I blew out a breath and lifted the mug of tea Annie had brought me to my lips. I focused on inhaling the warm, spicy chai before taking a tentative sip. It wasn't until I'd savored the heat and lowered the mug again that I tried to address any of their questions.

"Are you done?" I looked around at my siblings, my gaze landing finally on Charli, who was the only one who hadn't said anything. She smiled encouragingly, and I gratefully returned it. Andy had filled me in on how supportive Charli and Symon had both been the night of the incident.

With a deep breath, I explained how the solo camping trip had been the last thing on my list. Only Andy and Kane had known about it, both for different reasons.

"You knew?" Chase turned on Andy. "And you let her go up by herself?"

"Enough." I narrowed my gaze at my eldest brother. "He didn't let me do anything, because I am a grown woman who doesn't need anyone's permission to do anything. Just like I don't need protecting from—" I lifted my hands and dropped them again. "Well, anything. Now, please, if you could all drop this ridiculous overprotective schtick and just listen, I would really appreciate it."

I waited until they all leaned back in their seats, mouths shut.

"Okay," I said. "So the request was that I go on a solo back-packing trip and sleep under the stars." I looked at Steven. "I did that the first night, but then I decided to stay." My lips curled into a smile as I remembered why. "It was amazing up there."

Steven nodded knowingly. "He would be so pleased to know you stayed another night."

"But then..." I turned to Andy. "He came up to find me

and stayed, so technically, I didn't do it on my own. Does that—I mean—did I mess it up?"

I held my breath, but there was no need.

Steven shook his head. "You didn't screw anything up, Kat. Your dad appointed me to oversee everything and make the final decision if there was uncertainty. But the way I see it, there's no uncertainty here at all. The requirement was one night. As far as I'm concerned, you completed your assignment."

Relief flooded me, and a weight I hadn't even realized I'd been carrying lifted from my shoulders. Andy squeezed my thigh, and I shifted closer to him.

"I think it's important to note one thing," Steven continued. He stood and moved to the front of the room. "What Michael really wanted for all of you was your happiness. That's what this was all about. I can't pretend to know exactly what your father was thinking when he came up with this plan. But I did know him pretty well, and I can say with complete certainty that if he were sitting here right now, he would be so pleased to see what wonderful people you all are and the way you've come together. Also, I think he would be delighted to see how his family has grown, with so much love. But there's tension in the air today, and you all know as well as I do that he'd hate that."

He paused and looked at each of them in turn.

"Don't let misunderstandings or miscommunications get in the way of the bond you all have.

"It has been one of my great pleasures to do this final thing for your father. But now, I'm happy to say my time here is done. It's time for me to move on. I think the white sand beaches of Costa Rica are calling me. Thank you for allowing me to be an important part of your family for all these years."

Steven stood quietly for a moment, as if taking it all in, before clapping his hands together and turning to William, who sat ready to read out the details of our father's estate once and for all.

Chapter Thirty-One

ANDY

IT HAD BEEN A LONG NIGHT, and an even longer day. More than anything, I wanted to take Kat back to her apartment, run a bubble bath, and soak away the stress of the last few days with a glass of wine.

The meeting hadn't taken long. Michael Carlson's estate was divided up very equitably among the children, with generous amounts going to charity and trusts set up for his grandchildren, both living and future.

I, along with the other spouses and partners, excused myself as soon as it made sense, to give the siblings a chance to finish things up with William and Steven. Instead of joining the others in the kitchen, I snuck out to the backyard to get some air.

Things were still tense with the family, and it wasn't a situation I saw resolving itself anytime soon. I also had no plans to push the agenda. I meant what I said to Kat. I wasn't going anywhere. If that meant Craig, Asher, Chase, and any of the others were mad, that was on them. I loved Kat more than anything else in the world, and I was not going to put that aside just because they couldn't seem to get over themselves.

"Hey. Can I interrupt?"

I looked over my shoulder to see Symon with baby Poppy in his arms.

"She just woke up from a nap, which means she is not to be contained." Symon laughed and put the baby on the grass with a selection of toys.

I couldn't help but smile at the baby girl. She truly was a spot of sunshine in all our lives.

Maybe one day, there'd be a little red-headed girl crawling around too?

The idea of having a baby with Kat made me smile. No matter how far off in the future it was, it was definitely in our future.

"Shouldn't you be in Switzerland?"

"Just like you." Symon chuckled. "I pushed it by a few days. I get it if you need a few more. The team will be fine."

"I appreciate it." I nodded and leaned back on the grass. "I'm sure I'll be able to take off soon. I just couldn't go while she was…"

"I get it, Andy." Symon nodded. "I wouldn't have left either."

"What we do for love, right?"

"So you do love her?"

ELENA AITKEN

It was Craig who asked the question. I turned to see him standing behind us.

"Can I sit?"

Symon jumped up and grabbed Poppy, who squawked in protest. "I was just heading in." He was gone with the baby before I could object.

A moment later, Craig took his place on the grass next to me.

We sat in silence for a minute before I answered his question. "More than life itself, Craig." I didn't face him as I spoke. "I think there's always been some part of me that's loved her, but over the last few years, it grew to the point where I couldn't ignore it anymore."

"And you really went up the mountain in the middle of the storm for her? Hell, we didn't even know she was in danger."

I nodded. "I'd die before I'd let anything happen to her."

Next to me, Craig made a grunting noise. After another moment of silence, he said, "I know that feeling." He spoke softly. "That's how I feel about Lucy and Meri. I get it. I owe you, man."

"You don't."

Finally, I glanced over at my friend. We locked eyes, and Craig nodded before looking down again.

"I'm sorry I punched you."

"I'm sorry I didn't tell you about us sooner. I should have told you how I felt about her. Hell, I should have told *her* sooner."

Craig slapped me on the back. "You don't owe me an apology. But I do need you to accept mine. I really am sorry, Andy. I was out of line. For a lot of reasons. You're a damn good man. I just...I think I lost my head. When it comes to Kat, I've just always felt like I need to take care of her, ya know?"

"She doesn't need you to take care of her."

We both looked up to see Kat standing over us, her arms outstretched.

"She doesn't need anyone to take care of her. But she does need you all to love her." She laughed, and the happiness on her face made my heart squeeze. "And she also needs to stop speaking in the third person." She reached her arms out to both of us. "Now give me a hug. Both of you."

I let Craig get up first. I waited while brother and sister embraced and exchanged apologies.

"Now, you two." Kat tilted her head. "Hug it out."

I made the first move. I pulled Craig into an awkward man hug and slapped his back.

But it was Craig who tightened his arms around me and squeezed. "I love you, man. Can we move on from this?"

"You know we can."

Craig released me and took a step back. "You've always been like a brother to me, but I guess now..." He looked to Kat, who only laughed.

"One thing at a time," she said. "We only just made our relationship public...I don't think anyone is getting married anytime soon."

"I don't know about that, Kitty Kat." I grabbed her

hand and winked. "Don't worry, I won't propose right now. It's been a big day. But make no mistake, I'm going to put a ring on this finger." I kissed her hand. "I meant it when I said I can't live without you."

I couldn't resist any longer. I pulled her in for a kiss, but it only lasted seconds before Craig began to protest.

"Okay, enough already." He groaned. "I told you I was okay with it, but it's still freakin' weird. You can't just spring this on me."

"Or me," Asher called out as he joined us in the yard, followed by Chase, who was right behind him.

"Super weird," the eldest brother agreed. "But also, super awesome." He held out a hand to me as a peace offering. "Really, I mean it. I know you took us off guard, but you're a good man, Andy. There's none better."

We shared a hug before it was Asher's turn. He, too, apologized and embraced me. "Sometimes we can act without thinking."

"Sometimes?" Noa appeared by his side and rolled her eyes affectionately.

The rest of the family made their way out into the yard with bottles of bubbly and sparkling apple juice for the non-drinkers, and glasses that were passed around.

"I would like to propose a toast," Chase said when we all had a glass in our hands.

"Wait." Charli stopped him. "I think it's only fitting if Kat makes the toast."

There were murmurs of approval, and everyone turned

to look at Kat. I took a half step to the side, giving her space.

We all watched as she dropped her head for a moment before looking up with tears in her eyes. "Damn," she laughed, "I didn't think I could cry anymore."

Everyone chuckled.

"It's been a ride," Kat said. "And we've all been through it, haven't we?" She smiled and continued. "But I wouldn't change any of it. The last few years since Dad left us with our *instructions* have brought us together in ways we never could have imagined." She looked to Chase, who raised his hand in recognition. "We've learned things about ourselves and each other that I don't think we would have otherwise. And most importantly, we've all found love." Kat looked straight at me. "And learned how to open up to that love."

She blew me a kiss before continuing. "I don't know if he intended for any of that to happen, or if he thought it would just be a fun parting gift for us all." A few people laughed. "But whatever his reasons, I'm sure glad for it because I don't know about the rest of you, but I love this big, happy, totally dysfunctional family." She raised her glass high, and everyone followed suit. "To Dad."

"To Dad," everyone chorused.

"And to family," Kat added. And then to herself, "Always."

KAT

"Just when I thought this day couldn't get any better." I rolled over into Andy's arms and snuggled into his chest. "You proved me wrong."

"Was it the first orgasm? Or that last one?" He kissed me on the nose, making me laugh.

"All of them. I want them all."

His arms wrapped around me, and he held me tight. "Kitty Kat, I'm happy to make you purr anytime. And you know the best part?"

I propped myself up on an elbow to look him in the eye. "Is that we get to do it again later?"

"Definitely that." He wiggled his eyebrows. "But even better, we don't have to hide from your family anymore."

"Oh." I pretended to look surprised. "I think maybe we should keep all the orgasms private still."

"You know that's not what I meant."

I giggled and dodged him as he tried to tickle me.

But I knew exactly what he meant. Now that my family knew about us, I felt like I could finally take a deep breath. No more secrets. Especially not when it came to Andy. Never again would I try to push down my feelings for this man.

"I know exactly what you mean." I settled myself back into his arms. "It feels good not to have secrets, doesn't it?"

He trailed his finger down my bare arm. "It feels so good. You know what else feels good? This bed."

I laughed. "Better than sleeping on the ground?"

"Much."

We fell silent and for a moment, I thought he might have fallen asleep. "Andy?"

"Uh-hmm."

"You're not really going to move into that studio, are you?"

He tensed a little. "I can sell it."

"Or…"

"Or? Don't tell me you've had time to think about what I'm going to do with my new apartment with everything you've had going on."

"You'd be surprised what I think about."

He laughed. "I know that's true." He nuzzled into the base of my neck and trailed kisses. "So, tell me your plan."

"The rental market is pretty hot right now," I said. "I bet we could rent it out without much trouble. And…maybe we could rent this place, too."

"But then where would we live? Because, just in case it wasn't clear earlier, you're never getting rid of me now."

I had no plans of getting rid of him. Not now. Not ever. "I was thinking that maybe it was time to get a real house."

"A house?"

I smiled to myself and nodded against his chest. "A few bedrooms and a nice bright kitchen." I bit my bottom lip. "Somewhere with a yard," I continued.

"A yard?"

"Somewhere big enough for a swing set." I held my breath.

"A swing—what? Kat. What?"

I rolled away from him and turned on my side so I faced him.

"Are you saying you want kids? Because I do, too. One day I'd—"

"When you say, *one day*…"

He narrowed his eyes. "Wait? What *are* you saying?"

"I'm not really saying anything except my period is late and—"

"What? But how?"

"I think you know how." I laughed. "But seriously, we did get a little lax with the birth control a few times." I shrugged.

"Wow." Andy sat up and the sheet fell in a pile around his waist. "You…we…"

"Nothing is a hundred percent." I sat up and grabbed his hands. "And I don't actually know anything for sure. I might not be."

"But you might be."

"I might be." I smiled a little. "But I didn't even do the math until after we got home from the hike. I've been so busy and more than a little preoccupied that I wasn't really paying attention. And I need to tell you, I didn't drink any of the bubbly tonight…I had apple juice." I swallowed hard, the worry that had been playing at the back of my mind taking over. "But I did have a few sips of my dad's whiskey the first night while I was camping under the stars and—"

"Kat." He held my hands in his and scooted so he sat closer to me. "It's fine. If you are…" He blew out a breath and shook his head. "That won't matter. I promise. We'll go see a doctor just to be sure, but it's fine."

I nodded. "And you and me?" I asked, suddenly uncertain. "Are you okay with—"

"Oh my God, Kat." The smile split his face. "Are you kidding? I'm shocked, yeah. But, wow. I couldn't be happier, Kitty Kat. Remember what I said earlier about putting a ring on your finger?"

Oh, I remembered.

"I don't plan on spending another day of my life without you as my partner. Forever. As long as we're together, it doesn't matter what life throws at us. Because we've got this. No matter what. You just keep on loving me, Kitty Kat, and I'll keep on loving you. Deal?"

I'd never been happier or more content as I answered him. "Deal."

Epilogue

KAT

THE SUN WAS SHINING, and even with the nip of cold in the air that threatened an early winter, Mother Nature had cooperated with us for our moving day.

My family had insisted that there was no need to hire movers and they would all be happy to get it done for us. I was pretty sure they were regretting that decision by the time we were done, but for now, I was happy for the help.

"Kat. Put that down. You shouldn't be lifting anything in your condition."

Okay. I was mostly happy for the help.

I rolled my eyes when Asher wasn't looking before totally ignoring him. "I'm pregnant, Asher. Not an invalid. I'm sure this box of pillows won't hurt."

"You know I'm just looking out for you, sis." Asher

walked past me into our new living room, carrying two lamps. "I'm not trying to be overprotective."

"Sure you're not." I laughed and blew him a kiss so he knew I wasn't upset. Some habits died hard, and although my brothers had been making an effort not to be so overbearing, once Andy and I announced we were pregnant, most of those efforts had gone out the window.

"Which room should we put this in?" Chase and Craig appeared, each holding the end of a mattress. "Oh, Kat. You probably shouldn't be carrying that," Craig added when he saw me holding the box.

"You're right." I sighed and tossed the very light box that only contained a few throw pillows in it to the ground. "In fact, I should probably just sit with my feet up while someone feeds me grapes."

All three of my brothers stared at me, but no one disagreed.

"She's fine." Andy appeared. He set his stack of boxes down and kissed me on the cheek. "Kat knows her body, and she knows just how much it can handle."

He winked at me, and I worked not to laugh because earlier that day I'd used those exact words with him when he, too, expressed concern with my helping.

"Thank you." I put my hands on my hips and turned to Chase and Craig, who were still holding the mattress. "You can put that one in the primary bedroom."

"Ha!" Asher laughed. "You're carrying their bed."

I stared at my brother, who'd apparently turned into a teenager in the last few moments. "It's just a—"

"Oh, hell no." Craig dropped his end of the mattress, causing Chase to do the same.

"Hey!" Andy jumped to grab the mattress before it fell over. "What are you—"

"Look." Craig held his hands up. "I'm good with you two, but it's still weird and come on…that's my sister. I can't be carrying around the bed where you two—nope. Not doing it."

"You are being ridiculous." I crossed my arms and swallowed back a laugh. "Chase?"

My eldest, and most reasonable, brother shook his head, too. "You know what? He's got a point."

"Fine." I looked at Andy. "I guess I'll have to do it."

"No!"

"Kat!"

I burst into laughter and just to further make my point, rubbed my hands over my barely swollen belly and said, "How did you guys think your little niece or nephew—"

"Enough." Craig put his hands over his ears and stepped forward. "Let's just get it in the bedroom so I can stop thinking about it."

I laughed while everyone got back to work.

In the kitchen, my sister and sisters-in-law were making short work of unpacking—all except Lucy, who was almost ready to burst, sitting with her very swollen feet up on a chair.

"Wow. It's really looking good in here, you guys. Thank you so much."

"You know we're happy to help," Lucy said. "Not that

I'm much help. But I'm getting pretty good at pointing out empty cupboards and drawers."

I laughed. "I feel like I should be feeding you grapes."

"What?"

"Never mind. Just something I mentioned to the guys, who all think I'm doing too much."

"You know they mean well." Charli aimed a smile in my direction. "We all do."

"I know it. And I love you all for it. I really don't think there's going to be much for me to do once you leave."

"Oh, I'm sure there will be one or two things for you to take care of."

"There always is."

"True. But some things can wait." I let my gaze travel to the backyard and the exact spot where I wanted the swing set to go. "At least for a few more months."

ANDY

"There's still so much to do." Kat plopped down on the couch next to me. "Moving is so much work."

"But we don't have to do any of it right now." I pulled her down so her head was resting in my lap. "Today has been a huge day."

Moving always was. Even with the entire Carlson family helping all day, it had been a massive undertaking getting us from Kat's apartment, and the storage unit where I'd been keeping my own apartment's worth of things, into our new house.

But it was work worth doing. The house was perfect.

As if Kat had just read my mind, she looked up into my eyes. "I love our house."

"I love you." I kissed my finger and pressed it to her lips.

"Obviously I love you, too."

"I don't get tired of hearing it."

She flipped over on the couch and crawled up so she was in my lap. "I love you, Andy Fisher."

I closed my eyes and grinned. "Oh yeah. That's what I love to hear."

"I love you and this house that we're going to raise our kids in."

"Kids?" My eyes popped open. "Plural?" I raised an eyebrow. "Is there something you're not telling me?"

Kat laughed. "It's not twins. Not that I know of, anyway. I was just thinking that now we have all these bedrooms to fill."

I blew out the breath I'd been holding. "Why don't we just focus on one at a time?" I wrapped my arms around her. "We're already doing everything totally out of order."

She shrugged. "I like our way of doing things."

"I like you." I kissed her. "And do you know what else I'd like? A lot?"

"What's that?"

I reached behind me in the couch cushions for the box I'd stashed there earlier. "Kat Carlson, I'd really like it if you'd be my wife."

I held out the box and flipped open the lid to reveal my mother's diamond and emerald ring.

"Andy." She covered her mouth with both hands.

"I'm sorry it's not an elaborate, over-the-top romantic proposal, but I felt like it was fitting to spend the first official night in our new house as an engaged couple." I lifted the ring from the box and hesitated. "That is, if you say yes."

"Oh my God, yes." She flitted her hands in the air. "A million times yes. I would love nothing more than to be your wife."

I slipped the ring on her finger and cupped her cheek before kissing her on the lips.

"My brothers are going to—"

"Be so excited that I finally asked you."

She stared at me, open-mouthed. "What do you mean? Did they know?"

"Of course they knew," I said. "I sat them all down ages ago and made sure they would give me their blessing. After everything we've already gone through, I wanted to be sure they were all on board."

Tears sprang to her eyes. "You know I'm my own strong and independent woman, right?"

I chuckled. "I sure do."

"But I love that you asked them."

"I know that too, Kitty Kat." I pulled her close so her head was once more resting on my chest. I pressed a kiss to her forehead and held my fiancée close. "I know."

I hope you enjoyed Kat and Andy's story and all the rest of the Trickle Creek books.

But the love in Trickle Creek isn't finished yet. The Lyons brothers grew up in Trickle Creek, but they haven't found love...yet.

Keep reading for a sneak peek of From Grumpy to Forever, next.

From Grumpy to Forever

Please enjoy this sneak peek into another Trickle Creek family.
She needs a husband. He needs a job. What happens when their convenient arrangement becomes inconveniently real?

Reid

THE ONLY THING worse than ripping out century-old hardwood floors from a heritage house was doing it for a privileged asshole and his plastic trophy wife who'd just moved to my quiet, small town with plans to "modernize and improve" things.

And there was no way I was going to do it.

To hell with the fat paycheck that would come with the job.

Never mind that the money these assholes were willing to pay me to destroy their beautiful house and turn it into a McMansion with no soul was enough to buy me a new set of woodworking tools.

And maybe even my own workshop, too.

"Not fucking worth it," I muttered, pissed at myself that I'd even considered taking the job in the first place.

I tugged my gloves off and shoved them in my back pocket before grabbing my toolbox.

"Off to get supplies?" The bottle blonde with tits almost as big as her head stopped me before I could make my escape. She wore skin-tight jeans and something that could barely be considered a bra the way she spilled out of it, with a silky plaid shirt tied around her waist. No doubt in an effort to look *small town.*

"Changed my mind," I told her. "I can't take the job."

"Sure you can." She wiggled herself closer and pulled her shoulders back to give me a better view of her store-bought assets.

"No." I turned away and headed for the door, almost sorry to leave this beautiful house, knowing that soon it would be a whitewashed, sterilized version of its former glory. "I can't."

I wasn't an idiot, and I also wasn't the only handyman in town. Someone else would take the job. Of that, I had no doubt. But it wouldn't be me.

"Stop!" the woman shrieked, when she finally figured out I wasn't playing. "Phillip! He's leaving!"

I had already loaded my toolbox in the back of my truck, when Phillip caught up to me. "Where do you think you're going?"

"I'm not taking the job."

"You already did."

"Then I quit." When I turned around, he was so close, I almost bumped into him. If he was trying for intimidation, it wouldn't work. He might have more money than me—by a lot —but I was at least half a foot taller, with a good fifty pounds of muscle on him. Not that I actually thought this man had ever used anything but his wallet to get what he wanted.

"You can't quit."

"Already did." I put my hand on the door handle. I was already done with this conversation. "I'm not going to be part of you destroying this gorgeous old house just so you can turn around and sell it to some other outsider for double market price. I won't be part of it."

"We're improving the property." Phillip obviously didn't like to be told no. His face turned a very unnatural shade of purple. "And this entire backwoods little town. You're an idiot if you don't want to—"

"What did you just call my town?" He cowered just the way I knew he would when I took a step toward him. "Call me whatever you want. But you don't fuck with my town, got it?"

The man nodded and swallowed hard before I stepped

back and swung the truck door open. "Do yourself a favor, Phillip. Spend your money on your wife's next boob job and leave my town alone."

His bravado returned the moment I fired up the old truck. He was yelling something about me never working in this town again as I peeled away from the curb and the entitled asshole.

Okay, I might have gone a little too far with that last comment about his wife's tits, but I couldn't stop myself. It was people like Phillip and his plastic wife who would be the end of our town and everything that made it special.

It was bad enough with the ski resort and the new fancy golf course drawing in tourists both summer and winter, but now the city folk were starting to buy up properties. Things were changing in Trickle Creek, and I didn't like it.

I was still simmering in my shitty mood when I pulled up in front of the hardware store. The last thing I should be doing was tool shopping with my bank account looking as anemic as it did, but it was the one thing that would make me feel better.

Well, maybe not the *one* thing. But the odds of me finding a woman willing to put up with my mood was even less likely than me walking out of the store with the new thickness planer I'd been eyeing.

"Reid." My twin brother, Grayson, greeted me the moment I stepped through the doors. He'd been more or less running the store for the last few years since Old Man Holbrook broke his hip. "What are you doing here? I thought you took that job over at—"

"I don't want to talk about it."

"Don't tell me you got fired again."

"Actually, I quit." I glared at him. "And I'll have you know, I didn't get fired from the job up at the Carlson condo units either."

"Oh, right." Gray didn't even bother to hide his smirk. "I suppose you quit that one, too. It had nothing to do with Asher telling you it wasn't okay to be rude to the guests?"

I didn't bother to answer him because he wasn't entirely wrong. Although it was more of a mutual understanding between Asher and me. Still, Grayson's comment pissed me off.

"Listen, Reid. I know you don't like it, but the tourists are here to stay." Grayson moved around the counter and started to walk down the aisle toward the plumbing fittings.

Against my better judgment, and my lack of interest in listening to a lecture, I followed him.

"And whether you see it or not, it's good for the town."

He wasn't wrong. A fact that pissed me off even more. The Carlson family had done a lot to build up the tourism industry in Trickle Creek, effectively saving the town from ruin after the old mine closed and so many jobs were lost.

But it didn't mean I had to like it.

"You know," Grayson looked at me while he reached into a box and started restocking a bin of parts, "maybe instead of fighting it, you should try embracing the change. You could do really well here if you stopped fighting with all your potential clients."

"But they're all such assholes."

Grayson shot me a look and leaned past me to greet the new customer the bells over the door just announced. "I'll be right with you."

He dropped the part he was holding back in the box and looked me in the eye. "You know the other perk of all the new faces in town?"

"What's that?"

Grayson wiggled his eyebrows and chuckled as he gestured with his head toward the front of the store. "A lot of those new faces are beautiful women."

Instinctively, I turned around. My gaze landed on the firm, round ass of Grayson's new customer, bent over looking at something on a bottom shelf. My long-dormant dick twitched to life. "Fuck me."

My brother laughed. Before he walked past me, he turned. "You know the best part, Reid?"

"What's that?"

"If they're new to town, they don't know what a grumpy asshole you are yet."

Read the rest of From Grumpy to Forever NOW!

About the Author

Elena Aitken is a USA Today Bestselling Author of more than fifty romance and women's fiction novels. The mother of 'grown up' twins, Elena now lives with her very own mountain man in the heart of the very mountains she writes about. She can often be found with her toes in the lake and a glass of wine in her hand, dreaming up her next book and working on her own happily ever after.

To learn more about Elena:
www.elenaaitken.com
elena@elenaaitken.com